Rod Van Blake

Nyumbani Chronicles :

Draconian Tribunal

Mahali Pengine Ent

Nyumbani Chronicles : Draconian Tribunal is a work of fiction. The characters, incidents, and dialogs are products of the author's imagina-tion and are not to be construed as real. Any resemblance to actual events or persons, living or dead, is entirely coincidental.

A Mahali Pengine Ent Edition

Copyright © 2022 by Rod Van Blake
Cover art by Jordan P. Jackson
Hardcover Edition published by Mahali Pengine Ent
http://AncientIllumination.net
ISBN 979-8-9875664-3-5 Hardcover
ISBN 979-8-9875664-2-8 Paperback
ISBN 979-8-9875664-4-2 E-book

9 8 7 6 5 4 3 2 1

Prologue

Hurtling headlong through space towards Nyumbani, Olofi contemplates ending the illusion of him having the appearance of a meteor. He thought of ending the guise again after breaching the atmosphere as he was sure he was far enough away from Izulu so the other Orishas would not notice but refrained for fear of startling the inhabitants any further than he already would once he made planetfall. He did not understand Olorun's need for secrecy of his plan to keep an eye on developing troubles down below. The further away he hurled, the intensity of the bond with his disrespectful higher aspect waned. Their connection was not lost, but it felt weaker. Perhaps that was for the best right now. Olofi was not amused. Weaving his way through the clouds, he continued to tumble and picked a mountain range above what was usually a sleepy fishing village, but even from high above he could see there was plenty happening and from the billowing smoke stacks near the village it did not look good.

There's an unmistakable clap as Olofi breaks the sound barrier in route to the ground racing towards him. There's another thunderous boom as he collides into the mountain side far above Tanji. Briefly eyes raise towards the mountain ranges at the noise distracting them from the frenzy caused by the appearance of beings from the shadow realms suddenly showing up resulting in chaos. Dusting himself off after being unceremoniously thrown from Izulu to hurtle through space to the surface of Nyumbani, Olofi quickly takes account of all he surveys. Ducking into a cave, Olofi contemplates what appearance best fits an innocent observer. His celestial and godly form he had been so used to while wondering on Izulu would likely draw too much attention. He went through a selection of appearances until settling on the body and visage of a wizened old man dressed in tattered priestly robes from a long-forgotten religion. A cane materializes in Olofi's hand as he peers out from the cave remembering to dampen the light in his eyes until they're a more mortal looking deep brown.

A small hand gesture brings about a veil of invisibility over his form as he steps out from the cave. Once he is sure there is no one around that would be taken aback by his sudden appearance, Olofi does away with the veil and begins making his way down the mountain towards Tanji. Remembering to act like an elderly man gingerly traversing down the mountain only disturbing occasional wildlife on his travels. Halfway down that changed. At first Olofi was perplexed by what he sees crawling. It looks to be a Djaemon, heavily scarred but discolored to a drab grey. It looks to be male and someone or something had cleaved it in half. Walking around the animated flesh Olofi could feel the power that was keeping it mindlessly moving but could not quite place the source. There was a strange familiarity that he could not narrow down. With a wave of his hands Olofi's eyes once again glow as he severs the connection holding this battered body and it slumps to lie motionless as it should have been after whatever trauma it had obviously went through. The vibrant red color blossoms back into the fallen Djaemon's skin as he looks up in relief and gratitude just before the last light leaves his eyes. "Rest now warrior. May Serat embrace your final tribute." Olofi says continuing on his way down.

Well, that was a disturbing thing to encounter the god thought. Thinking on it further there was a mixture of a seemingly familiar power and corrupted magic that he felt. Meaning this could be some sort of collaborative effort leading to the mayhem here. Olorun may suspect one of their own, and this may be the reason for his methods orchestrating the precipitous fall of his own aspect to observe. Olofi almost chuckled inward at the pun. Upon reaching a lower plateau, his introspection is interrupted as he is approached by three behemoths from the shadow realm. Dark as night with glowing eyes and hair of what looked like multicolored flowing flames, but there was no heat coming from them. Looking them up and down Olofi asks, "What are you doing here? This is not your domain."

In response the center most creature takes up a nasty looking scythe and springs towards Olofi. With a snap of his fingers Olofi sent him back to the shadow realm. The other two pause briefly in confusion before beginning to lunge in unison with other strangely crafted weapons of their own. Olofi rolls his eyes and reveals his godly form hoping it would give these creatures a glimpse of who they were actually dealing with. They didn't break stride. Feigning a yawn at the last second, he snaps again and they too are sent instantly back to their home realm. Once again taking the appearance of an elderly man from a long-gone religion, Olofi hides himself under a veil so he can levitate and take stock from a high vantage point and sees small fissures or tears in reality which may explain why beings from other realms would be here, but to find out how that came to be he would have to do more investigation.

It would be faster to simply fly down the rest of the way but he wanted to enjoy the journey. After all it wasn't often, he was able to be here, in this manner pretending to live and travel as mortals do. Not to mention there could be other clues along the way. Feet firmly back on solid ground he looked himself over once again before stepping off. Occasionally he would wince in pain or pretend to be tuckered out by the rigors of climbing down what would have been treacherous terrain for someone the age he appears to be. The rest of the trip down was uneventful and he eventually makes it to the base of the mountain and has the small fishing village in his line of sight. Reaching out he can feel the sickness spreading throughout the lands is present here but it's not as prevalent as it is in the grasslands. There are however a lot of scars from rifts that had been opened fairly recently which partially explain the fissures Olofi felt before. Unfortunately, from both high and low vantage points he could see no clues as to whom was responsible for them.

Some of the tension in the air at least had dissipated as whatever the cause for the commotion he felt on his way planet side from Izulu must have found a peaceful conclusion or at the very least stopped for the moment. He could see in the outskirts of the village fires being put out as both people and damaged equipment were being healed or repaired respectively. No doubt the beasts from the shadow realm had something to do with this, but the question was why? More importantly the question was who would be foolish enough to bring them here? Olofi rolled these questions around in his mind but it was blatantly rhetorical and he knew the answer. Some man or woman here was obviously the fool or fools in question because any being that knew what dwelled in the shadow realm would never dare. There was some rustling in a patch of bushes that made the god pause before moving on to the village.

"Come out and identify yourself. I'm just an old man, no harm will come to you." Olofi stated calmly. After what sounded like whimpering coming from the bushes in question a young man with a shorn head and a somewhat underdeveloped beard wearing ill-fitting armor crawled out from them brushing himself down. Seeing that it was in fact an old man he introduced himself "King Daniel, at your service. What are you doing out here? There have been shades and all manner of strange creatures lurking about. I lost my men while out on patrol." A glint comes to Olofi's eyes as he replies "A king no less! Over which lands do you rule?" Stammering Daniel quips "None now, sadly the cataclysm many seasons ago destroyed them. Who might you be good sir?"

Now it was Olofi's turn to be hesitant as he had not thought of an alias to present to the people he ran into here. Hesitantly he responded "Ah…Lofin my friend. I was having trouble with my pastures and came here to see if there was any news of why the lands were in decline when I spotted evidence of even more trouble here, but I would think a king with no lands is no king at all." Anger briefly flashed over Daniel's face but he quickly composed himself. "Despite your insults

Lofin, I shall escort you into the village and see if there's any word of my men. These are indeed strange and dangerous times." Smirking Olofi allows Daniel to take him into the village and they both get a closer look at the damage and carnage that had occurred there. Things looked grim. From the brief encounters in the mountains, Olofi could see why the people here would be scared and on high alert.

A host of fishermen were inland now to help with the repair and cleaning efforts going on in Tanji. To Olofi's surprise there was a young girl leading a small cleanup crew comprised of fishermen, and city shields that had come from Kemet to help. Olofi hobbled up to the tall girl with tight braids the others were taking direction from despite being her elders to ask, "Child, what happened here?" Confused by the question and looking in the direction the two seemed to come from Kezi replies "Baba what are you doing out there with Daniel no less?! There was an attack of sorts but we don't know where they came from or why. My father says it's because the cursed boy has returned to us." Following the girls gaze at the last comment Olofi could see that her focus was on a boy that was a bit younger than she was. He was a bit odd but not cursed as far as Olofi could tell.

Daniel obviously had a less than stellar reputation here for reasons Olofi could easily guess. The young boy in question was highly gifted as Olofi could see his aura beaming. The boy had absolutely no hair from head to toe with cream-colored patches that disturbed his otherwise brown skin in places. There were three older adults with him. A couple and a one-armed Magus. Olofi could tell they had been through quite an ordeal recently. To Daniel Lofin commented "Those two, bear watching, Daniel the Lesser." Indignantly Daniel responds, "It's King Daniel!" Lofin cuts him off, "King of what exactly? A king with nothing or no one to rule is king of nothing. That young girl didn't seem to hold you in the esteem of a great warrior…so until you can show me what you are king of, I shall address you as Daniel the Lesser."

Grabbing his cane Olofi stepped off leaving Daniel speechless as the conversation was obviously concluded. Together they watched as an eclectic group of people gathered to fix things in the aftermath of recent events. Olofi watched and listened occasionally urging Daniel to pitch in. Begrudgingly the man did so. He wasn't sure why he followed the directions of the old newcomer. From listening to a small group of the fire forged present Olofi learned there was to be a hunting party put together in Kemet to seek out and find the person supposedly to blame for all or at least a significant number of problems in the area. The suspected culprit was rumored to be in the dead marsh, and elder dragons were said to be leading the party. This all sounded interesting, and Olofi wanted to make his way to Kemet as soon as possible. "Daniel the Lesser! We must make our way to Kemet." Confused Daniel stops what he was currently doing to ask the old man why he felt he needed to make such a journey.

"That's a few days journey for a person in good shape, and you seem a bit long in the tooth…no offense." Daniel quipped. Looking Daniel up and down obviously scrutinizing the ill-fitting armor, the scraggly beard and no true weapon to speak of and the fact that when they met Daniel seemed to be hiding in the bushes. Without speaking a word Daniel guessed he had been measured and came up short. A twinkle came to the old man's eyes as he asked "I need a proper escort. Can you handle my protection?" The subtle vote of confidence in the old man's look was enough to influence Daniel to stand up a little straighter and puff his chest out a bit as he replied "Of course I can protect you! I was more worried if you should take such a trek in your condition." Shaking his head Olofi states "Don't you worry about that. From what I'm told Kemet is not a long journey. All flat land, correct? It's not as if we are trapsing through the dead marshes."

Thinking it over Daniel had to concede that it was true. They would be going through mostly flat terrain which in his mind was part of the problem. The sun was heading down meaning they would be making the trek at night when the nocturnal predators would be on the hunt. The old man had somehow made his way down the mountain on his own which was a mystery, but if they had to move fast Daniel doubted, they could outrun a pack of Inja Enkulu, a stray dire panther or worse. Without another word Olofi walked into a bait shop and came out with some provisions. Seeing the bounty of supplies Daniel perked up. "That had to be some hefty coin you spent. Anything you can spare?" he asked.

Wrapping up the large satchel of supplies Olofi says "Stick with me and do right on this small journey and the creator shall always provide Daniel the Lesser. Look alive!" The old man threw the satchel to Daniel who struggled mightily under its considerable weight. Confused and somewhat off balance, Daniel tries to keep pace with Olofi as they step off in the direction of Kemet. The sun was beginning to dip beneath the horizon to give way to a luminous moon. It would be a fairly straight shot but animal noises began to permeate the air as they made their way through a shortened grassland. Daniel began to wilt beneath the weight of their supplies and was also being affected by the sickness that had seeped into these lands. The sickly-sweet smell of the bad grasslands certainly offended Olofi's nostrils but did not nearly nauseate or unbalance him as it was doing to his travel companion.

Just outside the affected area they could hear predators off in the distance fighting over carcasses or possibly just fighting for the rights to the area. Either way once they stepped out of the nauseating grasslands, they would run into whatever it was that sounded much larger than they were. Daniel was sweating profusely and worried this might be the end of his tale. Olofi could see the man would not make it much longer. He stopped and urged Daniel to set the satchel down to take a breath. Skeptical as he was still feeling sick but grateful for the brief respite, Daniel sets the satchel down and closes his eyes to compose himself. The grasses had fumes coming off of them. Daniel tried to rip a large strip of cloth off to cover his mouth and nose with.

As his eyes began to tear up blurring his vision Daniel swore there was a strange glow coming over the old man. Had to be a trick of the moonlight, the fumes and his headache the man thought. Seeing Daniel, the Lesser was about to pass out, Olofi decided it was best to simply teleport but he needed a point of reference. Nudging Daniel, he asked "The front gates to Kemet should lie North East of here, correct?" Through a fit of coughing Daniel nods that is indeed correct. Looking around to see if anyone could be watching Olofi bends down to scoop up the unconscious man and the satchel before teleporting them a little way in the desired direction. Once he felt they had gone far enough, Olofi peers out of the pocket dimension he had created for them and spotted a copse of elder trees a fair distance from the front gates to Kemet. The good news was that they were far from the grasses that had come down with whatever the ailment that was ravaging the lands here. Olofi made sure he still looked presentable as an elderly mortal man and gently laid both Daniel and the satchel down.

He decided to set up camp for the night so they could explore the city in the morning. Daniel slept most of the night and didn't even stir when they were eventually approached by lurking predators, but Olofi quickly scared them away by briefly showing his true self before screaming at them. Daniel finally began to stir as the sun rose. He shielded his eyes and attempted to roll over to hide from the rays of light. Chuckling Olofi nudged him with a foot admonishing "You've slept long enough. We need to get into the city proper to get our bearings. I want to be around when the gathering begins at the citadel." Still groggy from their brief stint through the poisoned grasslands Daniel squints in confusion as he realizes they had journeyed nearly to the city gate of Kemet. He had no recollection of leaving the putrid grasslands. "How..." he began but was cut off by Olofi "Don't worry about it. You rested then safely escorted me here after your head cleared. Luckily, we were not accosted by brigands or predators as you feared."

Try as he might, Daniel recalled none of that and it bothered him. Getting up to dust himself off, the man could still feel a slight haze as if there were remnants of the fumes in his lungs. Looking to the gates they could see the changing of the guard as two city shields relieved the night shift of their post. The looming silhouettes of tetsuo blades slung over their backs was unmistakable. Gesturing towards them Olofi asks "Will they be a problem getting passed?" Shaking his head as if to clear it Daniel responds, "Tensions are very high right now, but as long as you're not a revenant or strange shadow realm creature they should let you pass easily." Nodding his understanding Olofi confidently strides towards the gates with Daniel rushing to catch up once he noticed the older man had stepped off.

The fresh sentries noticed them coming almost as soon as they left the cover of the trees, they had made camp within the night before. Olofi noticed Daniel's demeanor change the closer they got to the gates as if he were trying to shrink himself. As they got closer, they could see one of the guards wearing the armor and sigil of the city shields was a rather large woman with deep ebony skin and long ropes of locs trailing behind her. Nudging her partner who was by no means a small man, they both turned in the traveler's direction as they approached the gates of Kemet proper. The male guard seemed to be a bit older, still heavily muscled beneath his armor most likely with an air of boredom in his eyes despite the times. Raising a hand, the woman stated flatly "State your business, trading has been postponed until further notice." Surprised by her gruffness Olofi replies "I am Lofin, and this is my assistant Daniel the Lesser. We are here to have council with the fire forged." It was true that more and more of the scattered so-called fire forged had been migrating back to Inciniba since some of the true descendants had come back to replace the group of impostors but the mention of Daniel caught the attention of the male city shield.

The two shield members briefly huddled before they both began chuckling and pointing. When they had composed themselves, the older guard asked "Isn't this the one who claimed to have a throne in some land nobody's heard of? Weren't you run out of here for your lying tongue?" Daniel stood silent trying to absently adjust his armor. As he looked into the city shields eyes a slight glow came to Olofi's eyes as he said calmly "Whatever his transgressions were before, I will vouch for this man now. May we pass?" The smirks on their faces vanished when they saw the power exuding from the old man. Stepping aside they let them pass but Daniel was still frozen in shame until Olofi once again nudged him. Sheepishly he followed. Daniel noticed how they regarded Lofin differently as they passed but looking on him as they walked, he could not see what had changed. He internally vowed to pay better attention as he had obviously missed something back at the gate. Something was definitely off with this old man, but he could not quite put a finger on what it was.

True to the words of the city shields the market place did indeed look to be shut down at present, but the city was still bustling with foot traffic as people were gathering supplies in what must be preparation for this hunting party Olofi heard about in Tanji. Off in the distance just north of the city the parapets of the citadel could be seen. Atop the building three elder dragons were also in evidence, one silver, one gold and the third black. All were preening themselves as onlookers gawked in amazement. Once again Daniel seemed rooted where he stood as Olofi noticed what appeared to be a tavern of some kind. A sign over the top of the entrance said "Salim's" "Come Daniel the Lesser, you look like you could use some libation at the moment." It was obvious that Daniel did not have the greatest reputation here which shouldn't have surprised Olofi given how he was regarded in the smaller village of Tanji. Once again, the man looked as if he was trying to physically shrink as they approached.

Touching him lightly on the shoulder Olofi gestured for Daniel to lead the way. Suddenly Daniel for reasons unbeknownst to him felt a jolt of confidence. Opening the door to Salim's the man's shoulders were held back, chest and head high as he surveyed the other patrons there. Many he had a hard time seeing as plumes of varying smoke permeated the air. No doubt the place was packed though. They made their way to a table. Leaning over Daniel mumbled "Unless something else happened during our travels I am pretty sure I am still short on coin." Olofi waived away his concerns and gestured for the proprietor to come serve them. The god in disguise noticed a changeling doing a horrible impression of a Djaemon was one of the servers and nobody else seemed to notice. There were soldiers no doubt trading war stories real and imagined as some recounted recent events. The owner after a while came to greet them "Hello! Welcome to Salim's! My name is Akachi, what can I get for you?" she said with a dazzling smile.

"What a lovely creature you are! We would like two of your most potent drinks, whatever the meal of the day is and likely lodging if you have anything available." Olofi said while producing a small pouch that thumped heavily on the table. Before Akachi could scoop it up Olofi asked "What currency do you accept here?" Raising an eyebrow, she said "Naira, what else would there be? In some cases, a proper barter could be acceptable. Olofi nods and lets her hand go. Almost imperceptibly there was a small flash of light that caught Daniel's eye beneath the old man's hand during the brief exchange. Akachi opened the small pouch and seemed satisfied with its contents and went about filling their order. When she was out of ear shot Daniel grinned as he asked, "Are you a grifter with a little bit of unesiphiwo?" Confused and then finally understanding Olofi shakes his head and replies "Daniel the Lesser, do you take me for some two-bit conjurer looking to swindle these people because you have a slippery tongue that has a hard time doling out reality when you choose to wag it?"

Seeing that those words had stung Olofi reassures him "I know that was harsh but that's why you are now Daniel the Lesser. Seek to achieve what you previously boasted about being and you can at the least be respectable again. I am not what you think I am and I doubt you would believe me if I told you. Keep your head down as you have been. Try to keep that mouth shut and when it is time to act, do so with integrity. Do just that and you shall be fine." Just as Daniel was thinking of responding the drinks and meal came. K'mbo the server who looked like an unhealthy Djaemon heaved two large plates of bedrahin steaks and some kind of buttered tuber. Two tankards of ale were slammed on the table as the red skinned server stepped off saying, "Enjoy the dragon's piss!" Perplexed Daniel said, "He's joking right?"

Placing a hand on the tankard Olofi closes his eyes briefly before opening them and laughing before taking a healthy swig "It is indeed a jest, or maybe the name of this particular brew?" Relieved Daniel takes a sip himself and briefly allows himself to relax as the headiness of the drink takes over after the initial burn. They tucked into their food with gusto and Daniel was amazed by not only the amount of food the old man could put down, but the speed with which he devoured it was unbelievable. He jokingly hooked an arm around his own plate as if to protect it. An abnormally pale shin and thigh were in Daniel's face unexpectedly. Daniel the Lesser found himself staring at a strange tattoo of a tusk on the intruder's leg. He refused to follow the lines to where the base of the tusk lead. "I'm Eron White friend, but I think you knew that already since you were run out of this city seasons ago, correct…King Daniel?"

Once again Daniel tried to shrink within himself taking a long pull on his drink. Everyone seemed to have stopped their revelry to see how this was about to play out. With subtlety Olofi tapped Daniel on his elbow as he reached for some seasoning before diving back into his plate. Daniel's head snapped up to meet Eron's eyes finally. "Just because very few or your kind are allowed to walk amongst us freely doesn't give you the right to badger me. I successfully escorted this old man here through packs of Inja Enkulu, revenants and even some beasts from the shadow realm. Let us eat in peace." Incredulous Eron looks back and forth from the two at the table. When Olofi didn't immediately confirm Daniel's tale he broke out in laughter. Many of the other patrons joined him causing Daniel to sweat. Pleadingly he looked at the old man continuing to scarf down food at a ridiculous clip.

Eron continued "I have fought alongside many here against hordes of Djaemon warriors. Held off swarms of drakes when someone decided it would be a great idea to light ukutshaya leaves near a nest making them awake in a frenzy. Faced a mighty Ibhere on my own and lived to tell the tale. The difference between my tales which sound tall and yours? I have usually had witnesses to my feats. Your charge here doesn't seem to have experienced what you say. Much like your non-existent kingdom, or other adventures. Hopefully he didn't swindle you out of too much good sir." Olofi took his time wiping his mouth and taking another healthy pull on his drink. He wanted Daniel to sweat and learn his lesson, but would not leave him hanging in the end. Shaking his head Eron turned to leave. As Daniel's head began to hang low Olofi spoke up for him "What the lad told you is true."

He continued "I tasked him with getting me here safely from the small village of Tanji just south of here. You all know at least in part of what these lands have been going through and I am here to convene with the fire forged to see if we can remedy some of that. Now I know Daniel the Lesser has spun some crazy yarns to some of you before and you may feel the need to distrust him for that. I cannot blame you. I only ask that you judge him by his actions going forward and we will work on that wagging tongue of his." With that most of the patrons in Salim's roared again in laughter. Some even came to pat them roughly on their shoulders. Eron simply raised his tankard to them and went back to his party. Leaning in Daniel whispered his thanks to Olofi who nodded and mumbled so only they could hear "Confidence is good, but bragging without the deeds to back it up can be dangerous. I would think you had learned this lesson a long time ago Daniel the Lesser."

Grateful for the old man's support Daniel just couldn't help but ask "When will you stop calling me that?" Chuckling he replied "When you become greater Daniel…greater than the lies you told, and when you truly stand for something greater than yourself. Now who is the golden boy with the tattooed legs?" K'mbo brought them fresh drinks and cleared the plates but looked to Olofi and said, "You are not as you appear." In response he took another healthy sip before adding "Now that is irony at its finest. Almost as if he was about to burn under the old man's gaze, the server quickly dashed back to the kitchen.

Daniel caught the exchange but was confused as to its significance so answered the original question "That blonde wonder is Eron, the silver-tongued savage. The rest of his people are pretty much banished from these lands because they have a reputation for not respecting the people native to them. Most have been exiled back to the isles from whence they came." Looking around Olofi could see he was indeed the only one of his complexion in evidence here, but thought it curious that this lone example was allowed to stay while others were not. That notion was shattered when three more city shields walked in escorting two more similarly colored folk along with a true Djaemon warrior, but something seemed off about the latter as well. Following the eyes of the old man to the new arrivals Daniel stammered "I am not lying

Lofin! These are indeed strange times. Up until recently Eron was the only one of his people given leave to move about freely here. By the look of the escort detail with them, they will be heading back to the Ilses soon."

Waving away the young man's concern Olofi studied the Djaemon of the group more closely. He was tall, broad shouldered and heavily muscled like most of his kind. What was unusual was the fact that his skin was nearly unblemished by scarring as most Djaemon would be at his age. The three city shields had tetsuo blades on their backs. Two males that were nearly identical but it was hard to tell as the bottom half of their faces were covered, and a tall woman that was obviously in charge by the way the other two regarded her. Something was also odd about one of the exiles legs. More specifically one of his legs. It looked to be made of a strange metal, and Olofi could feel a strange energy coming from it. In fact, he was sure he could hear it but no one else seemed to notice. The female exile had strange armor on but they seemed to have been stripped of weapons for now.

This group would indeed bear watching but Olofi felt that as peculiar as they seemed, he doubted they had caused the ailment spreading on this world for which Olorun decided it was necessary to send an aspect of himself to witness personally. He was about to ask if there was any information on these people when a loud roar erupted from the citadel that could be heard from the Mulanje peaks. At that just as fast as they appeared the city shields and their three exiled escorts got up to file out of Salim's along with most of the patronage. Signaling Akachi Olofi asks when she came over "Where is everyone going?" Disappointed at most of her customers storming out she replies, "That was Kibo making it known that they were about meet to decide on the hunting party to catch this…Motu?"

Olofi had never heard the name before and from the quizzical look on Daniels' face he too was unfamiliar. "Ah, I see. I guess that's our cue as well then. You never said whether lodging was available?" Akachi assured him that they would have a room available by the time they returned before going to tend to those that remained in the tavern. Olofi got up and went out to head to the citadel with Daniel in tow. They just followed the crowd out of the city proper to the looming tower of buildings just north of them. Most impressive were the three elder dragons perched on metal outcroppings that were clearly made for such a purpose. Daniel was unsure but it looked as if all three looked in their general direction as soon as Lofin was at the base of the citadel. At this distance the man felt he could easily be mistaken though and ignored it. The elder dragons roared again this time in unison making all but Olofi and the fire forged present flinch. They were stopped at the gates and told only fire forged or those part of the hunting party selection would be permitted inside.

Olofi stepped up and explained "I am Lofin from a long line of fire forged far north of here. This is my ward from a small boy and my protector now that he is able. My sight wanes from time to time in my old age but I should be allowed to enter." Before they could question his legitimacy Olofi opened his hand to produce a small flame to prove he did indeed have the ability to practice ilangantye. With that brief display the guards let them pass. Luckily Daniel noticed that the previous inhabitants looked to have been replaced so hopefully nobody would remember him. Gone were the pompous men and women in ridiculous robes and armor skulking around with an air of superiority. He had heard rumors that the true fire forged had returned, but didn't believe it until now. Daniel had no occasion to enter the Inciniba until now. Slowly they made their way up to the rooftop where the dragon perches were.

There was some spirited debate when it came to who was going to go on this mission. Many of the fire forged wanted to go in addition to some of the city shields. A delegation of Pantu tribesmen and a clan from the Gcina Okubomvu in the red desert were also putting their bids in. The elder dragons it seemed had their own ideas and wanted to simply fly and get the suspected culprit themselves. Olofi had not spent a lot of time on this world but he knew that if things were dire enough for the Djaemon to be here cooperating with mankind, things had to be extreme. He tried to nudge his way forward to hear more of the conversation. He felt he may have gotten a little too close when all talking came to an abrupt halt. For Daniel there was no doubt this time as three sets of huge draconian prismatic eyes were all staring intently at Olofi.

The black elder dragon Kibo craned his neck as if to scrutinize the old man before greeting him "Sidibene kakuhle, I am Kibo, this is Shira, and Mawenzi. What brings you all the way down from grand Izulu?" Murmurs of confusion rippled through the gathering as Olofi tried to avoid the attention but it was just not possible so he simply greeted them in return "Sidibene Kakulhe. I am Lofin, and I wasn't sure any of you knew of Izulu's existence down this way. I am here to merely observe and to take account since there was a pall sweeping the lands here." Kibo's eyes narrowed at what was obviously a false name but if the orishas had sent a representative here they must have their reasons so he would not be the one to oust them. The elder dragons all felt and recognized this one's power and true nature regardless of the appearance. The fire forged were curious as they had never seen the elder dragons pay this much respect or deference to any human before, especially a newcomer. With few exceptions Kibo looked more likely to bite your head off than speak to you. Here he not only greeted this old man officially but then went on to introduce the other elder dragons. Yasuke, the leader of the fire forged took a mental note of this as he had never heard of Izulu or where this land was, but obviously Kibo had. He would have to remember to ask him later when they were alone.

Kibo sensed that Lofin was trying to maintain a low profile and so he would not press him here. Thinking on it a god could be useful if this magus they were after could open rifts into other dimensions. The elder dragon would have to think on how they could make use of that option if Motu tried to escape as he had before, but he didn't know if Lofin would indeed only catalogue what was happening here without truly getting involved. The Pantu tribesmen, city shields from Kemet and even the Djaemon were all trying to tag along which could complicate things. The only group that wanted nothing to do with this hunt surprisingly were the Elinanye. They had apparently gone back to their precious woodlands and walled themselves off from everyone else. A selfish act to be sure but given the results of messy situations in the past, Kibo understood. They were wrong to think they could insulate themselves from the malady of the world when this corruption had seeped into the crystal conduits these elder dragons had constructed deep within their lairs. The Elinanye had no way of knowing that though. It wasn't like they had stayed to hear everything that had transpired.

Rolling his large eyes Kibo vowed to humor those wanting to come along knowing they would cover the distance long before anyone here could make the journey southwest to the dead marshes. K'Ain the ruler of the Djaemon contingent present was determined to go and the elder dragons knew they could do nothing to stop them. The Pantu tribesmen would be riding their dire panther mounts but the ability the Djaemon had to sandcast would be the fastest overland travel method second to flying. As it was the elder dragons would be the tip of the spear so to speak. Hopefully they would have Motu well in hand by the time the other groups arrived. Sensing how annoyed Kibo was becoming with this entire situation Mawenzi the golden elder dragon had an idea so she addressed the Djaemon ruler "K'Ain, you are aware of the so-called necromancer's ability to dimension hop?"

Surprised at being addressed directly by the elder dragons K'Ain nods that he does in fact know of this variable. Mawenzi continues "Good. Your group may be the fastest behind us. He may use that ability to escape our net. We may devise a way to communicate with you in case we have to improvise our strategy. We know from researching that he has turned a lot of your kind into his minions.

Some he fought against with the group of magi he formerly belonged to and later he apparently gleaned from scattered clanless who do not follow the teachings of Serat, your blood god." Kibo interrupted remembering something he discovered through the brief connection with Motu when he attempted to control the conduit crystal in his lair "The Magus has more than just Djaemon revenants now. Wild beasts, some long forgotten priests from a temple near your lair Shira, Iigbin, and possibly Bayaka as well. I know he unleashed some denizens from the shadow realm but to my knowledge they are not under his control."

It was obvious the elder dragons did not agree with the other groups tagging along but there was no stopping them as all felt they had a stake in the outcome of this hunt. Politics aside Zaniah and her city shields just wanted to get to work, capture this criminal for the damage he had done and go back to normal city policing and security measures. This was taking time and effort away from their normal duties and she was sure that street level trouble makers were taking full advantage while their attention was elsewhere. The groups traveling on foot and mounts overland went about preparing for the trek. Kibo and the other elder dragons agreed to give them a head start. Olofi saw the city shields from earlier heading back to their barracks with the exiles in tow. There was tangible tension between one of the largest members of the Djaemon clan members and the unscarred Djaemon grouped with the exiles. Most of the gathering dispersed until only the elder dragons, Yasuke, Olofi and Daniel remained.

They stood in awkward silence before Yasuke said, "Anyone want to tell me what I am missing here? It's obvious you are more than you appear. Kibo didn't treat you as the lowly vermin the rest of us seem to be to him most of the time. Who are you really…old timer?" Expectantly all three elder dragons once again fix him with a glance curious to see if he would actually reveal his true form to the men present. Daniel also knew something was different but felt this old man was nothing but a fellow grifter with a bit more talent than he or many others he had come across. Looking up Olofi asked, "Kibo, Shira, and Mawenzi lend me your wings for a bit to hide from prying eyes?" As the elder dragons and Yasuke approached the old man signaled for Daniel to step away and keep an eye out. Disappointed he acquiesced as the huge creatures came down from their perches. The roof thudded mightily when each of them touched down but held firm to everyone's relief.

Yasuke was a bit confused but crowded in as the elder dragons spread their wings to form a sort of winged tent hiding Olofi as he revealed himself in his godly form to Yasuke explaining "As you already know Kibo I am indeed from Izulu. Olofi is who I am but while here address me as Lofin. The creator, the sky god wanted to know why the world here has been changing as it is and sent me to be boots on the ground so to speak. I am as far as I know only to take account of what's happened and then report back when summoned. Things have become dire but I am not to aid you or remedy any ills here. Some of us have simply become…curious. Tell no one else of this." The elder dragons seem unimpressed as they could see his true form all along.

Yasuke on the other hand was dumbfounded. Breaking out of his trance he asked, "Does your boy Daniel know?"

Changing swiftly back into his mortal disguise Olofi answers "No, I want to ensure he acts as if he is traveling with a mortal man to ensure his intentions remain true to his real self. Knowing there's a god in your midst can change how one acts and feels. I am interested in guiding him yet not influencing too much. I could of course make him do as I wish but where's the fun in that?" With a nod the elder dragons knew they could reveal him again and went back to their perches. Daniel pretended not to be looking in their direction although he had been trying to peek the entire time. All he got was muffled conversation and hints of light. Looking out they could see the Pantu Tribesmen with their panther mounts preparing for the journey along with a platoon of city shields, and the Djaemon. They planned to ride out in a days' time.

Chapter One

Back in Tanji Mael, Simon, Jamaal and Kanaa are still helping out with clean up duties so the villagers can go back to normal life. Mael is struggling to hold in his disdain for this place. The place that took his mother and rejected him is now where he and his newfound family are lending their hands and talents. Simon thinks this could be therapeutic for the boy. He has grown a bit since they last saw him, and no doubt the kid's prowess in battle is likely a hot topic. Anyone wishing to oust him again will think twice. When it's announced that there are more revenants and creatures from the shadow realm milling about aimlessly near the river and at the base of the mountain ranges Kanaa quickly volunteers to head out with the city shields from Kemet who remained with the local fishermen and warriors. Jamaal gabs his huge tetsuo blade and follows suit.

Mael wanted to go as well but the slow negative head shake from Simon told him to stay behind. "Let them go. They're still processing their loss in all of this chaos." The old Magus reminds him. Mael knew this to be true but he also knew that part of why Simon wasn't following was because Kanaa at least partially blamed him for that loss. Part of her likely thinks if Simon had not come back into their lives, their daughter would still be alive. The fact that the extreme conditions affecting the lands and magic conduits according to the elder dragons were caused by someone else would not focus her ire anywhere else.

They all had history that Mael was curious to know but also did not want to cause more pain by prying open old wounds. Disappointed he stayed behind doing menial cleaning and repair jobs helping people he knew were whispering behind his back.

Meanwhile at the village entrance Kanaa and Jamaal were waiting to be assigned to a team to go route out undead fiends and random agents of chaos from the shadow realm that were still popping out of seemingly nowhere. "If this other magus was the one who brought these creatures into our realm, then why are they still appearing long after he is gone?" Kanaa whispered to Jamaal. The large man simply swept back his grey locs and shrugged leaning on his tetsuo sword.

Finally, a burly villager with a sour look on his face waved them over. "I am Otemu, head fishermen and one of the leaders here in Tanji. As grateful as we are for the help some of the others have reservations about heading out on patrol with you two. You're stuck with me I'm afraid. Up ahead on the river bank there are the walking dead and now something else has recently appeared. Two creatures like the others from the shadow realm but much larger. If you can stay at a distance to annoy and distract them, when an opportunity comes you and I will bring it down. I hope that blade isn't just a large ornament."

With that they split off in various directions. Jamaal, and Kanaa followed Otemu towards the river bank while the other groups went to the flatlands prior to the mountain base from whence the revenants had come from before. Kanaa was curious as to why any of them would be wary of teaming up with them but she had her suspicions that their association with Mael was the source. It would have to wait. A knowing look from her husband told her he had the same thoughts. With a flourish and a shake of his head Jamaal crept forward. Soon there were staggered sounds of something being dragged through sand, a pause then continued dragging.

Initially the tall reeds and willows leading to the river front hid what was moving but once it made its way into the foliage that had grown tall, they could see it shifting as the creature lumbered through. They all froze waiting for whatever it was to come out. When it finally breached the shrubbery, they were all aghast as an Iigbin revenant crawled out with a partial arm grasping for purchase with each pull. The other arm was completely missing and it was supremely obese. Otemu went to swing down with his long spear but Jamaal cut him off "Save your strength, only fire seems to get rid of these things permanently. You'll just create a bunch of little creepy crawlies." He advises.

Placing his tetsuo blade in the ground Jamaal pulls out a gourd that should not have fit in the seemingly small pouch at his side. Kanaa gives him a disapproving look as she realizes what it is. The revenant begins flailing about when he pours the liquid on it. They all step back as Kanaa figures out what he has planned. She nocks an arrow into her small crossbow with a cloth tied to its head. On second thought she takes the arrow head off completely leaving only the material which Jamaal douses in the fermented drink from the gourd.

Kanaa briefly turns her head as the pungent aroma causes her eyes to water. With a small fire-starting kit Jamaal produces a few sparks then a flame that immediately catches when it touches the doused cloth. Kanaa then aims at the still moving Iigbin revenant letting the headless arrow fly. The velocity of the headless arrow is still enough to puncture it, but most importantly the liquid poured over it bursts into flames causing the lethargic movements to become frantic. There's a horrible screeching before the creature finally goes still. The smell is abhorrent, and it takes a monumental effort for them all to keep from emptying their bellies.

The group moved further down the bank but kept near the reeds approaching the water to obscure their approach while also letting the foliage notify them of movement towards or around them. What they came upon next would not hide well in any environment. The ground shook mightily as huge beasts from the shadow realm stomped about. There were indeed two of them but luckily, they were not in the same area. Hopefully they would be able to take one out without the other coming to its aid. "That last encounter was strange." Jamaal commented.

Whispering to remind them to keep quiet as possible Otemu replies "How so? Isn't this all a bit…strange?" Thinking on it Kanaa agrees "Right, when they came to attack our home east of Kemet the revenants never made any noise that I can recall or even so much as winced when further damage was done to their already mangled bodies. The city shields and Djaemon we spoke to also commented on their relative silence when being visibly injured. Makes it a bit creepier." Nodding his concurrence Jamaal adds "I don't think that thing was calling out in pain but perhaps it was warning others of our approach."

Peering out from their cover they could see there were more revenants gathering to mill about near the river front they were making their way to. Then the stomping intensified as the larger shadow creatures began picking up the pace trampling groups of revenants and they soon realized why they were so mauled when encountering them. Truth be told it was a bit of a relief as they were inadvertently helping Tanji and Kemet out. The downside was that they too would have to be taken care of. Signaling to the other groups in the distance that they could see, Otemu makes sure they all wait for the shadow beasts to disable a majority of the revenants. At worst they would have to come back to ensure the mangled moving corpses were burned properly later.

Jamaal was studying the shadow creatures lumbering movements. Noting when it swung the large blunt weapon that was dragging behind it, and the stomp patterns. Waving a hand, he says "I dub thee Shadow Harbinger." Kanaa shakes her head at how clever Jamaal thinks he is right now. The newly named shadow harbingers are very similar to the other creatures from their earlier battles. Long hair that looks to be blue or orange flames but no discernable heat coming from it. Unfortunately, in order to confirm there was no heat they would have to venture closer. Their skin was black as dark night and their eyes glowed to match their hair.

The huge clubs looked to be trees they had stripped of most branches but none of them recognized the species. Perhaps they were native to the shadow realm as well. When a majority of the revenants had been stamped nearly into oblivion posing no real threat Otemu decided it was time to begin their assault as a group. The party nearest the further shadow harbinger was obviously thinking similarly as they hurled spears at it. The beast turned at the attack, faster than anyone had expected given its size swinging low and horizontally catching nearly all four individuals. It sent three of them flying clipping the fourth with multiple sickening bone crunching smacks. The one that was merely clipped hugged his ribs slithering backwards into the foliage hoping to hide while the shadow harbinger angrily looked around confused.

Otemu saw the three villagers land lifeless a good distance away and hoped not to repeat that scenario. Whispering again he asked, "Are you a great shot with that?" Offended Kanaa answers "I am but with the size of that thing I don't have to be." Waving away her bristling at him questioning her prowess Otemu continues "Keep to the cover but create some space between you and that thing before taking the shot. We will try and get its attention when it faces us try and hamstring it if you can. I know that may be a tall task with small bolts and the size of it. When it turns in your direction, we will go in."

Otemu runs off whooping and making strange noises to get the beasts' attention. The harbinger slowly turns to track where the sounds are coming from giving Kanaa a chance to seek cover a fair distance away and waits for it to begin walking towards the head villager. The shadow harbinger starts running slowly at first but picking up speed and momentum despite dragging its large club. The ground was shaking with each step, and at the last moment it stopped suddenly using some of the built-up momentum to bring the club overhead for a massive downward swing.

Otemu rolls barely escaping the fate of becoming paste on the ground. Hoping she was a far enough distance away Kanaa aims in and lets three successive bolts fly from her crossbow. They whistle hastily through the air and there are three quick thuds eliciting a monstrous roar everyone in the area felt in their bones. Otemu takes a breath as the beast has its attention towards where Kanaa was hiding in the underbrush. Clenching its weapon, it begins to lumber to where it thinks pain was delivered from. Seeing he has an opportunity to attack from behind Jamaal runs in with his tetsuo blade trailing behind him. The harbinger began to turn back towards him just as he got close.

The reaction was surprisingly swift but would be too late to avoid or prevent the impending injury. With a horizontal strike Jamaal was able to slash at the back of the harbingers leg cutting deep partially severing the huge knee and hamstring of the left leg. The blood curdling howl brought the unwanted attention of the other shadow harbinger who was now rushing to see what could have harmed its companion. This gave Otemu a chance to check on the status of the other group they witnessed get swept away initially. Two of them were beginning to stir thankfully but the others remained motionless. Otemu realized he had to get back to his group to ensure there were no more casualties.

With the harbinger Jamaal slashed looking back attempting to mash him with a two-handed smash having dropped its club altogether, Kanaa put two bolts in the base of its neck. The ensuing howls soon turned into sickly gurgling sounds as it grasped at its neck. While still in pain and confused, Otemu throws his spear catching it in the shoulder but that stopped the other shadow harbinger in its tracks. Not wanting to lead it back towards the already downed villagers, Otemu resumes screaming and flailing while running towards the mountain base searching desperately for cover.

As the hamstrung shadow harbinger unsuccessfully fumbles to dislodge the spear, Jamaal uses the collapsed leg to spring up and swing with all if his might cleaving through muscle, sinew and bone of its neck severing the head cleanly. The huge head of what looks like blue flaming hair thuds to the ground while the body is felled slowly like a large tree. The dust settles to show that Jamaal successfully rolled to avoid being crushed under the weight of the beast. He and Kanaa turn to look to where the other shadow harbinger was in pursuit of Otemu.

Kanaa lets three successive bolts fly hitting the second shadow harbinger in the back of its legs but did not hit the knee joint this time. Howling and enraged the beast did not break stride in pursuit of Otemu who was now in a panic. Twirling the huge club over head while running the shadow harbinger shakes loose what might have been thorns or shards of wood from the alien tree. Otemu shrieked in pain as black barbs slashed into his skin. It was obvious Kanaa and Jamaal would likely not reach them in time to stop a bludgeoning the head villager would not recover from. Improvising Jamaal slung his tetsuo blade overhead and behind him. Taking a bit of a running start he lunged forward to sling his blade sending it flying end over end.

The loud whop whop sound caused the shadow harbinger to turn around just in time to catch the blade square in its large chest sending it tumbling to the ground effectively impaling it in place. The weapon seemed to be a normal size in comparison to the downed monster but its confusion was evident when it struggled to remove it. Kanaa kept a watchful eye on it as Jamaal went to check on Otemu and the other downed villagers. Otemu sat up hastily picking shards out of his skin. The pain seemed to intensify each time. Jamaal went to help but he waived him off as it had become, unbearable.

When he was able Otemu stood and went to check on the others now that the situation was somewhat under control. Two other groups further down river had successfully burned the revenants to lifeless ashes, but losses were minimal. The group just ahead of them had not fared well. As suspected only two of their number would make the trip back to Tanji and they were severely injured. The other villagers began to gather discarded weapons and their dead and infirm further down. Once they were sure the others would be fine with cleanup duty Otemu and Jamaal went back to the fallen shadow harbinger still struggling.

This one's hair and eyes were flame yellow and orange which contrasted wildly with its deep darkling skin. The grunting stopped and its terrifying eyes bored into them. Two city shields were approaching but neither answered their hails which made Otemu nervous. Jamaal thought he recognized them from their trip into

Kemet and he relaxed placing a hand on the head villagers shoulder offering "I believe these two are mute. City Shields who ride often with their commander." When they got closer, they could see the masks covering both of their mouths and the tetsuo blades along with their armor was further evidence that they were at least not enemies.

Akil and Rahil signed to Jamaal but he did not understand apologizing "I am sorry my friends, but I don't understand. I cannot retrieve my blade until that beast is killed. Can you do us a favor and end its suffering?" Nodding their understanding they took their blades off their backs and went to the last downed shadow harbinger which had stopped struggling as it realized its fate. Akil signaled to his brother he would handle it and Rahil put his blade away. Closing his eyes Akil picked up his tetsuo blade holding it overhead and behind him. Raising it high, he leaned back and sprung forward into a somersault coming down hard on the beasts' throat cleanly separating head from body.

The huge hands that were previously fumbling with the hilt of Jamaal's tetsuo blade stuck firmly in its chest went limp. There was a sickening sound when Jamaal leapt atop the beast and pulled the heavy blade out. He laid the blade down and began wiping the ichor from his weapon before applying some much-needed oil. Coming to kneel beside him Kanaa comments "How many seasons had we been living in relative peace with that thing standing as a lawn ornament in our front courtyard?"

Otemu limps over to them. "You two fight well and seem like good people. We are grateful for your help, but that boy…" Kanaa cuts him off before he could finish "Is a child! Was a child when he was forced to leave here by all accounts. I know that boy also lost his mother here and has no idea where his father is. I know it's a sore subject and we don't like to pry. I question his judgment with some of the company he keeps but he has been a good boy since we have known him. You judge him because he is different and has qualities that you cannot truly know or understand. For that you shunned that young man? If I find out you were the one to take his mother from him…" Jamaal reaches up to gently grasp her arm.

Nervously Otemu limps off followed by the other residents of Tanji who had come out to patrol. Akil and Rahil waited for Jamaal and Kanaa before they all headed back to the village. They reunite with Simon and Mael there. Mael is taken aback when Kanaa runs up to embrace him. Still racked with pain she begins to sob. Looking up Jamaal comes over to join them. Simon desperately wants to join in, but knows he is still on thin ice with Kanaa so he simply watches before gathering food for them all prepared by grateful village people, happy to have strangers helping to rebuild the damage done and help protect their borders from encroaching revenants and creatures from other realms.

Watching them from a distance was Otemu. Grateful as he was, he still did not like the idea of the boy returning here. It was thought the child was a bad omen when he was born and not long after his return another disaster strikes. The head villager did not believe in coincidences. No matter how passionate the woman was about this child. Otemu had a duty to protect his people.

Chapter Two

Deep below the dead marshes, Motu and Masindi lick their wounds having narrowly escaped from Kibo's lair. More accurately Motu was looking after his wounds, Masindi was relatively unscathed. The young dragon taken from the ether of magic from a commandeered conduit earlier than he should have been was indeed worried. The magus, a magus in training and the fire forged that have resurfaced did not instill fear in him, but the elder dragon was a very different matter. Being born into this world prematurely he was not fully developed and his abilities to fly and defend himself were severely underpowered if confronted by a fully actualized elder dragon.

Motu was still a bit disturbed yet intrigued with his new limb after having to improvise by fusing an arm to his newly acquired nub to make him whole again. He swore the Djaemon who had taken his arm would pay dearly when they met again. His skin was a deep mahogany brown yet paled in comparison to the limb he took from a fallen creature from the shadow realm. The residual pain from the ordeal had lessened a bit and he now had full control of it. There was a dull ache and felt as if his new forearm and hand were constantly vibrating but not so much that it was visually evident.

Looking closely, he could see small hairs with touches of orange, but one had to examine them closely or shine light to actually see them. The skin was so dark it seemed to swallow light. More importantly, now that his dexterity was coming back, he should be able to spell cast as he had in the past. With some spells pronunciation was not as important as the movements that went along with them. Motu had practiced the art of thought casting for spells that could be particularly difficult to say so long as the caster knew what it was supposed to sound like. An added bonus was that in battle hearing a magus preparing to attack was often an opportunity to get out of harm's way or to counter before they finished.

The hand flourishes were nonnegotiable. They had to be correct unless you were profusely gifted. There were some schools that thought innate talent was all that mattered and those that held to believing verbiage or movements had little to do with efficacy. Masindi watched as Motu practiced rather simple spells at first. Holding the hand palm facing upwards "Ukukhanya" Motu says. A small globe of light sprang to life floating there. "Eqaqambileyo!" he exclaims and the light intensifies. Closing his hand with a flourish the light disappears. Nodding more to himself Motu says "If they come, I will be ready. The side effects of this abhorrent fusion have started to diminish. They will have to dig deep to get to us but I will have G'Orn and the others continue to fortify this place until another option comes along."

Masindi sauntered over to the magus and hissed "It is not a matter of if, but when they come. You and the mighty Kibo are linked as you moronically trifled with his personal conduit as if it were some simple bauble. No matter where you go, he will soon follow." Looking around he continued "We are in the dead marshes, yes? The land here is soft and there are more than one elder dragon coming now from what I can tell. All of which dug into varying land masses to build their lairs. Let's not forget you unleashed the shadow realm on this world, and we have no account of everything that is now roaming about. That limb of yours may attract some of those denizens as well."

All of this was true yet the chastisement gave Motu an idea so he inquired "When you were last alive in this realm before being recycled into the magic ether, did you have a lair of your own?" Thinking on it, Masindi replies "I…am not sure. The tail end of my previous incarnation is a bit hazy to recall. I am not sure what stage of maturity I reached and I certainly did not make it to elder status. That may come as I grow. We retain a lot of our knowledge but not all." Motu had set revenant birds of prey out to patrol far above the dead marshes in hopes to see any overland approach coming in advance while they prepared.

If running through various portals was not an option as Masindi claimed, then time indeed was not on their side. Truth be told there wasn't much they could do with elder dragons being the main threat coming. Still marveling at his new limb, Motu went to G'Orn to see how the deep underground construction of battlements, traps and other obstacles to incoming encroachers were coming along. The myriad of revenant Djaemon, Iigbin, Inja Enkulu, shadow creatures and former tetsuo blade masters sworn to protect the ancient temple Motu discovered were all furiously digging and scraping at the direction of the two the magus had left sentient.

Motu could feel the undisguised contempt from the Djaemon siblings under his control but did not care as long as they did as he bade them. He was long past sentimentality. Suddenly the ground all around them began to quake furiously and the magus closed his eyes to peer through the eyes of the birds in the area under his sway and saw nothing near them or even on an approach vector. Confused he opened his eyes and exclaimed "What treachery is this?!" Looking at G'Orn accusingly thinking the Djaemon had found a way to circumvent his influence and betray his location somehow.

Fearing a reprisal G'Orn just threw his hands up shaking his head negatively as things continued to rumble even harder. Angrily Motu pounded the floor with his staff magically reinforcing the underground cavernous fortress he had built for him and his hopefully soon to be revived love still encased in her own makeshift mausoleum for the time being. Before he could ask again a rather large head bursts through the ceiling of the chamber, they were in. A forked golden tongue sprang from a black and gold crenelated reptilian mouth full of jagged teeth. It was obvious there was more to this beast when the neck still within started to vibrate quickly causing the rumbling sound, eventually freeing it for them to observe.

Motu and the gathered revenants all stood briefly frozen as the creature was fully revealed. Shaking the moist sediment of dirt and rock from its body, it slid from the confines of what it just burrowed through to get there. It screeched menacingly sending the sound echoing throughout the lair. The rumbling began anew announcing that it was not alone. Intrigued but wary Motu sent a blast of green energy into it from his staff and mentally commanded the revenants to attack but held the Djaemon chieftains of his sordid army back. He wanted a glimpse of what these beasts could do before eliminating them.

As part of the revenant work crew approached it, many were quickly swept aside after lashes from both a long neck and tail. When a few were able to get close golden talons lashed out making bodily chunks decorate the walls, floor and ceiling. From many directions more of its kind joined in the dismemberment of revenants. Hearing all the commotion Masindi quickly slither walked his way down to find the cause. "What in all of Esihogweni is going on?" he shouted.

Having seen enough Motu replies "A pod of Ninka Nanka I believe we may have disturbed a nearby den with our work here. Wound them but don't ruin them completely if you can. They may be useful in fending off our next visitors." Aiming his staff, the magus sends green strands of energy into the first invader making it screech and convulse until it lay still. G'Orn and his sister began weaving in and out ducking talons, vicious tail swings and snapping jaws using their black blades to hamstring or otherwise incapacitate the creatures. Although mindless, the former testuo guardians showed prowess above the other revenants but were less effective than Motu's two Djaemon lieutenants.

Masindi found himself surrounded but rolled his eyes at having to involve himself in this fracas reluctantly spewing a gout of noxious gas at them resulting in them seizing. Soon all was under control. Motu went around to turn fifteen or so of the salvageable Ninka Nanka into more revenant servants. Many of the original group he brought there had been turned into useless squirming bits that would need to be removed and burned. A moment later the two great serpents slithered in. Eyes narrowing Masindi asked "Were you two on break? Your timing is impeccable."

The basilisks simply stared in reply. Motu and G'Orn took stock of their casualties but ascertained that these additions were actually better at digging than most of the mindless revenants doing so before. All was not lost, and perhaps these beasts could be a deadly trap to spring on others that may attempt to dig their way in. An elder dragon would have no issue of course but for the city shields from Kemet, fisher folk from Tanji, Djaemon and Pantu tribesmen and remnants of the fire forged, these beasts could pose quite a threat. Especially if they don't know they were here waiting for them.

Masindi shook his scaled head and slunk off muttering while G'Orn, and the rest of the revenant army renewed their efforts to fortify the cavernous lair deep below the swampy dead marshes. Motu closed his eyes concentrating on reaching out to his avian revenants patrolling the skies around the dead marshes or perched in the trees. Through their sight he could see as quiet as it was now that they survived the Ninka Nanka intrusion, it would not remain so for long. An assortment of warriors were now gathering where the foothills ahead of the Mulanje mountain ranges gave way to the entrance into the swamps.

The advance group had arrived to set up camp, survey the lands and likely begin planning their siege. Motu desperately wanted to attack them now before their plans were set but knew the elder dragons would not be far behind. Coming out now would only reveal his location faster and if Masindi was right about his direct connection through the conduit in the black elder dragon's lair, being caught out in the open too soon would be a death sentence. It was highly likely that end result was unavoidable either way but the magus would make them work for it. Motu could not only see through his avian minions for their bird's eye views, but he could also hear.

A sound was signaling the coming presence of Pantu tribesmen and their mounts, marching in from the west. Word had spread fast from Kemet and Tanji. The rhythm of the tribesmen as well as their footfalls resounded along with their voices announcing their impending arrival. Using revenant eyes Motu looked to the west and witnessed long lines of Pantu Tribesmen on foot flanked by their superbly trained and famed dire panther mounts. There was a sonorous call and response between one of the leaders riding his mount at the front of the procession, and those filing in behind him.

The other groups gathering on the other side of the dead marshes could not help but hear them. "Yo hey da lo! Yo hey da lo! Yo hey da lo! Yo hey da lo apantu!" …" Yeka!" The sun was setting as the Pantu tribesmen halted after wading through the dead marshes. They began to feed and water their dire panther mounts and the leader went to greet his counterparts from the city shields of Kemet, and Djaemon clan from Gcina Okubomvu. Motu noticed that the Elinanye were conspicuously missing. He wanted to listen in but couldn't risk sending the revenant birds closer without drawing attention. Opening his eyes far below the gathering forces, the magus muttered mostly to himself "Quite the entrance for the grassland guardians."

Although it was true a large group of Pantu tribesmen and their mounts all moving in perfect step, cover and alignment was very impressive, the next arrivals would indeed upstage even them. As the sky was darkening, parts were lighting up with fire, ice and cosmic energy. The mobilizing forces look skyward to see Kibo, Shira and Mawenzi in formation occasionally spewing their projectiles. Keen eyes could spot Yasuke, the leader of the resurfaced fire forged sitting where the base of Kibo's neck met his gigantic black wings joining in the fun by practicing ilangatye midair adding flames to the elder dragon's projectile energy.

Frantically the eclectic gathering of forces moved to make way as it appeared three elder dragons were about to land amidst them so some scattered to avoid being inadvertently trampled. As if they were in aerial formation, they made a simultaneous landfall without disturbing so much as a blade of grass. The pantu tribesmen appreciated the precision movements and even the slight jump scare it gave to those closest to the where all three large creatures set down. The three majestic creatures slowly fanned their wings to settle into a comfortable position giving strong yet still gentle gusts of winds to them all.

They had all arrived and time was getting desperately short. Kibo lays one of his wings at an angle allowing Yasuke to slide down from his perch. As if he knew he was being watched the entire time Kibo's prismatic black eyes begin to glow as he speaks directly to Motu through their magical link. "By now, you know we are here. I can feel that you and your…collection of ill created abominations deep below the boggy marshes we stand upon. You could save us all the trouble of digging you out, but I know you shall not. You will pay one way or the other for the rot you have unleashed upon these lands, the corruption to my and my sister's conduits as well as the deaths you have caused. What say you, magus of ill repute?"

The Djaemon, Pantu tribesmen, City shields and others gathered heard the words of the elder dragon but were confused as to who they were addressing seeing that there was no magus in evidence. Peering into the marshes for a glimpse of the culprit they were all here to see brought to justice, they soon came to the conclusion that Kibo could communicate with the magus by means that were not apparent to them. Yasuke and the lead representative from each of the groups went about strategizing where the best dig sites were cross checking with the elder dragons to see if they would be effective given the relative position only the dragons could pinpoint.

Yasuke approaches Kibo waiting for a chance to speak with him alone. When the last of the delegation heads left, he asked "If we catch the magus here, will we seek justice by eliminating him or will we take him for judgement?" Thinking on it for a moment Kibo replied "Mawenzi and Shira feel the same as I do and would like nothing more than to turn this bastard into ashes, but we may need his help in undoing what he did. Taking him for judgement is a far better way to assess the damage he has done when others gather to tell their tales as witnesses to his unscrupulous use of his unesiphiwo. We may also learn who helped him do it. If all we wanted to do was immediately abort his existence, we need not have gathered you with us."

Contemplating all that Yasuke had to agree that was all true. If the elder dragons had the location of the magus narrowed down accurately and wanted to kill him, they could simply do so without risking any of those gathered. The idea of forcing this criminal to undo or fix this corruption sweeping the lands was commendable but unrealistic to the leader of the fire forged. With the amount of destruction and mayhem caused by the fell magus it was obvious these were not the deeds of a sane person, and therefore it was unlikely they would turn around and act according to reasonable or justified demands of his captors.

First things first, they had to actually capture him. They had staked out three sites surrounding the dead marshes where each of the elder dragons would dig almost meeting in the middle. The idea would be to delay when they started forcing those hiding below to be funneled into one of the others. The moist terrain was proving difficult at first as the initial strategy was not proving very effective. One problem was that once a sizeable hole was dugout, the surrounding mud and slag would collapse into it.

Yasuke came up with an idea that might work but would take all three elder dragons to begin the process. Kibo listened but was not impressed with his role. "Why am I the only one clawing my way through this muck?" he snarled. Shira and Mawenzi were silent but looking very amused as Yasuke answered "You said so yourself that you don't know what your breath would do the new caverns we create, but you are big and strong enough to dig a large hole, Mawenzi can bring forth fire taking away some of the moisture and solidify the walls as Shira follows up with ice to ensure they stay that way for our journey down there."

It made sense but the black elder dragon didn't have to like it. He looked around to ensure there was nobody directly behind him and even wagged his tail back and forth to emphasize he needed room. Then he began to dig furiously into the sludge sending mud flying behind him until he was halfway into the large hole. Springing out of it he yelled, "Mawenzi!" As soon as he cleared the breach the golden elder dragon leaned her head into the hole and emitted a huge gout of flames so intense even those that thought themselves far enough away felt it despite the fire happening underground.

When she was done Shira inhaled, stepped in and exhaled to freeze the new cavern over. Yasuke tentatively walked into the opening and it looked like it would hold, but if they were making a way for them to make their way down it was obvious the dragons could not go all the way without risking taking out some of their own when the fighting began. This would be a long tedious process and the elder dragons went about repeating the process at each chosen site. In the end the Djaemon, city shields and some of the Pantu tribesmen would go pursue the magus below ground while the dragons would wait at their chosen tunnel for Motu or anyone the magus might have down there with him fleeing the pursuit.

Far below Motu didn't have to use the sight of his avian revenants to know what was happening. He could feel the sediment above rumbling as the elder dragons disrupted things digging ever closer to the magic barriers, he constructed to keep marshes from caving in on him. At first, he thought perhaps he could take away those magical barriers and trap some of them, but feeling what was going on above let him know they had a way to stabilize the loose mud and dirt as they went along. "Oh well Kibo, come do your worst." Motu thought.

Chapter Three

Back in the Kemet dungeon, Zaniah interrogates Max and Sparks who stand accused of being exiles from the Isles of Esikrwada. Argos is being detained with them which seems strange since he is recognized as a Djaemon who may simply be clan less. Max and Sparks were reluctant but voluntarily came back after helping these people fight the strange invasion that took place. Sarcastically Max states "You know this is a funny way of expressing gratitude." They did not have them in a cell out of courtesy but it was obvious they were not free to leave until they figured out where they came from.

Zaniah took a different approach once she figured the silent treatment wasn't forcing them to confess that they were in fact from the Isles. Oluso raised an eyebrow when she began to shrug out of her heavy city shield armor top revealing a leather singlet beneath. Leaning her tetsuo blade against the wall she approaches Max. Both Argos and Sparks are confused but curious. Sitting down in front of Max Zaniah leans in close to say "What proof do you have that you are not from the Isles? With no proof eventually we will have to send you back to the lands you came from."

Shaking his head Oluso walks over to where Zaniah placed her blade. Purposefully taking off his greatcoat, he reveals gleaming ornate plate armor beneath that was obviously custom made. Form fitting and too pretty for Zaniah's taste she offers "Don't tell me that's what kept you from being skewered earlier." Making a show of taking what looked like a small pouch from one of the coat pockets Oluso replied "Yes in fact it is, and it was forged from the same ore that produced those wonderful blades some of you carry." She looked as if she did not believe him but figured that was a conversation for another time. Turning back to Max and Sparks she continues "Congratulations…back to you two."

Before either had a chance to respond Oluso interjects once more "As you may not know commander, I repaired their suits of armor and his leg which like I stated before was not forged or created in any of the lands we know, and I can prove that much." Walking over to the assumed exiles he points to a pauldron on Max's left shoulder asking, "May I?" With nothing to lose Max merely shrugs and nods his approval. Surprisingly Oluso takes little time extricating it from the rest of the armor. Zaniah makes note of that fact "inquisitor for something you should be unfamiliar with that was done very swiftly."

Going over to where the city shields tetsuo blade and his armor rested Oluso asks "Commander how flame retardant are these walls?" Turning around as confusion fills her face Zaniah abruptly says "This installation is well prepared for protection against flames. Why do you ask?" Nodding he unclips the hidden clasps of his plate armor and sets it next to her tetsuo blade before producing a flask that looks much too large to have been in the small pouch. Shaking it a bit, it begins to glow slightly while he explains "This flask holds what I think is the blue dragon flame from a long dead elder dragon if my recollection is correct. That pouch can be…confounding. Everyone should get to the other side of the chamber for this. Ask one of your shields men to fetch the garrison's smithy if you please."

Still unsure of where this was all going, Zaniah walks over to the chamber door opens it and signals to the guard outside that they need their smithy. With that done she goes to the opposite side of the wall her and Oluso's armor sits against along with her blade watching with no clue how this pertains to Max and Sparks. Looking towards the tetsuo blade and armor sets Oluso opens his stance as he takes hold of the stopper to the flask, pointing the aperture at the top towards the items. There's a strange popping noise as he removes the stopper.

Simultaneously the chamber door swings open as a long thin blue line of flame rushes out of the flask. "Why would…?" Zaniah begins but is interrupted as the loud whooshing sound reverberates through the chamber as the smithy enters having his eyebrows and facial hair flashed from existence. Max, Sparks, Argos, and Zaniah all raise their hands to shield their eyes from the bright flames as they wash over the blade and armor sets. Struggling Oluso tries to quickly replace the stopper extinguishing the flames, falling to his knees as he did so. Zaniah rushed to see if the smithy was injured. He quickly waived her off stating "I am fine dear one…look at your plates and blade!"

They were all red hot but not melting as Zaniah feared. Strangely they also cooled surprisingly quickly evidenced by Oluso walking over to pick his plate mail up without scorching his hands stating, "This gear was forged using itsimbi ore, a nearly invaluable material for arms and armor, however this is not." Holding up the pauldron taken from Max's strange armor, Oluso goes back into the pouch. This time producing a large crucible cauldron setting the shoulder plate in it. The smithy scrambles to put on a protective helm with an eye slit covered by super-heated sand covering that protects him from flying sparks as Oluso repeats the steps to unleash the blue flames.

Bracing himself again he unleashes a gout of blue flame into the cauldron, but in a more controlled manner this time. Falling again as he closes the flask, Oluso quickly stands asking the smithy "Do you have a skimmer with you?" Lowering his hands to protect his face from the heat of the flame the smith nods that he does before reaching into a large pocket in his apron. Handing the long-handled tool with holes in the disk-shaped cup at the end to Oluso as the others gather around to look in the cauldron where the pauldron had been turned into shiny liquid goop. Slowly the Inquisitor begins swirling the skimmer around in the melted down pauldron.

Zaniah kept an eye on them as Oluso tried to skim for slag to catch impurities in the ore. With everyone's attention on that she examined Oluso's plate armor more closely and was surprised when she could not budge it, not even in the slightest. Impossible! She thought. The city shield commander figured the man was bluffing about his armor being forged with itsimbi, or at most that it was merely plated with it over some other less rare ore. Oluso saw her struggling but ignored her efforts as he swept finding no slag or other impurities. Turning to the smith he asks, "Judging by the smell, and the lack of slag where would you assume this ore was mined from?"

Zaniah came over as the look of confusion contorted the smith's face as he tried and failed to recall where he had run into ore that gave off this pungent antiseptic odor or that lacked an abundance of impurities from the surrounding rock or mineral deposits from which it was mined. The man was stumped. Shaking his head "I cannot." Was all he could offer much to the dismay of Zaniah. Max and Sparks sighed in relief but the commander wasn't convinced. "This means nothing. The world is a large place Oluso. This may prove their gear is made of another rare ore but nothing more." She countered.

Confidently Oluso turned to the smith, silently asking him to confirm. There was still some residual heat coming from the tetsuo blade of the commander and the armor of the Inquisitors'. The smith approached them and looked to be sniffing each. Pointing to the sword he said, "This was forged by the monks at the very old monastery just past the grey moor woodlands across the Ulwandle Olumnyama, and the armor likely at the monastery in the red desert." Shaking her head in disbelief Zaniah went to protest but Oluso cut her off.

"You don't need to confirm that is where you had your blade forged but can you deny it?" he asks. Max and Sparks didn't understand the distinction but awaited her answer anyway. Zaniah simply answered, "I cannot deny it." And continued "That still doesn't prove their origins just because our smith cannot identify where their gear was forged. Oluso waves them all over as he once again stirs the melted ore with the skimmer explaining "Most smiths, yours included I assume is taught to recognize the ore they work with to determine the worth of the armor or weapon. They do this so they know what to charge for the work. The itsimbi ore is a tightly controlled commodity that also has moral implications as you well know. This has a strange smell to it but the most telling thing is that there are absolutely no impurities to be found in it."

They could all see it was true but the smith was the most confused of them all. Oluso went on "Where they come from a lot of their gear and weapons are not forged as they are here. They are created under unnatural circumstances by what they call machines. Likely this ore was not even mined but in fact artificially blended together from many different metals, improving the tensile strength yet making it light." Max shook his head and had to ask, "How could you know that?"

Everyone watched the inquisitor as he began putting the flask away in his pouch, looking around as if he was figuring out what to do with the cauldron before nonchalantly answering "That's simple...I've been to your dimension. My duties require me to travel often, and not all the answers can be found here." Shrugging back into her armor it was obvious Zaniah was not very happy about this new information. Some of it may stem from the fact that their own smith couldn't find fault with Oluso's theory about the stranger's armor and weapons. She thought perhaps they had simply found a smith on the outskirts of known civilizations who could have forged it for them.

The look she gave them as she gathered her blade said that this was not the end of her belief in them being exiles as she stepped out of the chamber. After a few moments the two mute city shields men that were often with the commander came in with the rest of Max, Sparks and Argos's gear. Setting it down they made their exit as Max and Sparks nervously inspected their kit before nodding that they were ready to depart. Argos said nothing as he sheathed his ornate blade on his back. Looking them over Oluso took a box out of the seemingly impossible pouch that was obviously much roomier than it appeared to be.

Opening the box Oluso then struggled to pour the melted remnants from the cauldron into it. Curious the smith helped stabilize it until the contents were in the box looking as if it were cooling rapidly into a solid block. Oluso then closed the box and after a brief moment there was a flash of light that shined through followed by some wisps of smoke. Max, Sparks, and Argos crowded in to see the results after an audible pop Oluso opened the box to reveal the pauldron in its previous form as it sat on Max's armor. Max was dumbfounded and stood there shocked as Oluso reattached it.

Looking him over Oluso asks "How is your repowered leg holding up?" Bouncing slightly to test if Max replies "It's good to go so far, and the armor readouts in the heads-up displays are in a language we don't recognize but everything seems operational. What was the power source you used? There doesn't seem to be an added battery. We were curious in case it runs out. Might need a way to replace it." Sparks nodded her agreement awaiting an answer as Argos looked on and the smith was now uncomfortably close to them examining their armor. Oluso continued packing as he put his own plate armor back on as he casually answered, "A soul".

Both Max and Sparks stopped what they were doing as did Argos who noticed their sudden apprehension. "So, you're just going to drop that little bombshell and not follow up with an explanation? I mean you also powered my EV suit and armor up as well. I'm grateful since I can fiddle with things to make the internal temperature controls work despite not understanding the strange glyphs that flash by on my wrist console or HUD inside the helmet. Souls were not exactly the alternative energy source we had in mind. You are starting to sound like the magus, warlock wizard guy everyone is all up in arms about here. Are you one of them?" Sparks asks.

Going over to check the smith for injuries he may have been ignoring Oluso shakes his head negatively saying "No, I am no magus. I am…something else. I have no unesiphiwo, but I am very attuned to it. I can sense its presence or when it has been used. Often when others investigating fail to find answers for crimes or just nefarious actions towards others, magic is what was used. It's also easily hidden from most city shields men, trackers, scouts or others who don't deal in the realm of magics. When I fully understand what I am…I'll let you know. For now, gear up. I feel another large disturbance or disturbances coming from the shadow realm. They may not trust you and think you are a couple of exiles because of your skin, but keep doing the right thing and they may have no choice but to leave you to go where you will."

They didn't like the sound of that as it seemed they could still possibly be deported to another strange land where the reception might be worse if the inhabitants thought they were traitors of some kind. Argos was not fully accepted yet by his people but it looked like that may be changing. The crazier things got, the less guilty she felt about the trouble she had gotten them all into back home. At least the galactic civil war between mankind and mutants she could wrap her head around. Elder dragons, magically animated undead revenants and holes being ripped in between planes of existence introducing other dangers trumped anything she had previously experienced. That was likely the same for Max and Argos. Now she just learned her armor was powered by a soul.

There was a resounding boom that made the very walls of the city shield barracks shake. "Jesus! That must be the disturbance you were talking about." Max sarcastically stated. Nodding Oluso replies "Indeed. I suggest we get above ground lest we be buried down here." They needed no further prompting. All of them hurried out of the chamber, running up to the street level exit where Zaniah was conferring with her other officers. Turning to them as they approached there was a hint of scorn in her eyes as she explained "There's been another dimensional breach, the largest creature we have seen yet from these phenomena. Many of our contingent that would normally be here are in the dead marshes with the Djaemon, Pantu tribesmen, along with most of the fire forged that would normally remain at the citadel. I still don't trust you lot, but unfortunately, we need all hands-on deck available for this."

Right on cue there is another thunderous boom. One of the city shields men came rushing to his commander screaming at Zaniah "The front gates won't hold for long! We need to get another unit around to distract that thing, Commander!" Thinking things over Zaniah then orders her shields men to take a group through the smaller portcullis at the north end of the city opposite where the huge invader was banging at the front gate. From the sound of things, it would not last under the onslaught. Not wanting to be first in line to get smashed by whatever was trying to get through the city gates Max, Sparks, Argos, and Oluso followed the city shields men to the smaller rear entrance hoping to get a glimpse at what they were up against before engaging.

The shields men went to a large turnstile with handles connected to a pulley system that raised and lowered the portcullis gate. Five of them took the handles and began to rotate it slowly raising the gate. Once it was high enough to let the rear guard out, they held it in position while the rest of them skulked out hoping to go unnoticed. Breaths were held with each creek and groan of metal, and there was a collective sigh of relief when the gate was then lowered without incident. Oluso walked over to Max and began dripping a strange smelling lubricant on the joints of his prosthetic leg and on parts of his armor. Noticing Sparks, he did the same to her armor.

When they were about to protest the inquisitor whispered "You both trudged through the red desert to get here. There may be sand and other grit that will cause your gear to make noise at a time we need to be silent. I have no idea how sensitive the ears of this huge beast or beasts are." Max agreed with the strategy but also figure if these things had eyes, they likely also had noses, and this stuff was pungent. They also noticed the two mute city shield men that usually stuck pretty close to their commander. Oluso figured Zaniah probably sent them along to keep an eye on them.

Once they started to creep around the outskirts of the city making their way to the front entrance it was obvious Akil and Rahil were likely sent for another reason entirely. Everything about them lent itself with silence in mind. Their movement was less than whisper quiet even when leaves and rocks were underfoot, and they communicated nonverbally. They took point and scouted out the areas before coming back to get the main group. Meanwhile from the sound of things the siege was continuing at the front gates. Soon they were nervously close. Stomps and ferocious snarls could be heard around the corner. Akil and Rahil were the first to take a look.

When they came back the look on their faces said it was horrifying. The looks alone froze the company in their tracks. Oluso was confused as were Max, Sparks and Argos. Max whispered "These guys have seen dragons and probably untold other crazy things. It cannot be that bad. They're playing us." Oluso and Sparks crept up to take a look for themselves. After a brief moment Max and Argos followed just as they got a peak from cover. "It's a lion." Sparks mutters under her breath. Max who came up just in time to barely hear whispers "See that's not so bad."

Terrified she turns to him and says "Yeah…no. Remember that ancient children's book Clifford the Big Red Dog? It's like that except it's a huge three story tall grey lion, and it looks pissed." Scooting up to get a look for himself Max replies "Oh…yeah when you put it that way. The book has a horribly different ending." Just then they could see the lion stop moving and begins sniffing the air before suddenly turning in their direction. Locking eyes with the group it starts stalking in their direction. Oluso interjects "We might want to back away now, slowly." As they cautiously do so Max whispers angrily "Says the guy who may have just sprayed us down with this world's version of catnip!"

Chapter Four

Sulking somewhere in the shadow realm sat Simba Kivuli as he had become known. Banished long ago, he was far removed from the likeness of his former self. Once a dashing, powerful magus from a renowned order, he was now an exile living in this drab realm. The skies were perpetually dark and ominous, and the place he had taken up residence in was veritably an abandoned catacomb. To some that would seem a strange redundancy. The only ones allowed here were by his own design. Simba Kivuli, the shadow lion had forgotten his true name many seasons ago. The special mirror through which he could look back into his home realm had gone dormant some time ago since he was effectively cut off from the unesiphiwo he was blessed with.

He was unsure of the cause, but figured the time away from home had simply dwindled the potency of his gifts, eventually nullifying his ability to power the mirror. Something had changed. Sporadically he would get glimpses at different landscapes familiar to him. He ignored them at first thinking they were just wistful dreams born of futile hopes. Then they started happening more often, and he definitely knew he was conscious when the images appeared, and he most certainly recognized the various biomes before his eyes…Nyumbani.

It was obvious someone had been tampering with the veil between realms by repeatedly opening rifts. It was also clear they either had no idea what they were doing or were desperate, and did not care to be wary of the dangers. It did not matter. Simba Kivuli was grateful for their foolishness. It provided him with an opportunity to come home, and when he did, his revenge would be glorious. It was suspiciously quiet out. His two favorite minions were nowhere to be seen. Closing his eyes, Simba Kivuli concentrated reaching out to see through their eyes so he could get an idea of where they were.

One of the grey Ingonyama Enkulu was approaching a city that was immediately recognizable to Simba Kivuli. The front gates to the renowned city of Kemet could be seen through its silver eyes. Simba reveled in the possibilities for his trusted minion, "Oh you will feast for days my friend if you get through those gates!" He whispered to himself since no one was there to hear. It seemed they had both hopped through different rifts. Concentrating he mentally reached out to find his other large shadow cat which was stalking towards the Luhlaza woodlands but something was off. The landscape surrounding the woodlands looked normal, but somehow the ground itself had risen up to encase the ancestral home to the Elinanye there.

Through the senses of the beast Simba Kivuli could also feel a great wellspring of power there as well. The eleven tribes of Elven communities were always especially gifted when it came to their potential concerning magic. The unesiphiwo being displayed here took a group effort and the shadow lion wondered what had come to Nyumbani that would force these people to insulate themselves in such a fashion. With the various factions and groups all scrambling to protect themselves against other threats, perhaps this was a prime opportunity for the banished former magus to return. The shadow realm had dulled his power. This involuntary hiatus may have worked in his favor.

Although magic had little to no effect on beings from the shadow realm, the dire lion from the place that had served as a prison to Simba Kivuli could feel the source of wild energy and yearned to crack open this domed partition of magically formed land mass. It made little sense to the banished one but he did not reach out to dissuade it. To be honest he was simply happy to see another environment that wasn't the dreary existence he had been forced to endure seasons ago. The Elinanye were an arrogant, pompous group who had voted for his banishment; therefore, this would be partial revenge for them taking part in the exile to this forsaken place. Simba Kivuli vowed to make a visit to the Luhlaza woodlands personally once a rift opened giving him a chance to return.

He could feel them opening sporadically so it was only a matter of time before an opportunity presented itself. Rummaging in his lair, the banished magus gathered his gear. From an early age he had showed a special talent with mimicry most associated with changelings despite being human. The source of his unesiphiwo was a topic of great debate amongst the already established Magi at one of the oldest Itempile Yomlingo. Thinking on these things angered him mightily and brought visions into his mind of his upbringing and eventual downfall.

For the life of him, he could not remember his birth name. Only the lion lived within him now. Simba thought it was best this way. The other Magi always expressed concern with him remaining in this anthropomorphic lion form for too long fearing that it would eventually become permanent. Those fears were unfounded yet he felt no need to revert to his old form now. He had transcended into a superior form. Why go back after finding the best of both worlds? The senses of a lion with the intellect of man, all while having the same spell casting capabilities afforded him.

They nourished and encouraged his talent until they felt it was being taken too far. As a young man Simba eventually had to go to many battles eventually having to participate. Many of his initial mentors fell and he was forced to improvise when some of them were incapacitated. The survivors had the nerve to scold him for using his gifts to change nearby wildlife into minions that could turn the tide in battle. The absurdity was emphasized when he was able to restore them to their natural forms freeing them. The debate was continued amongst the elder magi when the topic of Simba's price for using the talent was brought up as well as a possible price levied on the animals.

It was time to leave the past behind until he could make it right. Not a living thing here in this realm was responsible for him being here. Simba had also learned skills here when his talent with magic was made dormant for the most part. His affinity for bonding with animals for some reason remained as strong as it ever was. Gathering the special blades, he had forged for himself long ago, he ventured out of the catacomb lair towards the slate-colored beaches. Everything here seemed to have an ashen film over it, and this nearly drove him mad with depression.

The thirst for revenge was much stronger and he refused to give in to the malaise a place like this could have on a man. At first, he tried to give the various beasts and humanoid creatures here names but soon stopped. There was no need to catalogue and keep track because he would find a way home. A pair of large lizards saw or smelled him come out of his lair. They turned quickly in his direction. From the looks of it they had been languishing in the muted sun on dark rocks as the murky waters of the sea churned and broke waves on them.

It also looked as if they had missed a few meals. Huge ribs were easily seen beneath their dingy scales. Uncertain if they would understand him Simba remarked "I know I must look like a good meal, but I am not prey. Although it's been some time since I have swung these blades. Perhaps if you feel the need to lunge at me, I will have no choice but to defend myself." His comments were met with silence, tongue flickers and cold unforgiving stares from two sets of reptilian eyes that continued to track his every move. Still unsure if they understood, but it was clear that either way, their decision had been made.

More to himself than anything he said "Very well. It seems you disagree with my assessment, and that is likely because I have come without my friends who are usually by my side." Out in the distance he could see flashes of random rifts opening and closing. Surmising that his opportunity to journey back home through one of them may come at any time, it would be best to deal with these two now. Shaking off his old cloak which was little more than tatters now, Simba unsheathed two black blades that looked to be forged of pure shade. The pommels and hilts still had a silver glint to them.

The lizards were slowly circling, tongues flickering faster now as their tails began to swish back and forth. Simba was trying to see which would try to pounce first. Ordinarily large lizards like this would simply sit and wait for prey to come by while they were burrowed into the sand. By the looks of them, foot traffic must have become supremely low, and they have been forced to try a new tactic. The problem for them may be that their chemosensory system may be more efficient tracking at slower speeds.

Simba did not intend to be a stationery or slow target. He was also not unwise enough to make the first move and unintentionally fall into a trap he was unaware of. The beasts were at least maneuvering to be on different sides of him after all. It still didn't seem to him like this was a well-rehearsed dance. Only now was he thinking it might have been smart to study the flora and fauna more closely here. He and his two-lion pride had been the apex predators ever since he could remember since his exile. There was a bit of time before he came across them as cubs before he reached that status in these lands.

That was when the shadow lion was forged. The harbingers and tribal flame haired humanoid creatures all came for him as soon as he realized his unesiphiwo could not be fully utilized here. The utter confidence that was brimming from him from the moment he stepped through that shameful portal evaporated when he called forth energies to his hands that never came. Like sharks circling bloody waters they came. He went down in a bloody heap from the rain of blows, but did not remain down for long. The attacks awakened something within him. Something that tapped into his animalistic nature.

The creatures in the shadow realm had crude blunt objects. After the pummeling Simba struck back with such ferocity, they soon knew it wasn't worth the trouble, and he didn't have that much meat on him after all. Harking back to those days Simba's mind had to come back to the present just in time to duck a savage tail swipe from one of the huge lizards. Luckily the sand slightly slowed his movement as he rolled narrowly missing being in the grips of the other lizard's strong jaws. Foul breath assailed his nostrils as he struck out with one black blade grazing its cheek. The beast hissed in pain as Simba turned to cross his blades in time to block a flash of talons from his opposite side.

He was not lacerated across his face and body but the force of the attack sent him flying a hefty distance away. As he hit the sand hard the wind left his lungs, and he struggled to regain his feet. It took one of the beasts a moment to register where he had landed while the other shook off the vicious slash to its jawline from the black blade. Simba had enough time to regain his composure and dawn his leonine helm that was forged soon after the blades he wielded. These creatures were desperate and it would not do to be killed by them at this point. Smiling beneath the helm Simba mumbled to himself "When I die, it will be with more dignity and to someone or something much mightier than the likes of you!"

Once again as expected they did not heed his words and came forward. Today would be either celebrated with a meal or end in death. Simba believed he had an idea on how they moved as well as their relative speed and decided to go on the offensive this time. Rushing in he anticipated the tail whip and tried to sever the tip with one of his blades. It was a good thing he had in fact dodged the opening salvo from the tail as the scales there were much tougher than he expected. There was a dull clank as the blade bounced harmlessly off nearly numbing his arm. The other lizard had obviously not learned its lesson from the initial engagement lunging in for another bite attempt. Jumping up over the attack Simba thrust his blade into an eye.

A louder hiss than the last sent strange shockwaves through Simba's bones as he shook his other arm trying to bring feeling back to it not wanting to drop the weapon in his right hand. The sword that was in his left was stuck in the large eyeball he plunged it into. The beast scrambled back flailing as it attempted to dislodge it. Rolling as he landed in the sand; he stood just in time to see the lizard that favored its tail attacks coming in but cautiously as it saw and heard the reaction of its companion. Switching tactics, the large lizard attempted a talon swipe this time which was easily avoided. The exiled magus took his remaining blade into two hands swinging with all of his might at the middle joint in the beasts' arm once safely inside the sharp talons.

Now both lizards were hissing loudly and something about the sound vibrated through Simba's ears in an extremely unnerving way. He had to make it stop, and quickly. The beast with his blade stuck in its eye was on its back was still making a frantic yet futile attempt at removing the sword. Running over and jumping to avoid the wild movements of legs claws and tail, Simba swept the blade along its exposed neck. Luckily the scales there were softer than those on the topside of the animal and apparently the tail. After bleeding out quickly, it went silent. Finally retrieving the blade from the fallen creatures' eye, Simba went to end the suffering of the other lizard.

Sensing his approach, the lizard tried to scamper aways but its efforts were hindered by the nearly missing limb. Simba dodged as the animals' frenetic movements slung dark blood everywhere. It was obvious it was scared and no longer on the attack but the screeching hiss sound had to be ended. Slashing at its neck as the lizard attempted to rear back on its hind legs, Simba mercifully ended its suffering and the silence that followed was nearly blissful. Panting, the exile knelt down cleaning the black blood from his blades, and took his helm back off catching his breath. Looking at the two huge carcasses, he figured there may be some useful bits he could take along on his journey.

He went about his work quickly and efficiently before searching for where the next random rift back to his home may open up. Other large, deadly scavengers would show up soon curious from the smell of a recent kill, and if they were bigger than these two beasts, he had no desire to try and contend with them without his family. Lasekholo, and Lasekunene is what he had named them more to himself. He rarely referred to the Ingonyama Enkulu verbally most of the time, yet somehow the dire lions from this shadow realm seemed to know what he needed. Right now, he wanted to be reunited with them back in his homeland where hopefully the use of his unesiphiwo would be restored to him.

This hard-fought victory paled in comparison to some of the things he had defeated here, and it was excruciatingly obvious Simba was long out of practice since gaining dominance in this area some time ago. As if the realms heard his thoughts an incredibly large sphinx could be seen flying high off in the distance bringing up some legendary battles from the past, one where he had to outsmart a notoriously aggressive example of the mythological creatures. After making sure his bruised and battered form was not worse for wear, he gathered his scavenged lizard meat along with other useful materials.

It was also painfully apparent that he had packed on some weight over the seasons. Sharing kills with his small pack, taking his share to cook later while the Ingonyama Enkulu devoured the rest had its perks, and Simba had taken advantage over the seasons he had been stuck here. With more movement the armor would improve in reference to the fit. Scanning the area Simba found a group of peaks that looked to have more frequent rift flashes than any other surrounding place.

Sighing at the prospect of ascending to the necessary heights, he put his head down, and put one foot in front of the other dutifully until he stood at the base of the mountain. "Ah well if it was easy, everyone would do it. I can only hope in the end, it will be worth it." He said to himself as he began his ascent. The climb was grueling, especially with the assortment of gear he was now carrying in addition to his scavenged loot from the lizard carcasses. The sun here still somehow intensified in heat despite the constant overcast nature of the skies. Either that or it could have been a figment of his imagination given all the other variables.

Simba casts it all aside to focus on reaching the top. The gauntlets he had forged seasons ago had simulated claws in them enabling him to gain purchase on this treacherous mountain terrain. He still had a few close calls and nearly slipped and fell to his death multiple times. Finally scrambling to the apex, he rolled onto his back, and sat up catching his breath before looking for the rift flashes he needed. Being this high up would bring a different variety of predators. The respite needed to be short. The sun was also beginning to fall below the horizon. A vast majority of the wildlife here was dangerous. The nocturnal variety were even more so.

Almost as if on cue, there was a crackle and he saw as well as felt a rift open to his left a little distance away. Now the trick would be to predict when and where the next rifts would appear and see how long one would remain open. The time was obviously variable and he imagined the rifts his companions went through had to be sizable. They also had to have lasted a good amount of time in order for them to walk or leap through. Simba thought they would be initially cautious but it was possible he was wrong on that front.

Plus, the prospect of new hunting grounds may have been a temptation they simply couldn't resist. The universe must have heard his thoughts as one large rift crackles open before him just as some large avian species began circling him from above. With a bit of anxiety and trepidation hoping this rift would indeed lead him back home, Simba stepped into it leaving the perpetual gloom of the shadow realm behind.

Chapter Five

An intricate system of tiny bells within the boughs of trees throughout the Luhlaza woodlands begins chiming frantically. Under other circumstances when only a small amount of these bells chime from the wind or from unwanted would-be intruders unwittingly raising this subtle alarm by climbing to the heights needed to cause it, this would be a sort of pleasant sound. Currently with the very ground risen up to enclose the woodlands and the entire chime system going off at once, it was nerve wracking. This was especially so for Dambisa. She was resting. Her duties as leader of the scouts had run her ragged recently.

Queen Izibele had ordered the Elinanye to raise up a border to all outsiders until it could be determined what the cause was for the sickness sweeping the lands, and creating a disturbing variety of revenants that had become a nuisance to all. The queen was untrusting as it was unclear who was to blame for all this, and in times past when calamity struck Nyumbani all groups banded together to find a solution. The last few global incidents and more specifically the great cataclysm had taken a very great toll on the Elinanye. When the jungles, woodlands and other natural habitats entrusted to the elven tribes were hit the hardest, it was them, and them alone that went about repairing the wounds disasters left behind. Crazed dragons, gods on rampages and vicious tribal wars between the Djaemon and any number of other peoples not willing to brook their constant encroachment came and went.

After the Elinanye lent their bows and blades in times where allies needed them, they were there no matter the cause. When it was time to help clean things up, when those catastrophes spilled into the Luhlaza woodlands or Ephila and many other Elinanye territories, they were often left to do so themselves. The enclosed dome of dirt, stone and detritus magically gathered to form it amplified the chiming unceremoniously robbing Dambisa of her much-needed sleep. Something was attempting to breach their perimeter.

That something was trying to get in was not unusual. The fact that whatever it was could slam into the dome hard enough to force the whole chime system to ring out simultaneously, was very much an abnormal occurrence. Many a debate was had between Dambisa and Queen Izibele over not closing themselves off to the rest of the world during crisis. She knew her queen well. It was not just the fear of lives lost and desecrated lands. Queen Izibele feared herself. More accurately she feared who she became when forced to deal directly with conflict. The eleven tribes of the elves or Elinanye as they referred to themselves were widely known as a peaceful race. Circumstances often occurred when they had to give up on diplomacy and do what was necessary to defend their homes and people.

Dambisa sat up in a rush sweating through her bedclothes and sheets. Perhaps she was in the middle of some unremembered nightmare and the disturbance had merged into it. "Gods I am still tired." She whispered to herself as she swung her legs over to place her feet on the floor. Before she could shake the haze from her head the unmistakable glow from small iridescent wings began flitting towards her. The head Elinanye scout sighs asking "Jori, what in Esihogweni is going on out there?" Flying nervously back and forth at high-speed Jori replies "I was going to go out and see but was too afraid. Whatever it is…it's enormous." As if to emphasize that point the dome is rocked again as something was slammed against it. The thud was resounding as the myriad of chimes go off once again. The sound reverberates throughout the structure surrounding the woodland.

Hastily Dambisa dawns her heaviest armor set over her bedclothes and gathers her weapons. Once out of her quarters she could see the royal guards as well as other Elinanye scrambling to see what the cause is. They all stumble and Jori jumps at another loud bump shaking the trees. Flying frantically Jori exclaims "You won't believe what is at your barrier trying to pummel its way in!" Dambisa watches the small Aziza, wings flapping at incredible speeds showing just how worried she had to be and waited for her to clarify. After a moment the brown skinned fairy calms a bit and continues "It looks to be a very large slate skinned lion with silver eyes. I have never seen the like of it before."

Dambisa and a few of the Elinanye who had stopped to eaves drop didn't quite understand but figured they would when they confronted whatever it was on their proverbial doorstep. Unbidden, the rest of Dambisa's usual squad had already made their way down to the forest floor on the woodland. They were awaiting her orders along with the pack of Inja Enkulu. They had their hackles up as they were on high alert like everyone else. Jori flew down as well as the scout leader made her way to meet them. Dambisa ran to the border to the woodlands as the Ingonyama Enkulu from the shadow realm swatted the barrier with a mighty paw causing another resounding thud once again shaking the chime system.

Once they got to the border Dambisa and Jori could see a group of Elinanye guards that were clearly exhausted. With each attempt to cave in the enclosure they kept their hands in the dirt nearly instantaneously mending the damage before the cracks could develop into a large hole through which the creature could gain entrance. The Elinanye warriors that had come with her lent their efforts to the guards already present as it was obvious the efforts were draining them. They could not sustain this in perpetuity.

Dambisa could see this and everyone knew that someone would have to go out and confront this aggressor. Soon smaller attacks could be felt at different points along the improvised border wall. So, it was not alone in this assault. Something else was joining in making it more imperative that it be stopped. The difficulty would be getting out without letting the intruders in. Dambisa and the pack of Inja Enkulu came to her side as did two of her squad members, and three of the guards who had exchanged places with some reinforcements that had followed Dambisa and her squad. Sinking their hands into the ground they could feel the presences of the beings trying to break in.

The feeling wasn't as bad as when they had tried this while in corrupted land but it did have a familiar sensation from some of the intruders which were smaller than the beast from the shadow realm. Dambisa pulled her hands from the soil and could tell from the nods around her that they sensed the same thing. Revenants of corrupted denizens of Nyumbani were amongst the intruders from the shadow realm. The Elinanye were hesitant to use flames so close to their sacred Luhlaza woodlands. They would have to improvise as word had spread that fire was the best way to be rid of them for good. First things first, Dambisa thought. They had all felt where the most plausible gap was in the assault attempts.

With nocked arrows and unsheathed blades, the Elinanye warriors gathered at a gap far enough away from where the shadow realm invader was swinging away that they would be able to approach relatively unseen, and where none of the smaller revenants were making their own intrusion attempts. Four of the Elinanye placed their hands along the barricade wall of dirt, rocks and earthly materials magically raised to shield them from the rest of the world. An opening appeared and the Inja Enkulu slipped through first silently without so much as a signal from Dambisa.

She followed them out, waiting for the rest of the advance group to come out. When they did so the breach began to close as they placed their hands back on the barrier. At the last moment Jori flew through the hole just as it was closing her golden but nearly translucent wings catching the moonlight as she exited the dome that had been hiding them since the Elinanye retreated there. The thudding continued as they hastily made their way towards it from the outside now shredding revenants as they approached. Soon there were dozens of macabre scenes of severed body parts scrambling around aimlessly. Then they saw that the Dire Lion wasn't the only intruder from the shadow realm trying to enter their precious woodlands.

Reports had come back from other regions that the shadow realmers were not as susceptible to magic attacks. Dambisa silently signaled for them to save the use of their unesiphiwo before she let loose two arrows from her bow. They struck true violently puncturing the heads with almost flame like hair. Three others stopped their pounding at the sound of their companions falling. They looked up just in time to see large balls of fur and fangs leaping to tear throats from their necks. These actions were repeated a multitude of times as the Elinanye went most of the way around the barrier, cautiously avoiding getting too close to draw the attention of the huge grey lion from the shadow realm that made the Inja Enkulu look small in comparison.

When enough of the other intruders had been eliminated, it made it easier for the Elinanye on the inside to instantaneously mend the damage from the siege as it was only really occurring in one place now. The operation outside was swift, silent and deadly, but they were perplexed as to how they would tackle this next challenge. Dambisa was unsure if they could kill it outright with a bowshot, and getting close with a sword looked too risky. Shaking her head, she thought a Tetsuo bladesmen or women would be really useful right now. Sticking to the shadows and high foliage she signaled these thoughts to her squad mates, who relayed it to the others that were in her line of sight.

The stench of the nearby corrupted grasslands gave her an idea, and a plan was hatched. They recalled not long-ago trapping revenants with a smaller version of the dome surrounding their home simply encasing them inside which she hoped the Pantu tribesmen had come along and discarded later. That would likely not work on a beast this large that came from the shadow realm, but what if they encased it in corrupted soil? Their stomachs turned at the thought of it. They would have to interact with the corrupted land to even make the attempt to see if it would work. First, they would have to lure it in that direction away from Luhlaza. Kneeling down Dambisa nuzzled the pack leader of the Inja Enkulu who returned the gesture.

Slowing blinking her glowing red eyes, it seemed to know what was needed and sprinted off and the rest of the pack followed suit. The Ingonyama Enkulu could feel something was not right as it was now much quieter than it was before and briefly stopped swiping at the barrier. It briefly began pounding again when it smelled something unfamiliar yet familiar simultaneously. It was highly unlikely this beast had encountered Inja Enkulu in the shadow realm, but predators usually recognized other predators. Perhaps it was the scent glands on the approaching animals or it could have been the contrasting smell of mainly herbivores in the area. The dogs had fed recently. Blood may have been fresh on their breaths. Whatever the tell was, it froze in place after turning away from the barrier.

A low rumble built up as it growled warning off any who dared to approach. The pack sprang out from the grasslands and the lion rushed to meet them. The Elinanye had spread out watching the encounter from a distance with arrows trained on the beast. Dambisa whistled shrilly just before the pack leader reached it and arrows were loosed. Just as a huge silver-grey paw was raised to reveal razor sharp silver claws ready to tear into the pack leader, there was a multitude of successive thuds as arrows penetrated its hide. The roar that was elicited likely woke the dead. Dambisa was sure she felt the very ground shaking.

In pain and confused, the lion still managed to lash out at the hind quarters of one of the pack sending it spiraling through the air giving a yelp of its own. The rest of the pack darted away towards the corrupted grassland in between the Elinanye territory and the Pantu traditional home. The pack leader doubled back at the sound of one of her pups being injured. The black and white beast with the red glowing eyes met the silver eyes of the lion and growled threateningly before darting under an attempted swat, sinking her teeth deep into a rear ankle before turning once again to lead the now slightly limping lion towards the target area.

Both the Inja Enkulu pack and the Elinanye were now hiding within the uncorrupted grasslands but their movements made the grasses sway enticing the lion to head that way. Still in pain but not blinded to the ruse, the beast stops pacing back and forth at each provocation. It knows they're trying to bait it. Another arrow sends it into a frenzy as it bolts in the direction it came from. The pack dart in to nip at the lion making it continue to give chase until they're all in a patch of corrupted, fetid grass. The stench alone forces even this mighty beast to give pause. The huge lion began shaking its long mane and chuffing as if it could somehow rid its nostrils of the putrid smell through vigorous movement.

Dambisa's head was swimming and she could see that her brothers and sisters were also fighting nausea just being in the midst of this area. What needed to come next would only make things worse for them. The Inja Enkulu weren't fairing much better but stayed despite being adversely affected. Tamping down to control her turmoiled stomach, Dambisa bent down and thrust her hands into the tainted soil. The other Elinanye did the same and together they felt the full power of the land's sickness throughout their beings. The sensation brought them all to their knees, but they endured.

Seeing their friends in such anguish made the Inja Enkulu forget their own misery. They renewed their sporadic attacks to keep the lion from the shadow realm distracted while the Elinanye use their ability to manipulate the land in an attempt to encase it in the soil and grasses. The beast began to writhe as the dirt slithered all around it forming a sickly cocoon around it. After being slumped over the Elinanye get up, retracting themselves from the corrupted patch of grasslands and scurry closer to their border to stop feeling the effects of the malady within that area. Catching their collective breaths, they wait to see if the lion would remain trapped.

At first nothing happened and Dambisa as well the others present were astonished that their plan had worked. The pack of Inja Enkulu swarmed to Dambisa and her two squad mates since they were not as familiar with the other Elinanye. Tails began to wag as they too began to recover. The mound of grass and soil encasing the lion began to quake as it stirred beneath and it became evident the beast would not remain trapped for long. There was a crescendo as the vibrating grass, dirt and other earthen materials erupted.

The massive lion let out another ferocious roar before sneezing and chuffing again, sprinting away hindered by its arrow laden legs. Dambisa felt bad for whomever encountered the beast next but was relieved they would not be forced to deal with it now. The world was beginning to make less and less sense. She went over to the Inja Enkulu that was struck earlier. Jori was hovering over it along with the pack leader. Looking up as she flitted about Jori stated "It's bruised pretty good and the long cut over the eye should heal well enough. I think this one will wait next time to jump in after the pack leader has done so. They were supposed to only divert its attention, not engage it directly."

Luckily it could still walk and the scratch had missed the eye. Suffering mostly an injury to its pride, the pup should grow up to become a productive member of the pack. The Elinanye were mostly shaken from their interaction with the tainted grounds. They had wisely kept their distance from the worst of the would-be intruders. They swiftly policed the areas around their magically risen borders, taking extra care to gather scattered revenant parts that were slithering around. It was gruesome business, but Dambisa ordered them to compile this vile refuse together so it could be burned properly.

That was the only way to ensure it would not wander its way into a water source or be eaten by some starving animal with nothing else available, possibly creating another revenant. They were unsure of how all this worked so it only made sense to be cautious. When they were finished the Elinanye, Inja Enkulu, and Jori flying amongst them went back into the Luhlaza woodlands sealing the magic enclosure once more.

Jori was especially worried since it had been a long time since she went back home to be with others of her kind. Hopefully the revenants, corrupted lands and shadow realm intruders had not reached any of the Aziza enclaves spread throughout Nyumbani. Dambisa seemed more pensive. The fairy figured this was because this latest development would force her to advocate for joining forces once again with the other groups the queen had forcibly isolated themselves from. Queen Izibele could be stubborn, and they all knew she had her reasons. It was just that not everyone was privy to them.

Dambisa was trusted and in the inner circle despite not being high born. Her skill and intelligence buoyed her well beyond what some thought her station should be, and the queen trusted her judgement. Contrary to all of that the queen would ultimately do what she thought was best for her people, and refused to repeat what she felt were previous mistakes that cost an exorbitant amount of lives. If others felt she was being over protective then so be it. Dambisa took her time after going back to her quarters to bathe and wash the miasma from the infected grasslands away.

She was sure it was just a figment of her imagination that the smell was still clinging to her armor but that may have been a result from melding with the lands that were in such a horrible state. Some of the feeling stayed with them even after disengaging. The body, mind and spirit held onto that memory of nausea and despair felt throughout the grounds. If it was spreading, it would eventually encroach on their woodlands. The remedy if that happened may come from the minds of the magi, regular people or even the Djaemon.

Reluctantly mankind had formed a bit of a strained alliance with the Djaemon recently and Dambisa was confident that was part of the queen's hesitancy to seek cooperation with the other groups in addition to her own seemingly sordid, dark history with the red skinned warrior clans. Now that she was properly cleaned up, she would report to her. Stepping out she mumbled under her breath "My Queen, you may have to simply get over it."

Chapter Six

Three very large slanted holes had been dug by Kibo, incinerated by Mawenzi, and then flash frozen by Shira to keep these pathways stable so that the main hunting parties could go down into the depths of the dead marshes to capture Motu, and his host of defiled, twisted revenant slaves. The three elder dragons would have to wait at the surface for the others to either catch their quarry below or they themselves would do so when the wayward magus tried to escape. The elder dragons could also feel the presence of at least one distant relative below. It would seem there was a lot going on far below.

When Yasuke saw that Kibo, Mawenzi and Shira looked satisfied with their work, he nodded to the black elder dragon before calling a small flame to his left hand in preparation for the descent to the underground lair. It provided some light but not enough for everyone. Hesitantly the Djaemon warriors filed in behind him followed by Pantu tribesmen who would eventually have to get off their mounts as the ceiling and walls narrowed. Some of the others pulled out torches and lit them as they did not have the same gifts Yasuke displayed. Bringing up the rear was a small contingent of Tetsuo blade wielding Shields men from Kemet.

There was an eerie sheen on the walls, floor and ceilings on the downward path they were traveling. The hastily dug, singed and flash frozen moist muck that made up this long impromptu entrance.

Yasuke was confident the structure would hold for their trip down, he and some of the others were more worried about the return trip to the surface. The trek was quite a bit longer than any of them had expected by the time they got to an area that looked untouched by the efforts of the elder dragons.

The air down here was damp with a hint of moldy desiccation. They begin to hear scratching and skittering which prompts low growls from the dire panthers. The Pantu tribesmen do their best to calm the beasts as the Tetsuo blade carrying Shields men get a bit apprehensive about the situation. A stampede back to the surface would not be a pleasant experience. The armor of the shields men would prevent some injuries but these were dire panthers after all. They simply hoped the Pantu tribesmen had as good a handle on the beasts as was reported.

The search party arrives at an area that looks to have been recently excavated. Yasuke bends down to inspect the ground, paying particular attention to the scratches and other strange markings. Having tracked animals in and near the woodlands as well as the areas surrounding Kibo's lair, the leader of the fire forged had a hard time recognizing these markings. He stands to shine the light from his personal flame on similar markings on the ceilings. A couple of the panthers seemed interested in what looked like splashes of blood but quickly snorted and backed away as it must not have been to their liking.

Cautiously Yasuke moves to pet one of them before changing his mind saying "There was a fight here, and recently by the looks of things. Any of you recognize what animal could have made these markings?" A few of the tribesmen look over various markings but shake their heads negatively. The shields men don't even try. Most of them had spent a fair amount of time within the city walls of Kemet. It looks to be claws of some kind that made the marks, but they're too thin to be dire panther claws. The group is stumped but press on hoping they are progressing towards their quarry.

Yasuke figures there may be another group hunting this magus or perhaps there was a mutiny from animals who broke some spell of control. Either way someone had been wounded. Perhaps it was someone or something from the shadow realm. That may explain the revulsion the dire panthers had to the blood. His musings and those of the group were all interrupted by sudden quaking as the grounds above, below and all around them began rumbling. Luckily the path had opened up into a larger area so they were not so packed together as the agitated panthers' tails swished as they growled and looked for where danger could be coming from.

Before Yasuke could give the command, all weapons were unsheathed. Simultaneously the walls, floor and ceilings seemed to erupt. Some of the personal flames from the other present fire forged were extinguished as black reptilian arms lashed out with golden claws. Multiple screams of agony rang out as flesh was sliced from limbs. Amidst the blood spray the dire panther's eyes adjusted quickest to the dimming of light and sought out the attackers as their handlers looked to protect themselves while trusting the instincts of their mounts.

The shields men in the rear fared better being more protected by their heavier armor. They had also smartly formed a phalanx with their tetsuo blades shielding the group and limiting the direction any ensuing attacks could come from. A pitiful yet alarming hissing sound reverberated throughout the underground structure as some of the panthers successfully latched onto limbs of the mystery beasts. The hissing turned to shrieks as powerful jaws clamped down and bones crunched audibly.

The assailants quickly slithered back from whence they came in various directions giving the search party time to recover. It was obvious they had made it into portions of this structure that was created long before their arrival. With no idea what had caused the bloodshed prior to them getting here, they soldiered on to their objective. Yasuke stopped momentarily to investigate the partial limb one of the dire panthers had chomped off. Some of the others gathered to get a closer look as well. As they stepped off one of the Pantu Tribesmen took the limb from Yasuke examining it.

Yasuke lingered with the man and held his personal flame close as they both trekked along. The rest of the group went ahead as one of the other fire forged took the lead igniting a flame of their own to partially light the way. The limb had black scales with hints of gold flecks, and the claws were extremely sharp golden protrusions. Plainly reptilian but they were hard pressed to determine what specific species this was. The tribesmen offered the limb back to Yasuke who shook his head negatively. The man shrugged and stuffed it into a pouch at his back before whipping out a wicked looking khopesh at hearing the walls tremble once more.

Marching into a large underground hall with sconces along the walls, the fire forged no longer needed to produce lights of their own to help the group see. At the end they saw the magus they were hunting for surrounded by a mixed group of revenants Djaemon, Iigbin, and shadow realm invaders. In front of them were a smaller group of newly converted Ninka Nanka. Looking at the large reptiles, Yasuke guessed that to be what variety of severed limb the Pantu tribesmen had. These, however were not burrowing, just sitting with tails swishing back and forth seeming to await orders.

There was also a hint of the ghostly green glow coming from their eyes that also came from the magus's own eyes. So, it looked like he had set up a gauntlet of sorts for them to get through in order to apprehend him. Yasuke also noticed a smaller wyvern like creature coiled around the magus's neck. The leader of the fire forged believed he recalled seeing a similar beast with him at Kibo's lair. If this was the same creature it had grown significantly in a relatively short time. Stepping forward Yasuke addressed the magus directly "Motu, I presume. You need not waste our time or yours. There's no escape for you, and your…minions here will do no more than delay your capture."

Chuckling maniacally Motu leans forward off of the sarcophagus like structure behind him that Yasuke was late in noticing. Studying one of his hands which seemed much darker than the other Motu conjured a green globe of energy which transformed into an emerald flame that continued to build as he replied "I have no desire to be captured. I only wish to bring my beloved back to me. The elder dragons that led you here could easily delve into this structure, capture and likely kill me in the process but you all would be collateral damage. Since they have not already done so, that lets me know they want me alive for some reason. I guess you will have to pay the price for that frivolity."

By now the green flame had grown considerably and with the formality of the parley over, Motu hurls it at the search party. In response Yasuke and several other fire forged produce flame projectiles of their own and throw them nearly simultaneously. They meet between the groups exploding spectacularly sending a shower of green and orange sparks flying. With a subtle flick of his wrist Motu sends the revenant Ninka Nanka charging in. The dire panthers had been waiting and needed no such prodding from the Pantu tribesmen.

Before the panthers could intervene some of the search party was indeed caught off guard as there were more large reptiles within the walls and ceiling of the cavern that burst in around them making quick work of those caught unawares. The Pantu Tribesmen who had been fully apprised of what was happening waded in blades scything through black and gold scales as an onrush of revenants joined the fight. Motu sat back watching things play out mentally moving the revenants like pieces on a board game.

The Kemet city shields men and the fire forged began to work in tandem having experience from facing revenants during prior battles. As a throng of revenants came forward, they are met with quick, decisive slashes from huge tetsuo blades halving the foremost of them. Before the severed remains have a chance to hit the ground to continue wriggling towards them the fire forged step up releasing gouts of flames incinerating them to lifeless ashes. Motu watches this all unfold knowing it's only a matter of time before they break through his defenses. Determined not to give up, he mentally commands the two basilisks to get involved. The Djaemon joined in the dance wherever they fit in, hacking and slashing where they felt needed.

The Ninka Nanka both the revenants the magus had turned and the natural group trapped within the underground construct he had created were now either destroyed or had fled since some of the magical barriers Motu imposed were faltering with him concentrating on the battle at hand. Regardless the fire forged were making a concerted effort to turn all remains into dust and ash to stop it from reanimating and coming after them. Both groups continue to clash together as attrition dwindles their numbers down. The advantage is still with the search party.

Stopping to catch his breath amidst the action Yasuke sees a large serpent spring from one of the holes created by the Ninka Nanka quickly to swiftly curl around a Pantu tribesmen who strayed too far from the main group. Before he could shout a warning, the other serpent burst through the grounds and began encircling itself around Yasuke. Across the underground cavern Motu smiled cruelly thinking this was his chance to turn the tide. With the leader gone the magus felt he could handle the remaining warriors himself. The problem was that he had no means of truly escaping if his new young wyrm was correct that the elder dragons could track him through some magic connection.

The air was leaving Yasuke's lungs at an alarming rate, and panic was setting in. Through watery eyes he could see that the other basilisk had successfully overcome the Pantu tribesmen he hadn't warned in time. Panic gave way to acceptance briefly before determination boiled up in Yasuke. The others were fighting fiercely and had not noticed what was happening to the group leader. As the basilisk's mouth was just about to close over his head, Yasuke closed his eyes and concentrated to summon all of his unesiphiwo that he could muster. One of the Kemet city shields men finally noticed what was happening too late and would not be able to traverse the cavern in time to do anything.

She informed some of the others that had been fighting in her specific phalanx and they tried to fight their way through the chaos to try anyway. Yasuke allowed himself to go half way down the beast's gullet when at last he released a powerful display of ilangatye. Flames burst out of the large serpent rendering it headless as the tail thumped lifelessly to the ground leaving them all to stare amazed at a nearly naked Yasuke floating above the ground with cooked gore sliding off of his body. He slowly lowered himself to the ground. The momentum was once again in their favor, and they advanced towards Motu who was more or less resigned to the incoming defeat. The basilisk that had taken the Pantu tribesmen had slithered off after its counterpart was destroyed. The remaining Djaemon looked disappointed.

That did not mean he would go quietly. The magus sent all remaining forces at his disposal forward in a last-ditch effort to repel the enemy. G'Orn and his sister who still had their wits intact went against their will as they were still reanimated through Motu's touch had no choice but to join the fray. Motu looked for weaknesses in formations. Spaces between armor slats in which he could hurl harmful magic energies into effectively eliminating some of the tide rushing towards him. The revenants he had created from the tetsuo blade wielding guards at the old temple ran into their more contemporary counterparts from Kemet. The skills were still evident in these warriors and they were just as well armored.

However, since they were spiritually disconnected from being able to carry their blades, there was no contest when up against the shields men who dismantled them quickly with the legendary oversized weapons of their own. Yasuke was weary from his latest use of his gift and sorely needed to end this quickly. It was obvious the magus would drag this out for as long as he could to inflict the most damage. Seeing that he was laboring a bit one of the Pantu tribesmen came over with his mount and quickly offered a wrapping from his saddle bag so the fire forged leader could at least cover up before getting back into the fight. While wrapping up as fast as he could, Yasuke thanked the man and his eyes were drawn back to the sarcophagus in the rear of the chamber.

Signaling to a few of his fellow fire forged they began hurling flames towards it. Motu was quick to notice and began hurling magic of his own to deflect or block the flames being thrown at his love. With his concentration elsewhere the coordination of the revenants dissolved into disarray and the Pantu tribesmen, Kemet shields men, and fire forged overwhelmed his revenant forces handily until only a few of his Djaemon revenants and Motu himself were slowly retreating towards the sarcophagus with him occasionally blocking balls of flame with his very body. G'Orn and his sister were busy locking swords with the advancing Pantu Tribesmen as the fire forged and Kemet city shields men were content to slowly back them up while protecting their flanks and rear.

More and more of the flames hitting his magical defenses were beginning to take a toll on the magus who finally collapsed at the base of the monument to his lost love. Screaming "NOOOOOOOO! You mustn't destroy her! I will bring her back!" At Yasuke's signal they stopped the flaming onslaught. Masindi tried to slink off into the shadows when Yasuke saw in his periphery. Throwing one more mighty blast of fire in that general direction, the fire forged leader exclaims "I don't think so! Kibo and the rest will want to know what part you played in all of this as well." Moving slowly out of the shadows Masindi begins to whimper and talk in what he assumes is baby like gibberish.

Tilting his head to the side Yasuke is slightly amused but not fooled by the ruse saying "I know you look young but you forget that I know your kind well. Your intellects are ageless. You are recycled into your physical forms at each incarnation. You may not know all that you have ever known, but you are certainly no babe without the ability to speak." Silently blinking at the group Masindi comes forward a bit more before muttering "It was worth a try." The Kemet city shields men quickly shackled a weeping Motu and stood him up roughly before they began the trek back to the surface.

There were a couple Djaemon revenants who did not seem mindless but had the grey pall in their skin, just watching them. Yasuke was taken aback briefly as he had no idea what to do with them. Instinct told him to burn them but seeing intelligence still in their eyes refuted that notion. As if reading his thoughts one of the shields men asked "What to do with these two?" They were not attempting to flee, nor were they attacking. Shrugging Yasuke ordered "Bind them and bring them along." Surprisingly they did not even resist when approached.

As they began to file back the way they came after checking on their dead and wounded Yasuke went up to the large male Djaemon inquiring "You two seem to have your wits about you. Is it by your will that you came to be in service to this magus?" Weapons were drawn as the grey warrior flexed against his bonds for the first time and they feared he may escape and attack as he screamed "No, your foul magus slew us and turned us into the perversions you see before you! Somehow our minds are at least partially intact." G'Orn calmed himself when he saw they were on the verge of cutting him and his sister down.

One of the Djaemon warriors approached them. Large as a wild bedrahin and scarred from crimson head to toe. Looking them up and down he muttered something in their guttural language. Yasuke didn't understand and looked to G'Orn for a translation since he spoke the common tongue. Understanding the silent request G'Orn says "He wants to know why we are smooth skinned. Our clan does not follow Serat, or any of the gods for that matter." That was curious as Yasuke assumed all Djaemon worshipped the blood god, and scarred themselves ritually in addition to what they earned in battle.

These two had plenty of battle scars but none of the traditional scars the red skinned beings tended to sport. That and the drab grey hue was the other detail that differentiated them. The discoloration was so jarring that he likely would have missed the lack of scarring, but obviously the clan from Gcina Okubomvu would not miss that feature. The tree-like warrior roughly pats Yasuke on the shoulder, mutters another unintelligible phrase and stalks off. Another questioning glance urges G'Orn to respond "he says our blood is tainted, and warns you not to spill it for Serat would not be pleased. Though I do not believe fully in Serat…I would have to agree. However, I ask that you take mercy on us and end this miserable existence."

If what the grey Djaemon said was true, Yasuke understood, and could not imagine being used against his will while still remaining conscious the entire time. The problem was they needed answers and it was not guaranteed Motu would be forthcoming. Perhaps in exchange for a permanent release, these two would provide some much-needed clarification. He would ask Kibo and the others when they reached the surface.

Chapter Seven

It had been a few days since the search party left Kemet for the dead marshes. With at least some information gathered Olofi decided to hang back and try to relay what he could to Olorun. The god was going to do his best not to influence too much of what was going on. His job here was to observe and report. Three elder dragons and the gathered forces going along should prove to be more than enough to apprehend a wayward magus. Going along might have put him in a position to do more than what was planned. Being amongst these people for long periods of time made some of the orishas empathetic. Besides, things had changed significantly here that the sky god would likely be interested in as well.

Daniel who was disappointed at first at not being amongst the groups chosen to go with the search party was now frightened by the prospect of being within the city walls that were being besieged by an enormous beast from the shadow realm. He and Olofi were given a room at Salims. While the god in disguise looked to be writing in a very strange and intricate looking journal, Daniel was huddled in a corner quietly whimpering which each roar or thunderous thud as the dire lion tested the strength of the front gates. "How can you be journaling at a time like this?" Daniel frantically inquired.

What the man hadn't noticed was that Olofi's eyes were closed, there was no pen or quill in his hands as the words were being transcribed into the magic journal. Simultaneously the words filling the blank pages below were also going into an identical booklet in Olorun's private chamber far above Nyumbani in Izulu. When the sky god returned for respite, this report would be awaiting him. Olofi finished the part where the magus was likely the catalyst for the spreading malady to the lands but he was sure to mention the power he felt coming from the undead Djaemon that was encountered on his way down to Tanji.

Surely someone else would be implicated in this business when all was said and done. The power felt was likely that of another deity. Olorun would not be happy with that portion of the news. Unable to concentrate with Daniel's incessant whining, Olofi opened his eyes, and stood to turn on the young man admonishing "Where is that infernal bravery you must have been bragging about prior to my unceremonious arrival into your life?!" Wiping his face Daniel started to respond "Lofin, I…" The man didn't finish seeing the old man's eyes narrow as he asked, "Are you crying?" Looking down he tried to compose himself. A look of shock came over him as the old man's journal seemed to close on its own accord, and place itself on a shelf.

The old man went about getting ready nonplussed by what just happened. Daniel wasn't sure of what to make of this elderly man. He wanted to press him but also respected the fact that if he cared to share his secrets he would do so. Not to mention this was the only person in years who seemed genuinely interested in his well-being without constant ridicule. "Are you not at least concerned? It sounds like this place is about to fall down around our ears!" he asked. Olofi nods his understanding as he finishes dressing so they can go downstairs to eat as the siege carries on outside the gates.

Opening the door to their room the disguised god says "Bravery is not the absence of fear Daniel the Lesser. It is doing what must be done in spite of that fear. Fear freezes people into inaction, and the truly brave among you force themselves to act in the face of what looks like insurmountable odds. No doubt some of the warriors and city shield men facing the terrible creatures from the shadow realm are afraid, but they do their duty anyway. From what I gather by the interactions we have had in this city and the small village of Tanji; you boast as if you should be among them. Don't worry about ridding yourself of fear, just the hold it has over your actions."

Rubbing his spotty beard as shame flooded into his being, Daniel stood up and tried to at least look the part of the warrior. Straightening out his clothes as best he could, he followed Olofi down to the tavern to get something to eat. His stomach however might not be so cooperative. Keeping the food down would be a task as his insides quivered with each reverberation that went through the city as something felt like it was shaking the very foundations of the place with each blow. Shakily he followed Lofin to a table and sat down trying to keep himself composed. Relief set in just a bit as Daniel realized most of the able bodies were out dealing with the danger at hand.

Akachi saw them coming down and went to set placings at their usual table. The old man seemed nonplussed with the drama and chaos happening just outside the city walls but she could see Daniel was shaken. Ordinarily she may have taken a jab at him verbally, but understanding that it sounded as if things could get dire if the city shields and other gathered defenders did not win the day. Besides there were very few patrons in evidence so it would not be wise to alienate the ones that were in attendance. The menu was limited in case a rationing of food was needed later. A good amount of the bedrahin steaks had been cut into many chunks along with some tubers and vegetables for a hearty stew.

When she offered them a couple bowls both men nodded that it was a sufficient meal choice. Ironically there wasn't that much else to choose from currently. She just shook her head and smiled trying not to remind them of the limited options or the potential danger everyone was in. As a favor she also dropped them drinks free of charge. The two tuck into their meals straight away and Daniel is struggling to swallow he's so nervous. Olofi looks at him with a slight twinkle of amusement in his eyes. "I know why you fret boy, but you shouldn't. Old Lofin will take care of you."

Trying to concentrate on getting what may be his last meal down, Daniel scoffs at the notion of an old man taking care of him. "How exactly do you plan to do that? You came here to find out what's been going on, and you just may have brought me here to my doom." Chuckling Olofi chides him "Whoa now son. I suggest you take some of that bass out of your voice and listen for a change. I did come to find out what's been happening in these lands because it may tell me my why mine were affected. These creatures from the shadow realm did not just mysteriously appear or the grasslands and other areas begin festering for no reason. I aim to find out what that reason is. Save that iron you just showed me for when you need it. We venture out soon. I arranged to have something made for you."

The thought of leaving while they were under siege was enough to turn Daniel's stomach again. He was curious as to what the old geezer had for him, but whatever it was, he doubted it would help much once whatever was pounding at the city gates began pounding him. "What is it?" was all he could manage between spoons of stew before taking a heavy swig of the ever more popular "dragons' piss". Wincing as the brew went down, Daniel's face appears quizzical as Olofi waves to a musclebound dark-skinned man who had just come to the tavern entrance carrying a large bundle.

The newcomer strides over to set the parcel on one of the empty stools at their table, he and the old man briefly lock forearms and share a brief but seemingly affectionate headbutt. Daniel notes the man's stature, build and confidence as he exits. "Who was that man to you? The thick leather apron over that barrel chested fellow marks him as a smithy, but I don't recall hearing about him when I last frequented this city." Daniel inquires. Waving the concern in Daniel's voice off Olofi replies "That's just one of my brothers. He is known to take on black smith work every now and again in different places. Open the package."

That didn't sound right to Daniel and he said as much while curiously prying the gift open, still skeptical of its usefulness or value given current circumstances. "Don't you need permission from the local guilds to ply a trade in most cities or villages, and how many brothers do you have?" The man's eyes widened when it was finally laid bare for them to see. Inside was a beautifully crafted set of plate armor. Akachi walked by and whistled when she saw it. Looking from the new set to what Daniel was wearing, she stated flatly "I would put that on if I were you. It looks to be…a better fit to say the least."

Looking down at what he presently was adorned with, he had to agree. Slowly Daniel took off the hodge podge armor set that he had cobbled together likely from fallen warriors of varying sizes throughout his travels. "I guess if I have to go out, why not do so in style." He murmured. Olofi got up to help him get his head through the top of the chest plate, securing the fastenings at the sides that held plates to protect his back and midsection tight. Then he locked the pauldrons in place before handing him the gauntlets

A set of cuisses, and greaves nearly completed the armor set. There was no helm and there were still gaps left unprotected, but this was obviously more protective than his salvaged gear. Not to mention it fit him perfectly. It was well crafted but not gaudy. Light, yet Daniel felt it may be able to withstand a good beating. Just as he was regaining confidence and started to stand straighter again another resounding thud shook the city walls. "This is wonderful, but I doubt it can stand up to…whatever that is outside. I am grateful though Lofin." Patting him rougher than anyone thought the old man had strength to display Olofi replies "Worry not! We shall only go observe what's happening. There must be parapets where we can observe from a high vantage point. I'm not asking you to charge into the beast trying to gain entrance."

As Olofi began to walk towards the exit Daniel blurted "What about a weapon? You have neither armor nor a weapon to speak of!" Laughing Olofi says "Ogun was right that you'd ask for a weapon! Remember we are not going to fight but to observe, and you've not earned a weapon yet Daniel the Lesser. What I've given you should protect you well enough for what I aim to achieve." Stepping closer he continues at a whisper "To be fair you haven't earned this, but I said I would take care of you. Come on."

With terror rebuilding within himself Daniel asks, "Who was right?" Olofi stammers to answer "Ah…my brother…Ogunlye. He knew you'd want a weapon to go with the armor." The god in disguise stepped out and Daniel reluctantly followed. Most of the citizens had made the wise choices of either hiding in their homes hoping their defenders would prevail, or fled through lesser-known exits once all the gates were blocked off. With all of his being Daniel wanted nothing more than to flee to a place of safety wherever that might be.

Something about the old man made him want to live up to this strange idea of who he could be rather than what he had always been. One seemingly lead laden footstep at a time, Daniel followed Olofi up to one of the high perches atop the city walls facing southeast, and when he got to a place where he could see over the precipice his heart leapt into his throat with fear. A lion it seemed was what had been banging at the north gates. This was no ordinary lion though. It was nearly half the height of the front gates with a grand grey mane shot through with dark streaks, grey fur with striking silver eyes and claws. The beast would be beautiful if it wasn't so terrifying to behold.

It looked to have been distracted by something to the south as it slowly turned away from battering the front gates as something else had drawn its nose. Chuffing and sniffing the air, the creature slowly turned in that direction just as Olofi and Daniel caught a glimpse of movement. Squinting Daniel could barely make out the silhouettes of whatever poor saps Kemet had chosen to send out to distract this monstrosity. Olofi produced a small looking glass and handed it to him. "Tell me who you see there, that has the attention of the Ingonyama Enkulu." He asks.

Surprised the old man had such an apparatus, Daniel did as he was instructed and used the device to take a closer look. Now with the ability to focus he exclaims "I think it's the exiles that were being escorted around earlier! A few of the city shields are with them, and I think an inquisitor that some have not been so happy to have around." Taking the device to get a peek himself Olofi mutters "Interesting. Exiles you say? Why does no one want these inquisitors around?" Before Daniel could answer the dire lion sprang forth swatting at one of the rear guards sent out to deal with it sending the man flying.

The rest of the group engaged so it could not focus on one target. Two of the city shields went in with tetsuo blades flashing. Their movements were nearly in perfect sync. At the first pass there was a strange silence as if nothing had happened only for that brief respite to be shattered by a thunderous roar. A Djaemon ran in with a bedazzled looking blade highly uncharacteristic for anyone of his kind to be carrying, and the others followed suit in order to continually harry the beast. They gave it no time to recover or strategize an approach. Slice after slice kept constant pressure on the huge animal.

When the word spread that this tactic was working, soon archers appeared at the battlements peppering it further. In between volleys ground forces boiled out of the city with the beast distracted to reinforce the brave advance group. After swatting a few of them despite the pain being inflicted, the shadow realm intruder began retreating but did manage to snag a city shield who lingered too close for too long in an attempt to land a blow. They all froze in horror for a moment as they could hear bone and armor alike crunch sickeningly as the powerful jaws made quick work of him.

One group of city shields formed a phalanx and began walking the creature back in coordination with volleys of arrows, forcing it to back away further. Rebelliously it took another large swat at the group advancing destroying the formation out of protest it seemed before the now bloodied beast looked as if it heard something none of them could. It turned and simply ran off leaving them all confused. Olofi moved faster than Daniel thought possible for an elderly person. They made their way back down to greet the defenders now heading back into the city.

It was decided they would keep the city closed in case any more shadow realm encroachers came along without warning. When they made it to the gates along with the other citizens who came out to express their heartfelt appreciation the city shield commander was being briefed by two of her lieutenants. Daniel made a face when he saw they were not speaking but signing to each other. "Are they trying to be secretive? He asked. Olofi smartly cuffed the young man upside his head. "No, you fool! Either she is deaf or they cannot talk obviously. I gather it's the latter from the coverings over the bottom half of their faces."

Daniel rubs his head as they watch the exiles and rogue Djaemon walk in. The woman has short blond hair and strange armor. The man with dark hair has similar armor in addition to what Daniel thought was a thick wooden leg but upon closer inspection it is made of a metal with eerie lights at certain sections. The man was complaining as they helped him move along. "Next time one of you can play Jerry to that big ass Tom of a lion! Max is not the one!" Seeing the looks of slight amusement on the Inquisitors face, the Djaemon and the woman in their company, Olofi and Daniel surmised that must have been the person who took that unfortunate first swipe from the dire lion.

Everyone's mood turned somber as they hauled in the mangled remains of the city shield that wasn't fast enough to avoid the gaping maw and horrid jaws of the beast from the shadow realm. As they were passing with his and a few other bodies the crowd spoke almost in unison "Sidibene Kakuhle", and the phrase is echoed as the bodies pass more groups of mourners. It was now Olofi's turn to be confused.

Looking to the young man he asks, "Daniel the Lesser, what does that mean?" Trying to hide the well of tears building up in his eyes Daniel replies "It's a formal greeting. It's like saying hello but in times of death it can also be a hero's greeting which also says well met, we shall see you again." They thought on that as the rest of the city shields filed in and secured the gates after they closed. Slowly the city folk went back to their homes to discuss the possibility of the city nearly falling to one beast from the shadow realm.

Olofi and Daniel stayed out a while longer before meandering about until they ended up back at Salim's. Olofi perked up when he saw the exiles were there as well. It was obvious there were always going to be eyes on them as they went about in the city but at least the city shields were no longer personally tailing them. Daniel nudged him after they discussed the seeming slight change of heart. Looking to where the man was nodding Olofi could see a group of burly men and women that had taken an especially acute interest in the two exiles and the rogue Djaemon.

It seemed as if some of the city shields had taken a new approach of surveilling them by eschewing their armor and tetsuo blades to be less conspicuous. It wasn't working. One of the exiles noticed the attention of the group as well as Daniel and Olofi gawking at them in addition. He limped over nearly dragging his strange metal leg. "I see you've noticed the plain clothes units following us around now that we're at least temporarily out of the clink." Confusion shown on both of their faces as Olofi greets him "Sidibene Kakuhle, I am…Lofin, and this here is Daniel the Lesser."

Bewilderment turns to consternation as Daniel nods in greeting as the man nods in return offering "I'm Max, that blonde firecracker over there is Sparks, and the big red guy is Argos." Sparks did not appreciate the intro but waived politely and Argos tilted his head almost imperceptibly. The Djaemon went back to admiring his bejeweled blade. Olofi waived them over and called for Akachi to bring them a round of drinks. Reluctant to join the two at first, that changed when the large flagons were put atop the table.

As they all bellied up to drink, Oluso entered the tavern and saw his charges sitting with the old man and a known fabricator. The mystical inquisitors' instincts automatically kicked in as his eye began to twinkle once it settled on the seemingly jovial elder statesmen. Finding a spot on one of the hard benches Oluso asks "Mind if I join you?" There's an awkward pause as Olofi can't quite put his finger on it but there's more to this inquisitor than meets the eye. Max breaks the tension as he asks, "You two gonna kiss or can we drink?" They erupt into uncomfortable laughter as Lofin says "Of course, of course! My apologies inquisitor. Old Lofin and Daniel would enjoy more company. Where might you all be from?"

Taking a long pull from one of the tankards in front of him Oluso replies "That's been a sore subject of late for this group. I will answer for myself, but would like to ask you the same in return. Quite sure you're not from around here…old timer."

Chapter Eight

Tanji was not yet fully restored to its former glory, but it was well on its way. News travelled fast about the presumed culprit being caught finally. Simon, Mael, Jamaal, and Kanaa listen to the latest gossip as they gather provisions before heading to Kemet. Otemu watched them closely as his daughter Kezi gathered their own provisions for a fishing expedition. The village chieftain was grateful for the help they provided but still had doubts about the boy. He had grown a lot since they last saw him. Kezi who was one of the principal teasers when they were little seemed to be in awe now.

Otemu felt the boy's mother was a trouble maker and though still a young boy, the feeling that he was the omen that always preceded bad news or tidings would not go away. The adults he was now in the company of seemed like nice reliable people. The storm that nearly destroyed their small village all those years ago was on the day this boy was introduced to the world. When he returns, another calamity happens. Thinning of veils between the realms, rogue magi, and reawakened elder dragons. Otemu understood very little of what was being described as the causes for the recent chaos, but he was familiar with cursed energy when he felt it.

A small part of him felt guilty that the boy had been orphaned at such a young age before being sent away. The boys' father was well respected before he went off to another senseless conflict. His disappearance was like many others who sought pay and glory on battle fields on which they didn't belong. Many of the fisher folk shared the superstitions and rumors surrounding the boy with the strange skin and inexplicable power. At the behest of the village midwife who also doubled as somewhat of a shaman, a blind vote was taken behind Otemu's back.

The vote enlisted assassins who were supposed to eliminate the boy, but the mother fought too fiercely. The burning of the home was supposed to make it all look accidental. The shameful looks on some of the village folk told Otemu that more were involved than he initially thought. No one would outwardly admit that they were involved and to this day there was a strange solidarity surrounding keeping those directly responsible anonymous. The village chieftain figured what's done is done. There was no going back and he could not truly rectify things even if we wanted to. That ate at him but he was still responsible for the village and his family. He still could not bring himself to look that boy in the eyes.

Taking a bundle of extra supplies, Otemu walked over to Jamaal and Kanaa, handed it to them and walked away calling for Kezi to come along. Simon and Mael saw the brief silent exchange and came to them. "What was that about?" Simon inquired. Kanaa went to inspect the supplies and from her head movements and sounds, she approved. To Simon she replied, "The villagers know they were wrong for how they treated young Mael, but this was as close to an apology as they could manage, I think." Anger was etched on the adults faces as they prepared to make their way to Kemet. Mael was unsure of how he felt.

Anger was understandable, and he felt that, but this whole homecoming experience had been a cascade of bittersweet emotions. He never forgot the looks of disdain and fear he got from the villagers or the mean-spirited taunting at the hands of their children. There was still some of that even now but it had evolved since he had grown up some and some of the people who had eagerly ushered him out of town, saw him in action. Some still feared and were repulsed by his presence, but there were also others who now revered him for his efforts along with the people he came with.

Kezi looked at him differently, and while Mael had no idea what it meant, it was obvious her father still held malignant feelings towards him. With a sigh that told the group this was a heavy subject to be tabled for a later time, Mael gathered up his belongings so they could be on their way. With a grunt, Jamaal hefted his massive tetsuo blade out of the ground and slung it on his shoulders letting the rest of them know that he was ready to move out. Kanaa sinched her pack, and leg quiver tight so they didn't move about in case they had to move quickly.

Simon looked to be done applying the awful smelling salve so he signaled they should step off saying "Let's see what all this fuss was about. The fool must be brought to justice, and I for one could do with a bit of brew from Salim's." Jamaal could not help but smile at the thought of a good drink which prompted Kanaa to elbow him roughly in the ribs. Mael stifled his laughter as he fell in line with his found family. Looking northeast towards their destination they could see they weren't the only ones making the short journey in anticipation of the coming event. That included some of the fisher folk of Tanji.

Mael's mind started to wander when he saw something off in the distance to the left of them cresting the foothills between the Mulanje mountain ranges and Inciniba. It was large but obviously low crawling in an attempt to keep a smaller profile. It wasn't working. Calling out softly to Simon and the others to get their attention without raising an alarm, Mael points to see if his eyes are playing tricks on him asking "Are you seeing this?"

Kanaa nocks an arrow just in case as she somewhat recognizes the partial silhouette in the distance as some kind of predator. Just as Simon prepares to gather his unesiphiwo and Jamaal nudges his massive blade off of his shoulders the animals' front quarters peaks out of the foliage it was partially hiding in. They notice what looks like a harness and a small reign bit in its mouth. Simon let out a small sigh of relief as this looks to be a tamed dire panther but the question is where was its rider? After a few tense moments, a slim dark-skinned man came out from the underbrush as well. He was using a khopesh to cut his way through.

When he saw the group staring in his direction with weapons drawn, he waived quickly to reassure them he and his mount meant no harm. "Sidibene Kakuhle! My name is Baaqir. Don't mind Sheba, I fed her a while back but she gets a bit restless if I ride too long." Simon quickly dissipates the burgeoning power he was holding and returns the greeting as many more Pantu tribesmen sprang from the long treelined area. It was interesting that there would definitely be a rather large yet diverse audience for the rogue magus when he arrived. "I am Simon, this is Mael, Jamaal and Kanaa. I take it you're headed to Kemet as are we, but where are you venturing from friend?"

Thinking on it he responds "I guess we are part of the advance group, but with the exception of a couple of my new red friends, we did not go down for the actual apprehension. The main group is marching the wayward fool over as we speak." Out of the brush comes a line of Djaemon, two very large males and a pretty impressive female who although isn't as stout as her counterparts is no less intimidating. All of them are heavily scarred. Mael is curious but also quite wary of them.

Trying to keep things cordial Baaqir introduces them "Simon, Mael, Kanaa and Jamaal? This is K'Ain, D'Na and T'Ome. They're from Gcina Okubovmvu in the red desert just a bit south of the Tetsuo monastery and west of the grasslands where my tribe lives. Life sure is crazy these days." Mael did his best to compose himself and gave a strange half bow and waive, immediately feeling self-conscious afterwards as the others greeted the other new arrivals. These were strange times indeed. Simon knew the boy was nervous but part of him was very proud of the way he handled himself in light of the new company.

Mael was absolutely mesmerized by the panthers as they strode in step with their handlers who walked beside them or the others being ridden by the Pantu tribesmen. Much larger than normal panthers these beasts had evolved to be large enough to take down a full grown bedrahin singlehandedly. Simply put these animals were loosely contained violence that could spring any second. The contrast was that they were also very beautiful to watch. The boy was amazed at the cool calm demeanor of the Pantu Tribesmen casually riding or walking along when at any moment one of the animals could literally rip them from head to hind quarters in a matter of seconds.

Baaqir noticed the boy's scrutiny and obvious curiosity. The young man's soul nearly leapt out of his body as the tribesmen had Sheba softly pad up beside him before asking "Would you like to pet her?" Mael had been staring intently at the other dire panthers unaware that when he turned around, he would be gazing into such luminous amber eyes. He nearly fell over causing Sheba to give pause and it was Simon and Jamaal's turn to attempt to hide their guffaws.

Kanaa was one of the few unappreciative of the moment, and didn't see the humor in scaring the boy. Mael quickly composed himself as the panther stopped at some nonverbal command Baaqir issued either with his hand on her neck or with his legs. Mael was trying to see how the command of such a creature was being executed but it was all too subtle for him to pick up. "Did you say its name was Sheba?" Mael asked. Quickly sliding off the panthers back Baaqir answers "Yes, Sheba is her name. She has been my companion since she was a cub. I had to wait until she matured some before, I could ride her. In the Pantu, you cannot have a herd until you have a mount. More accurately until a Pantu mount has chosen you."

At the repeating of her name the panther looks back and forth between Baaqir and Mael as if annoyed. While passing Kanaa comments "If she could cuss you out, she would." Baaqir smiles at the jest, before taking out what looked like a brush looping his hand through the handle and began brushing the panthers coat. After a few moments he handed the brush to Mael and motioned for him to give it a try. Cautiously he looped his hand into the brush as he saw Baaqir do. Then while looking at Sheba he went to brush her but stopped just short of pressing the brush to her coat. "Is she going to stare intensely at me like that the whole time?" he asked.

Chuckling Baaqir says "Of course, but you have nothing to worry about. Since I haven't reacted to you as a threat, she won't regard you as such. You are however about to physically touch her. She is watching in case my judgement is bad. If you were to try and harm her or me, she would make her own judgement at that point. For now, she is satisfied to keep an eye on you since you garnered my interest." Mael got over his hesitation and just went for it and began hastily brushing.

As he got more comfortable, he slowed down and noticed Sheba finally closed her eyes while leaning into the brush causing him to giggle and step back. "She likes it I think!" he exclaimed. "I think you're right, but I think we should keep moving. She likes you." Baaqir said before opening a hand to ask for the brush which Mael reluctantly returned. Sheba was still purring noisily as they continued on towards Kemet. The sun was setting as they saw the gates come into view. Mael wondered why a Pantu tribesmen had taken any interest at all in him.

Catching up with Kanaa he asked her "Why would the Pantu tribesmen have any interest in anyone like me?" Kanaa turned to the boy and half embraced him as they walked. He wasn't quite sure why but he allowed it and leaned into her affectionate gesture. He could see she was thinking of what to say until she finally replied "With all of the rumors going around, your name is among them. In small places like your birthplace, it may start with just how you look. Now that you've travelled a bit and done something, your deeds will fuel rumors as well. You are different and for those reasons alone people will talk. It's compounded by the fact that you also have special abilities, and some will be wary or even jealous of you if not outright afraid. The Grey Moors have a tale about you while we were at sea. The villagers of Tanji thought you were long gone only to have you return to help them in fantastic fashion. Your legend will grow young one. Don't let it go to your head…and don't let their ignorance dissuade you from your beauty."

Mael wasn't sure he fully understood the last part but he was grateful for the kind words. He extricated himself from her half hug and ran to catch up to Simon and Jamaal who were up ahead checking out the approach to the city. A long line had developed at the front gate, and the city shields looked to be keeping track of all who entered. As they drew closer to the gate the Pantu tribesmen and their mounts formed up into a two columned formation. Baaqir began to call cadence announcing their official arrival. At the gate they were told they could enter but would have to leave their mounts outside of the city. It was expected but some were still disappointed.

Simon, Mael, Kanaa and Jamaal waded into the sea of bodies trying to gain access to the city. A rather diminutive looking city shield approached Jamaal and informed him he would have to check his blade at the city shield barracks before heading into the rest of the city and on to the citadel where everyone was gathering to await the arrival of the elder dragons and Motu, so they could decide his fate. Mael noticed some rather large scratches at the front gates and more along the walls that he didn't recall seeing before. While Jamaal went to check his weapon, Simon ran into Salim's. Kanaa just shook her head in disapproval.

Surprisingly Simon didn't linger long in the tavern and came out with some news as Jamaal circled back to join them. At the quizzical looks he commented "Apparently, it's been lively a lot of places including Kemet. There was a Ingonyama Enkulu here at the gates after we left trying to force its way in and feast. The people that live on the outskirts of the city are trying to seek refuge within the city walls in case it comes back. So, it's not just the fate of a rogue magus that has boosted the population here."

Jamaal and Kanaa looked at each other briefly and Simon guessed it likely had to do with how they all left Kemet the last time they were here. The city shields as well as a mystic inquisitor had them all pegged as persons of interest in a wide-ranging investigation that started with an incident on their homestead involving revenants and a potential murder. Hopefully they had bigger intlanzi to fry. Just to be sure though they covered up as best they could and tried to keep a low profile. Despite the heat Jamaal and Kanaa dawned hooded half cloaks. Simon understood what they were doing but refused to hide and wore his cleanest set of ceremonial robes. It was all black with clean blue lines. It was a favorite of his that he had not worn in a long time. In case he was called upon to speak, he wanted to look the part.

After all there was a fellow magus at the center of a lot of the current strife, and troubles going through the lands. Huddling up with his group Simon asks them "Now that the miscreant is in custody, what would you all have done with him?" Tears welled up in Kanaa's eyes as she stated flatly "Death. He took our little girl from us. I would pay him back in kind." Coming closer to put an arm around his wife Jamaal nodded his agreement with her assessment. Mael was not as assured that the man deserved to die but he also went along with their decision.

There was a commotion as the search detail was now in sight of the western gates on the city proper and the crowds that had gathered at the north gates as well as within the city all came piling out for the chance to get a glimpse of the now infamous diabolical being that was somehow responsible for the sicknesses across the lands in addition to the recent shadow realm invasions. Not everyone was clear on how this all connected with the waking the elder dragons, but hopefully things would become clear when he was called to answer for his crimes.

A chorus of loud boos went up as he was paraded into the city in chains flanked by the city shields that went on the search detail. They were followed by the Djaemon. The Pantu tribesmen had broken off as soon as they caught Motu to give Kemet a heads-up of his ensuing arrival. A small carriage with a cage held what looked like a young dragon surrounded by the fire forged that went with the search detail on foot. Everyone's attention was instantly taken from the prisoner when loud screeching heralded the arrival of the three elder dragons as they flew to the apex of Inciniba.

Kibo, Mawenzi, and Shira took to their perches atop the citadel and waited for them to bring Motu and his remaining contingent of partially revenant Djaemon. There was some confusion as to what to do with them. The city shields in garrison had to come out to calm the crowd that had become a bit too rowdy in expressing their disapproval. Some began hurling rotten produce at Motu and the pale Djaemon who were under his sway inadvertently hitting some of the search party members. Relations between the Djaemon and mankind was always in flux. Things usually leaned into the unsavory aspects. A brawl between them and the citizens of Kemet would be highly counterproductive right now.

The city shields within the gate of Kemet came out to ensure things would not escalate to that boiling point. They calmed a bit but still let the magus hear them. Simon studied the man as he was walked into the city then he seemed to play into things by dropping to his knees forcing his guard detail to physically carry him to the top of the citadel where the elder dragons and leader of the fire forged awaited him. Mael was a bit confused by the sudden change in demeanor. "What's that all about?" the boy asked.

Simon leaned in and said "I think it may be a play for sympathy, and although he may have had a bit of experience with dragons seeing as he somehow got his hands on one, they are not the forgiving kind under even the best of circumstances. From what I saw of Kibo when we went to his lair, he will not take encroaching on his territory lightly. Not to mention the other things this man is supposedly responsible for." So far luck was on their side as everyone was paying much more attention to Motu, his young dragon and his revenant cohorts.

Nobody paid much attention at all to Simon, Mael, Jamaal, and Kanaa so they were able to move about pretty freely. They were even able to elbow their way close to where the proceedings were to begin. Simon and his friends got into perfect positions to hear Kibo address the rogue magus directly after hopping down from his perch landing with resounding thud. Fanning his wings as if he was trying to adjust blowing dust into Motu's face as he did so. The man was just left to kneel in front of the black elder dragon. The silver and gold elder dragons looked on as Kibo took the lead.

"Motu the necromancer…whatever shall we do with your pitiful self?" he snarled. Nobody would have been surprised if the dragon bent down to chomp the man in half, and many of them would have been happy with that result. At least two people were fervently hoping to see that vision come to fruition. They would be disappointed.

Chapter Nine

High above Nyumbani, Izulu reigns supreme in the heavens as the gods for the most part go about their own existences without worrying too much about what the mortals below have going on. Olorun walks into his private chambers and sees a special tablet he and his other aspects created to communicate with each other when the spiritual tether was stretched too far for telekinetic messaging. The thruster on Izulu blazed hotter than it ever had providing the surface with an unbearably hot day down below on Nyumbani. The Sky god and creator was wondering how Olofi was getting along on his information gathering mission.

He found it ironic and a bit amusing when words began to form on the pages. Just knowing one of his other selves was currently furiously scribbling away as he watched the detailed report materialize made him feel better. Some would say this was how it was supposed to be. Olorun was to rule, create and divine from the skies while Olofi was to be the bridge between both Izulu and Nyumbani. Something about the distance made Olorun feel uneasy. What outright irked him was the fact that some mortal was meddling with dimensional veils, spreading an ailment to the lands below and causing other problems. What's worse was that Olofi suspected one of their own was likely at fault for all of it.

Reaching out through time and space Olorun tried to strengthen their connection so he could feel the slippery yet all too familiar power Olofi described feeling when he was accosted by some poor mutilated Djaemon revenant soon after making planetfall. Olorun chuckled a bit at the thought of tossing his aspect overboard before the other Orishas could see what he was doing. The realization that came too late on Olofi's face was priceless just before he was thrown. Surely his aspect would not find the circumstances humorous in the least. Oh well, he'll have to get over it. Olorun thought.

Heavy footsteps could be heard coming towards his chambers. Quickly throwing some garments over the tablet Olorun goes to see who is paying him a visit at this time. By the time he got near the threshold to his entrance the power in the visitor was felt clearly. Power nearly reverberated through the walls. "Ogun, to what do I owe the pleasure?" Olorun asked as he opened the door. A heavy hand harshly claps the Olorun's shoulder as the god of war and iron chuckles heartily replying "The others told me you were here sulking. Something about tainted lands below. Why do you worry so?" Olorun was unsure if it was true the others were gossiping about him or if Ogun was using the notion as a ploy to fish for information.

There was obviously someone from amongst their lineage being too hands on with some of the denizens below. Suspiciously Olorun leans in and asks, "When was the last time you went down to the surface?" Laughing again and waiving off the creators' suspicions Ogun calmly states "It had to have been ages ago when I last used the core to smelt and plant some itsimbi deposits. Shamefully only a few have been able to discover and use any of it. I know how much of a stickler you can be about letting these beings evolve more organically, but let's be honest. They've been far more responsible than many in some of the other realms. I believe they would do nicely if I introduced some advancements. It's been so long and they're still swinging wildly with melee weapons. My itsimbi can be used for so much more!"

"No!" Olorun exclaimed a bit taken aback by the vehemence in his response. He did not apologize but Ogun could tell even the sky god was surprised by the outburst and was likely regretting the harshness in it. Composing himself by smoothing down his shimmering robes, Olorun continues "I know you are fervent in your desire to introduce technology to this realm, but we have seen the danger in doing so in a myriad of others where they have destroyed themselves or nearly so. I for one am not trying to have those mistakes repeated. It seems one of our own may have taken it upon themselves to meddle by knowingly augmenting a desperate magus's unesiphiwo, and the world below is beginning to pay for it. Not only that but the thinning of the veils may have already introduced a manner of tech from another realm to this one."

It was Ogun's turn to heat up…literally. Ogun stood with flames in his eyes that could heat the molten cores of a thousand planets. With more than a little iron in his voice he rumbled "So…one among us has taken to claiming one of my duties as their own, and you are only just now informing me?" Olorun met those flames with star fire of his own stating flatly "I found out only moments before you came to me. The thinning of the veils may have caused this technological intrusion from another realm inadvertently. I do not believe it was an attempt to usurp your duties or domain, but trust that my aspects and I will find the one or ones responsible."

Ogun did not look satisfied with that proclamation but said no more and left quietly enough. Olorun returned to look over the rest of Olofi's report and decided to see if he could learn if any of the other Orishas might have any information. It was obvious from Ogun's response that he was not the culprit. Perhaps this may turn him into an ally in finding the heavy handed among them not willing to let things progress on their own.

Stepping out on a balcony he took in the view of Nyumbani from on high. Even with the corruption spreading, it was still a beautiful sight to behold. Olorun was determined to keep it that way. Olorun understood why Ogun had taken offense to the idea of someone else even indirectly introducing tech to Nyumbani when the only source previously was Izulu itself, and the mortals below did not have access to the giant city ship the planet orbited. In fact, they believed the huge thrusters were simply the sun. The creator doubted any below could fathom they were revolving around a legendary civilization of deities. After what past experiences told the Orishas and other gods how technology in the wrong hands of mortals how things could go horribly wrong, it was decided to take things slow here.

Olorun thought they were all in agreement. Yet it seemed one or more may not concur. It may prove difficult in finding out who wished to dabble in sowing chaos down below, but the sky god was determined to do so. Hopefully it could be done without raising too much suspicion. Leaving his chambers Olorun decided to take a trip down to the gardens. He was not the only one keeping an eye on the situation. Babalu Aye was doing his own due diligence, and was nearby to hear the brief verbal conflict between Ogun, and Olorun. The new tension between them was something the god of sickness and disease hoped to take full advantage of by fanning the flames of suspicion and discontent.

Babalu Aye wanted more power and would do whatever was necessary to build upon what Motu an unwitting pawn had started. Since the other Orishas neglected to see his importance, it was up to him to ensure his rise in the order to take a more prominent position, whether it was up here on Izulu, or if necessary to forge a kingdom of his own below on Nyumbani itself. The one thing he would have to be careful of was the possibility that the magus would divulge the fact that a god had disguised himself as another in order to influence this gathering of power.

Yewa, the goddess of death would not approve of her likeness being used and the false promises given on her behalf. The deity of disease would have to find a way to throw the scent of suspicion her way in order to put her on the defensive. In his mind as long as no one was focused on him and his efforts, things could go as planned. By the time the truth came out he may be powerful enough that it would not matter. Deciding it would be better if he was not caught snooping around the sky gods' chambers, Babalu Aye crept speedily away heading towards the primordial gardens deep within the heart of Izulu.

There he could meditate and flesh out his scheme in peace without the threat of prying eyes, or so he thought. The primordial gardens were one of the most beautiful places any being could hope to find themselves in. There was flora from nearly every realm to ever exist, most of which were extinct in each of the dimensions they originated. The garden was deep within the city ship but the overhead ceilings in this great chamber were designed to look as if you were looking out into the abyss of space itself. Now that he was far away from the tension that looked to be building between Ogun and Olorun, Babalu Aye relaxed a bit. Being the target of either god's ire would not be a great position to have, but it would matter less if Motu continued to build revenants solidifying his power base down below.

The next step was formulating in his mind when something felt…off. The usually pleasant temperature turned cold rapidly forcing him to open his eyes leaving the meditative state he had just fell into for clarity. The ordinarily fragrant ambiance within the gardens soured and he felt an unfortunately familiar presence approaching. His lungs tightened and his throat felt constricted despite no one being around. He knew beyond any doubt who was approaching. Fresh morbidity clung to the air as Yewa seemed to materialize and Babalu Aye quickly composed himself to mask his rising fear. Despite her domain the goddess of death was still a ghastly beauty.

"Feeling a bit contemplative, are we?" she asked. Babalu Aye swallowed and narrowed his golden eyes as he replied, "Absolutely I am. Storms are brewing sister." She shook her head sidling up to him slowly to whisper in his ear "Would they be brewing as a result of someone stirring the pot down below with the mortals? Interestingly I have a few of my chalices that have gone missing." The patron of all pestilence and ironically healing feigned surprise. "Really? He lamely offered. Sweat began to bead on his brow as he saw she wasn't buying it. Looking around Yewa asked "Where are your two favorite slithering pets?"

Nervously he retorted "They have not been feeling themselves so I sent them to another realm to…recuperate." Confusion, anger then slight amusement flashed across the goddess of death's face as she finally stopped to inquire "Was that an attempt at humor? If so, it was a poor one. Now I gather it was either you or Esu but he has no need to guise himself as it's well within his power to emulate my likeness if he so chooses. I am betting it was you, and if I find that to be true, I will take your two basilisks as my own. They shall make fine decorations, and I am not convinced of your…candor in this matter. Olorun is in an uproar but not telling us why."

Babalu Aye did his best to shrug the accusation off, desperately clinging to an air of innocence, but knew she had no damning evidence. If she came with proof more would happen this day in leu of veiled threats. She could not embrace him in death, but that did not mean the others wouldn't vote to let her hold him for a while torturing his being for what would feel like an eternity as punishment. Indignantly he nudges her to get some distance between them. "I have no need of your chalices!" he protests a little more fervently than he desired.

Esu, the trickster god was an interesting prospect to deflect blame onto, but if word got back there would not be one but potentially four gods with grievances against him. As risky as it was Babalu Aye might have to venture back down to Nyumbani to see what the delay was. He could feel his power had risen considerably since putting his scheme into motion, but at the moment he was stagnating. He needed more, and he needed it before all the gathered deities were apprised of his machinations. Perhaps the other city ship that reigned over the night sky where most of the outcast deities spent their time could serve as a haven Babalu Aye thought.

He was not so foolish as to think he could overturn the hierarchy here but at least he could gain enough potency to have the other Orisha's true respect. Often, he felt like a mere afterthought. That had to change. A balancing of the scales was long overdue, and if the sky god, Ogun and even death herself could not see that then he would dig out his own fiefdom below or elsewhere once he had the power to do so with or without their blessings. Yewa studied him as she drew further away waiting for the facade to crack further. The fact that he was visibly nervous was telling.

If things went as she believed there would be much pleasure in breaking this one. She sauntered off accentuating her movements as if to allure him. "You are to be the balance in all things. You and I both are part of that. If you seek to tip the power scales more in your favor, what makes you think the others will allow for that?" With those last comments, she left him to his musings, but her aura seemed to hang in the air long after she was gone. Her power could still be felt. Flowers and other plants had actually wilted in her presence. Bablu Aye observed this and sneered "That is what I want. She is content as part of the balance because she has a measure of potency I was not afforded. There are no temples in my name throughout this world we have eked out here while the rest of my brothers and sisters have throngs of worshippers constantly bolstering them."

Angered at his reaction to death Babalu Aye scurries back to his domain on Izulu to gather his thoughts. There would be no surprise visits there. The basilisks were indeed not feeling like themselves. In fact, one had returned almost completely immolated. Further proof he might have to pay Motu a visit. Without the giant snake guardians to keep an eye on things down below, the god of sickness and healing was operating blind. That would not do. Something had to have gone wrong.

The power that was previously burgeoning as the magus raised the revenant army while the taint spread through the lands was now dwindling. His pets were on the mend and when they had fully recovered Babalu Aye planned to see exactly what was going on. Suspicions would point to him once he disappeared, but that could not be avoided. He desperately wanted to solidify his base of power before making any open declarations. Esu was likely the only god here he could openly challenge but perhaps drawing him in as an ally was the smarter play.

As cliché as it sounded, a trickster god would not be the ally of choice for most, but in any scheme, Esu would surely be the first suspected. May as well take advantage of that knowing full well betrayal at some point was just part of doing business with the likes of him. By the time any of these hypotheticals materialized Babalu Aye figured he would be well ensconced and insulated from any consequences. The only problem was that he would now have to seek him out. After the last encounter, he was not comfortable going out again. It was necessary though.

Throwing a cloak on uselessly, Babalu Aye headed out of the confines of his personal domain to seek out Esu in the trickster god's palatial abode. Disguises here had literally no purpose as all the deities could identify each other by the energy they gave off once in a close enough proximity. On Izulu there was no such thing as a seedy area, but there were places that were less opulent. Heading into the higher reaches that would be considered towards the northern pole of the ovoid shaped city ship, the streets were not as gold laden, but everywhere it remained to look like the height of modernity.

This whole place was a mix of technology and the depth of cultures that spanned untold millennia. Even having spent a considerable amount of time here as an immortal Babalu Aye could not help but marvel at this place. Many chose to fly under their own power, or take the many powered walk ways and bullet trains, but some like Babalu Aye chose one of the oldest modes of travel while here. He simply walked to take in the sights. Seeing the wonder brought up a bit of anger and jealousy. Angry that most mortal civilizations would never attain this level of achievement and after trying to sway things to his advantage it would be highly likely Babalu Aye would be ousted to live amongst lesser beings.

That would also come after being tormented by death. A concept he did not relish. The optimal thing would be to build his power base as planned and simply relocate on his own terms. This had become a home they all loved. Some more than others but the god of pestilence would rather have a meager kingdom of his own than to languish as a proverbial doormat of the power spectrum here in paradise. The other city ship destination was a glum place where Serat and a few others resided. Not the most pleasant of places. The blood god and the sycophants that entertained him would not be a welcoming crowd.

The streets had gone from a glorious golden hue to a drab but still metallic grey. Foot traffic of any sort had tapered off to nearly nothing and Babalu Aye knew he was close. As he neared the entrance the environment shimmered signaling that he was breaching an invisible membrane where Esu reaffirmed his status as a master of illusion. From the outside it looked as if this were simply the poorer side of the city, but once inside the ostentatiousness of the trickster gods' tastes shined through. Babalu Aye was trying to gather his thoughts to formulate how to proposition an alliance.

The feeling of another familiar presence let him know he would not get the chance to finalize the gambit. He would have to improvise on the fly. Seeming to appear out of thin air Esu himself steps out looking dapper as ever. "Hello brother. Curious finding you here. To what do I owe the pleasure, or displeasure?" he asks. Looking sheepishly Babalu Aye replies "Now why would my visit be the source of displeasure? I have no quarrel with you."

Suddenly there are a myriad of images in various garb of Esu all around, and with many voices they echo "Rumors abound dear Babalu that someone or something has been meddling too far into mortal affairs down below ruining that perfect jewel Olorun covets so much and we all know how he takes his precious creations. The hypocrisy of it is hilarious, but that's neither here nor there. Now tell me, have you come to discuss these rumors, or something a little more…interesting?" The images dance around before colliding into the true god standing before him. Esu shakes his head as the last of them morph into his body. "Ah, that's better! You were saying?"

Chapter Ten

He landed roughly as his momentum carried him through the rift leaving the shadow realm behind. The washed-out color pallet instantly changed before his eyes into a much more vibrant aesthetic almost hurting them. Things were not exactly as Simba remembered. Off in the distance he could see a pall hanging over the grasslands to the south of him. After a quick self-assessment and ensuring there were no injuries suffered during his brief rift hopping, the banished magus scanned the area looking for landmarks he recognized.

Simba soon figured out the hazy clouds had to be hanging over one of the Pantu grasslands which placed him just north of the Luhlaza woodlands. He could see the enormous dome that had formed over the Elinanye ancestral home. "I'll come back to dismantle you myself since it would seem my pet was unsuccessful in cracking that nut." He murmured to himself as he headed southeast towards the dead marshes skirting the Elinanye borders. The banished one wanted to make sure he was fully acclimatized before getting into any conflicts here.

It took time but as he walked, he could feel his unesiphiwo burgeoning. His powers were reawakening after remaining dormant for so long. He stopped as it gave him a feeling similar to a drug induced euphoria. The sensation distracted from noticing a gathering of Iigbin that had been tailing him as he approached the outskirts of the dead marshes. The bluish green skinned goblins had a clear numbers advantage but individually tended to be smaller in stature. Simba assumed they took him for an easy mark, but also knew they would likely wait for nightfall before attempting anything. Generally, their species had an advantage when it came to night sight over men.

The shadow lion was no ordinary man. When the heat of Izulu's thrusters that served as the sun here dipped below the horizon giving birth to the night sky, these Iigbin will be biting off more than they could chew. Needing to hone his skills further in addition to seeing how much practice he would need with regards to casting, Simba Kivuli decided to play along. The former exile gathered kindling to make it obvious he would be setting up camp for the night. The magus could only shake his head as he felt the various beady eyes boring fictional holes into him as he made a show of his preparations.

Moving around he was once again reminded of the paunch that had developed throughout the seasons spent in the shadow realm. Well at least with all of this combative activity that would be remedied soon enough he thought. Racking his brain, he tried to remember the proper incantation to summon a small veil of protection over his form so he could lay down and pretend to sleep. As the light finally abandoned the sky, it came to him. "Ukhuselo." He whispered to himself barely remembering the subtle hand motions. While lying down there was a brief shimmer that enveloped his body. With that done, he closed his eyes and rested next to the small fire hastily built to keep predators away.

Although it shouldn't have been a surprise given what he'd just gone through sleep actually took him quickly. The Iigbin waited thinking it was a ruse. Mentally Simba Kivuli was taken into the past via a deep dream state. The world he found himself in was a scene from his youth. Itempile Yomlingo was at the time one of the most prestigious schools of magic where only the best went to see if they had what it took to become a true magus. "Ayisosopho sodwa!" the professors would chant while the students meditated to find the pool within them where their power awaited to be tapped into.

The grounds were always immaculate. If the students hadn't known better, they would have sworn this was a pocket dimension kept pristine by magic to be untouched by anyone outside of the mystical ministries. This was a beautiful vision and from the lack of anything detected with his senses beyond sight, Simba realized this was a dream. It angered him that despite being transported to this place and era in his life, he still could not remember his true name. It was at the edge of his consciousness, and he could feel it but somehow lacked the ability to pluck it from this memory when it should have been fresh in his mind. He opened his eyes.

Strange as it was to do so now because he vividly remembered remaining in position as the other students had on that day. All eyes closed concentrating fully on finding their centers of power. All but two of them, and Simba recalled their names easily which stoked his frustration. Jamaal, and Simon as he recalled. An odd pair to be sure, and Simon didn't seem quite right. Some of the other students were surprised he was accepted at all to study at such a grand place. The professors were repeating the phrase from earlier which meant "It's not the gift alone.".

Simple Simon they had come to call him since the boy had a speech impediment. He and Jamaal became fast friends and Simba was always a bit jealous of that. Powerful though he was, his connections were strongest with beasts that most were terrified of. In dire times it was a talent he would exploit much to the chagrin of other magi. Leaning too far into this aspect would eventually lead him into exile. The dream was shattered as a nasty looking blade tried to end his life.

His eyes sprang open as a loud chime signaled something tried and failed to penetrate his veil of protection. The noise made the five Iigbin standing over him fall back. One clumsily fell into the fire screaming in pain as the flames engulfed his body. More Iigbin crowded in to beat the flames. As the flames were doused and the overhead coverage from the surrounding trees blocked the moonlight, darkness prevailed emboldening the Iigbin bandits. Simba closed his eyes briefly. When he opened them, his pupils were silver and blessed with the sight of many nocturnal predators he had come to know. Foolishly the group of goblin kind rushed in thinking his sight was impaired by the lack of light.

Day or night would not matter. The exiled magus was back in his home dimension with his connection to his unesiphiwo fully restored. Not to mention he had just spent many seasons in the shadow realm where dusk and night ruled heavily regardless of what time it was supposed to be. Standing to his feet, Simba only unsheathed one of his black blades as the throng of Iigbin came charging in confidently.

With his other hand he summoned a globe of energy. The attackers in the rear had a chance to hesitate, but those at the front were already committed and too close to reverse course.

A flash briefly lit the area as Iigbin bodies were turned to ash as they met the ball of magic bringing most of the group to a halt at seeing what happened to their companions. Simba leapt through the wall of ash while unsheathing his other blade. The surprise at what just happened wore off quickly. After he beheaded the foremost Iigbin while jumping through the lead assailants his blades were being blocked and reposted by multiple wicked or crude blades. These were a seasoned bunch to be sure. What they lacked in strength compared to some of the larger human or even Djaemon warriors they made up for with speed and coordination of attacks.

Simba's rustiness with swordsmanship was showing as a shower of glancing blows rang off of his armor. A few nicks to his midsection where he had outgrown his gear made him grunt in pain, but didn't slow him. "That's one way to lose the weight." He quips. Rolling back towards the now smoking fire remains, he quickly retrieves his helm dawning it a minute moment before another dark blade clangs off of it saving his life. Remembering that he wasn't some holy paladin wielding an enormous tetsuo blade, nor was he stuck in the shadow realm having to rely solely on his skills as a melee combatant, Simba dodged backwards to evade more incoming slashes exclaiming "Ukutshaya!" as he continued to retreat.

The Iigbin were confused as they were suddenly enveloped in clouds of smoke. Panic set in as they began swinging wildly often injuring their own inadvertently. Simba swept in slashing and eviscerating with deadly efficiency. Under nearly any circumstances or in any dimension this would have been an unfair fight. Simba had no mercy or sympathy. Had he been anyone else they would have heartlessly gutted him and taken what they deemed to be of use with no thoughts of anything but the results of them having some loot in the end. The Iigbin attempted to scatter out of the murky smoke. One ran right into Simba who casually placed a hand on his forehead whispering "Mdala." Before letting him go and vanishing back into the cloud.

The Iigbin's eyes widened as a few of his clan came upon him to watch in horror as he aged instantly going from a spry young fighter to a grizzled and desiccated corpse before their very eyes. Screams echoed through the night and they finally gave up. They scrambled into the dead marshes as quickly as possible. Simba did not give chase. Kneeling down to catch his breath, he felt the presence of Lasekunene off in the distance, and he could also feel that he was in pain. Closing his eyes, he telepathically reached out to the Ingonyama Enkulu currently locked in battle with the warriors and city shields of Kemet. "Come to me my friend. We shall return when you have healed."

He also reached out to Lasekholo but could not feel his presence at all. The shadow lion did not think his other companion was dead but that something was blocking or cutting off their link somehow. When Lasekunene came, he would be sure to search for his brother before beginning any conquests. Things had evolved here, and he would need his most trusted allies when the time came to exact his revenge. As exhilarating as it was to use his gifts after so long, it taxed him mightily. Simba once again applied a veil of protection to himself after finding a place to rest that was better hidden from prying eyes.

Exhausted, he laid down hoping no one else would disturb him before Lasekunene arrived. Sometime later as the daylight crested the horizon the injured Ingonyama Enkulu limped over to the slumbering magus and collapsed at his side. Simba thought he felt the beasts' presence while he slept but thought it was just his hopes creeping into his snoozing mind. Rising, he went to examine the damage done at Kemet. There was blood matted into the animal's mane and fur near his hind quarters. He tried to remember a healing incantation but they all slipped his mind. "Alright my friend. It seems we both need to recover. You more so than I. I guess we will have to help you the old-fashioned way." Simba Kivuli stated as he transferred the veil from himself to the huge grey lion.

Satisfied that no one would likely come before he returned, Simba stepped off to find the necessary horticultural ingredients to make a healing salve. Although Lasekunene was from the shadow realm meaning his physiology might not match up exactly with his leonine counterparts here in Nyumbani, the magus was confident trying would do no harm. If successful then his trusted friend and usual guardian would be on the mend faster. Then together they would seek out his brother Lasekholo. Thinking on it, gathering twice as much might be beneficial in case the other great lion had injuries as well. The last he knew, the other Ingonyama Enkulu was attempting to breach the barrier the Elinanye raised to reinforce the border to their Luhlaza woodlands.

Gathering up various herbs and other plants to grind up and adhere to a poultice covering the great lions' wounds he thought "As genteel as those pointy eared bastards pretend to be, they can tussle with the best of them." The added propensity for being very astute at using unesiphiwo might have made for an even harder challenge than what Lasekunene endured. Being that these were beasts, the Elinanye were also more likely to try diffusing the situation without harming these magnificent creatures. Simba tried to remember how long it had been when he discovered they were gone as well as the last time they had been fed before that. Magic barrier or no, if a dire lion from the shadow realm is hungry and it senses that there is food beyond that barrier, it will not likely just go away.

Violence may have been the only option he gave the Elinanye in order to stop him from tearing into their territory before eating his fill. On his way back to the boggy dead marshes, Simba froze hiding in the surrounding foliage to avoid another group of Iigbin that were no doubt on their way to one of many subterranean hideouts their kind were in favor of for housing. He had no doubt he could take them but was still not fully recovered from his most recent conflicts both before hopping into the rift to escape the shadow realm, and the initial skirmish near the entrance into the dead marsh itself.

Once he was confident that they were gone and out of ear shot, the magus made his way back to where he left Lasekunene. The beast was obviously worn out but it seemed that no one had attempted to disturb his rest, and the veil was unmolested. Simba removed the veil and then went about grinding his gathered ingredients, adding water before ripping some fabric from his tattered cloak beneath his armor. Combining that with s strip of reptilian hide he scavenged off the large carcasses he left behind in the shadow realm, he made a compress. This procedure would have to be repeated several times given the number of wounds he saw on his companion.

The lions' eyes shot open and he groaned while Simba Kivuli went searching through his fur and skin to find the worst of the sustained injuries. The low growls stopped as it realized who was examining him. "Apologies my friend, but this is necessary to see where I need to place the ointments." The magus said while patting him gently to reassure him. It was unknown if the animal understood, but at the least it calmed down and stoically endured the examination.

The worst of the injuries as suspected were at the hind quarters. A majority of the wounds were on the lower extremities. It looked as if they were trying to hamstring Lasekunene. A wise decision as most would try to avoid the slashing front paws and powerful jaws. The size and variety of wounds meant that the trek away from the city was likely a very painful one. Luckily nothing was too deep or life threatening. After preparing more ointment laden compresses, Simba went about placing them where needed and tying them where it was possible to do so.

At certain other areas he simply packed the ointment in hoping it would stay in long enough to heal the wound sufficiently. There were some problem areas higher up where it seemed arrows were embedded in the large creatures hide, but something had to be done to shed parts of the bolts or arrows. Knowing that this part would be unpleasant, Simba warned "You're not going to like this." The Ingonyama Enkulu shifted its weight once the magus began poking around trying to find a way to get a strong enough purchase on the partial bolts to pull them out.

Lasekunene just stared at him with his large intelligent silver eyes almost as if to say, "I'm not in the mood.", but unfortunately this was necessary. Leaving these foreign objects in the body could lead to infection, or the skin could heal over and the bolts could be causing problems internally that Simba would be unaware of, likely until it was too late. He could not chance that happening. Once he was confident that he had a good grip, he braced and yanked a partial bolt out. There was no way to unseat the barb towards the end of the tip. It was too small to simply push through in order not to deal with it.

Had the bolt gone all the way through the great lion's body it could have been a fatal blow. Lasekunene roared shaking the nearby trees and disturbing the wild life for great distances. They went through this process several times, and finally Simba Kivuli gave the beast some time to rest. By the time he was done, night was falling again, and they were both exhausted. The last wound would not stop bleeding and the magus knew of only one way to stem the flow. He started another fire and watched as the Ingonyama Enkulu seemed to relax once more after the trauma of the day.

He suspected the beast was only pretending to sleep when he placed the tip of one of his blades in the fire, setting it there until it was red hot. Slowly he got up to retrieve the blade only to turn around to find the animal staring more intently this time at him holding the heated sword. A low growl began to slowly build as the lion may not have known exactly what was about to be attempted but knew for sure it was going to be nearly worse than what it had already been through. Looking at the trail of blood still slowly leaking into the ground the magus said "I know, but this must be done. I'll give you some more time though."

He feigned placing the blade back down as the beast looked to understand this would wait, but at the last moment swiftly brought it up to lay the hot tip on the bleeding wound. There was a sizzling sound and Lasekunene's eyes shot back open. Simba saw a huge grey blur as a massive paw flew into his chest knocking him clear over the fire into a muddy patch of dirt. The beast stood abruptly roaring once more before wincing and collapsing back to the ground. The large silver eyes never left Simba Kivuli's direction as he collected himself to stand.

Waiving his hands placatingly and to show they were empty, he approached once more. The growls started up again and he did his best to calm the beast saying "No more, I promise. I think it's sealed now. We can both just rest a bit now if that's alright." Sidling up to the lion under the suspicious glances, Simba Kivuli leans into the animal and slides down to sit in the crook of its body, patting him reassuringly. Absently he places a veil of protection over both of them before falling into a deep sleep. It wasn't necessary. The roars of a dire lion had spooked any would be attackers or predators off for some ways away. Their slumber this night would continue without incident.

Chapter Eleven

Oluso listened to Lofin's tale of the farm town he had never heard of but tried not to let on that he believed very little of the old man's story. Something was off, his senses screamed that this man was not what he seemed. The amusing thing was that every time he glanced at Daniel; the guy looked guilty but it was plain to see the man didn't know what he was guilty of. Oluso made a habit of looking at him to either confirm or deny details of the yarn being spun. Max, Sparks and Argos were simply relieved that they for once weren't the target of suspicion.

Akachi kept the drinks and food coming and all were amazed by how much the old timer could put down. Time passed comfortably and soon others joined the table or sat nearby to listen in as it was obviously a stimulating conversation. An odd twinkle came to Olofi's eye as he turned to Oluso to ask, "I don't mean to be rude but what can you tell me about your parentage?" There was an awkward silence as everyone turned to the mystic inquisitor awaiting his answer. "Uh, my mother was one of the portal guardians, a mother of darkness tasked with keeping those pathways between the realms safe…my father." He began clumsily before the entrance of a well-known character saved him by interrupting.

"Max! You madman!" Eron exclaimed as he ran over to where Sparks, Argos and Max were sitting, wrapping the three of them up in an enthusiastic hug none of them looked to be willing participants of. The feat was rather impressive given that Argos was a fair bit larger than Eron, but the man still was able to include the red behemoth. Olofi was appropriately distracted by the large barbarian making his presence felt, but would couch the question for Oluso for the time being. Something within the man resonated with him. There was a wellspring of power in his aura, and the man did not seem at all taken aback being in close proximity to a deity. Yet it was obvious from his posture and mannerisms that the inquisitor could feel something different.

For those reasons Olofi was genuinely curious to know if Oluso was even aware of his heritage. He was betting the father likely had an abode above in Izulu. Further questioning would have to wait for when he was comfortable broaching the subject, likely with less people around. A supremely svelte looking Djaemon barback came to deliver more drinks as Akachi was now busy with other customers and Olofi was amused that no one picked up on the fact that K'mbo was obviously not a true Djaemon but a changeling disguised as one. Argos could be forgiven simply because if they were telling the truth, he had not grown up in Nyumbani with his kind, but was raised by Max in another realm.

Eron began regaling them with a tale of Max's bravery as he approached the Ingonyama Enkulu outside the gates, confirming Olofi's guess that it was indeed the suspected exile from the isles who was tossed a great distance away by a vicious paw swipe. Daniel of course was mesmerized by the conversation which he wasn't included in but at least wasn't told to beg off. Oluso looked to be deep in thought, no longer paying attention to the main discussion. Olofi took a moment to scoot a bit closer to him asking "If your mother was a portal guardian do you think she would have any insight to how the veils have thinned between realms in addition to this theory of one wayward magus being the cause of the shadow realm incursions?"

The query puzzled the mystic inquisitor who replied, "You have doubts of what the elder dragons stated?" Thinking on that Olofi replies "I have no doubt that is what Kibo believes, but there are always many possibilities. If the group you have over there is indeed from another dimension, then it's possible there is another source. This problem may eventually become more widespread and from a multitude of possible realms crashing into ours. I may not hold your profession but I would think investigating all avenues would be the prudent thing. There are realms far worse that the shadow."

He could see the possibility of invasions from more horrid places than what was presently churning through Oluso's mind. Olofi could also tell the fear was not just one from imagining, but this man had seen evidence of these other places existence. There were times when the imagination could often be worse than reality. It was obvious to the disguised deity that this man before him had set foot in realms that would give the most hardened battle worn warriors here nightmares. That realization intrigued him further about his earlier questioned heritage. Finally, after more thought Oluso stood and said "You're right. I'm not sure where my mother is at the moment, but I do know a good friend of hers who may still be at Al-Karaouine."

Eron, who had stopped boasting to do a bit of ear hustling clapped Oluso roughly on the shoulders declared "Ah! Al-Karaouine, one of the last bastions of education for those wanting to study the mystic arts. If you're making a trip there, I would offer my blade for protection. I have never been, and times are trying these days. One can never be too safe." Oluso didn't immediately respond. He was on board with seeking out the last remaining portal guardian at Al-Karaouine, but taking Eron the silver-tongued savage along may not be in their best interest. Especially since he would also have to take the suspected exiles. The commander of the city shields made it clear they were his responsibility since he vouched for them.

The thought of her seemed to have manifested her presence. Zaniah strode in confidently with Akil and Rahil flanking her. Their usually sparkling armor was caked with dust and blood. All three looked to be in surly moods. Oluso hoped news of him potentially taking at least one headache off of their hands for a while would make them feel better. Hesitantly he walked up and greeted them. He could have sworn beneath the half masks that Akil and Rahil had smirks on their faces. The gleam in their eyes gave it away. They knew that Commander Zaniah was still irked with what she felt was meddling in city business by a mystical inquisitor.

Oluso fumbled through the explanation of what he planned to do. She was predictably not impressed. Akil and Rahil forcibly looked away trying to disguise their laughter. Being mutes made it almost more obvious. Shaking her head Zaniah states "The search party and the elder dragons should be back momentarily with the culprit. Don't you want to be here when justice is meted out? You think Kibo is wrong about his connection through his conduit that proves this Motu to be responsible?" Nodding Oluso replies "I believe Kibo is right about the magus attempting to corrupt his conduit after invading his lair, but the veils between realms are not flimsy things. There could be more to this spreading corruption, and that may involve others. That possibility dictates me seeking other potential causes. You wanted me to trust you to handle the situation here. I'll do that while checking out another promising lead, and take this lot with me for now."

It was plain to see on her face that Zaniah didn't like it but could not refute his points. At least for a bit he would take the perceived exiles out of her hair while they dealt with more pressing issues at hand. She still didn't trust them and her trust of Oluso or more accurately his position was strained to say the least. She turned to Akil and Rahil and signed instructions to them which immediately changed their jovial expressions. To Oluso she added "I'm sending them with you to keep an eye on them. I understand your reasoning for confirming their claims but I say it's still to be determined. Akil and Rahil are skilled and can aid you on your journey." The twins looked crestfallen, and Oluso signed a vulgar phrase to them when Zaniah wasn't looking.

To her he asked "Wont' you need them here? I can handle myself and it seems so can Max, Sparks and Argos. Eron even offered his blade." Trying to contain her frustration Zaniah opines "That especially bothers me. If I heard you correctly, the old man and Daniel the braggart are trying to accompany you as well. Eron is indeed good when it comes to swinging iron around but the exiles and anyone else you can take along are not comparable to tetsuo blade masters. To be honest I want an account of what happens from people I truly trust. The rest of the garrison will return with the search party so we should be fine here." That she openly communicated her distrust of Oluso stung but he understood.

With that the Commander of the city shields left after abruptly downing a flagon of what was becoming the tavern house special. Oluso gave Max, Sparks, Argos, Daniel, Lofin, and reluctantly Eron instructions to get some rest and meet him at first light if they planned on making the journey with him. Lofin interjected "I agree that we not begin tonight as we have had a fair share of food and drink but perhaps, we can be on our way tomorrow as the sun sets to be out of the heat that will surely be upon us by mid-day."

Oluso was incredulous and retorted "We will need mounts at least one for you. I don't expect a man of your…considerable maturity to go on foot." They all chuckled briefly at the diplomatic attempt at the inquisitor calling out Lofin's age. The ancient one waived him off saying "Don't you worry about securing transportation just get some rest as you said, we can meet here when the light source begins to hang low in the sky. I will take care of any transport concerns." Oluso wasn't sure but didn't fight him on it at this time. If the old man could not make good on this promise, the mystical inquisitor would handle things himself. He was a bit worried about keeping a handle on this motley crew of travelers.

The twins, Eron, and the Djaemon he likely needn't worry about if they were attacked on their way to Al-Karaouine, but Daniel and the old man were sure to be liabilities. Something about the old man had Oluso less worried which was irrational but the feeling remained. He had come to trust his instincts and he definitely felt the hint of magic on him. Strong magic to be sure from the way his eye tingled. Thinking about that made him self-conscious. Occasionally he was told there was an almost imperceptible gleam to his left eye when he was out on other investigative calls. The glint often indicated he was near a source of magic or in a place where strong magic was used.

He didn't always understand it, but this was part of why he was so good at his job. Magic when used for nefarious purposes leaves clues that most local enforcers of law are just not used to looking for, or they would not even be aware of the evidence pointing to that possibility. This quirk made him even more efficient than a lot of his contemporaries within the mystical inquisitors who were trained to look beyond the normal methods of executing dastardly deeds. It gained him many allies and potential enemies with the jealous within their own ranks in addition to the criminals who were caught misusing their unesiphiwo and talismans.

Oluso begged off for the night and went to his room. There he put up his habitual protective wards and traps with various devices and tools he had come into possession of or constructed throughout his investigative career after not finishing his studies as a magus because it had been deemed that though there was some talent within him, it just wasn't enough to make him an effective magus. Although the latter assessment hurt, he did have an affinity for sniffing out magic which became very useful in what would become his next occupation. The fact that his connection to unesiphiwo was so strong, some saw that as evidence that he had to be immensely talented. Perhaps he was just a late bloomer some would argue.

Either way a decision was made and he was no longer accepted as a student to pursue that life. It still haunted him. Trying to put that out of his mind, Oluso laid down for the night. Tomorrow would bring its own challenges. After a while the others did the same and filed to their rooms for the night. The night flew by as most of them were sluggish from the carousing the day before. Max was glad they decided to wait for dusk at the earliest to begin their trek. The hearty stew Akachi served was greatly appreciated. Daniel the Lesser spent most of the day convincing himself he was a warrior worthy of being on this journey.

Max and Sparks saw this as an opportunity to get away from the scrutiny of the city shields. That was until they saw two of them would in fact be accompanying them. Argos was tempted to try and join the Djaemon clan but knew that although some of them had come to respect him, it wasn't likely they would accept just yet. He also still felt a deep kinship to Max whom he had known virtually all his life. Oluso made sure he had everything he came to Kemet with safely packed away in various hidden satchels beneath his cloak. Daniel once or twice swore he saw the man arguing with a small light source he pulled from a pocket briefly, but nobody else seemed to notice. Eron, finally showed up and the only one unaccounted for was the eldest member.

"Daniel the minimal, where's pops?" Max sardonically asked. Sighing Daniel replied "He was right behind me when I came down. Oluso looked on disapprovingly as Lofin finally made an appearance, and they all exited Salim's. Just as they thought perhaps the twins had changed their minds, the two city shields seemed to appear out of nowhere spooking Sparks and Daniel. Max observed "You know with weapons that big we should have heard you guys coming. Impressive really." Lofin just shook his head stating, "We should get on our way; the blaze overhead is almost sunk beneath the horizon."

Oluso confused asks "I thought you were arranging for transport? I don't expect you to be able to make such a trek on foot regardless of how well you've maintained yourself over the seasons." Max decided to chime in "I hate to pile on but I agree with Baron Mordo here. You won't make it very far." Sparks gave him the dirtiest of looks but kept silent. Lofin waived their concerns away saying "There will be transport once we are away from the city. Once we are away from prying eyes you will see."

As the elder of the group confidently strode away the rest of them were left no choice but to follow. None of them looked too confident, especially Oluso who felt something had to be amiss. The twins silently flanked the group, Daniel followed dutifully behind Lofin and Oluso. The mystical Inquisitor often looking back to ensure they hadn't lost anyone. Argos hung in the middle of the group with Sparks who looked contemplative. Max tried to hang back with Eron who seemed happy enough to be going on an adventure.

A look of pure bewilderment was on the only true islander among them when Max asked, "So how were you the only one invited to the cookout?" Another icy glare from Sparks influenced Max to quiet himself for a while as the marched on. Soon they passed the city gates headed south east towards what looked to be a dormant portal. No mother of darkness or portal guardian had resided here for untold seasons. When Oluso noticed where he thought they were headed, he communicated as much.

"Why would you bring us here when you know this portal lies in disuse. I hope this wasn't the transport you spoke of earlier." Oluso said sternly. Lofin paid him no mind and kept on walking at a surprisingly fast clip for a person of his seeming age. Oluso sped up to catch him. Frustration did away with all politeness as he yelled "Old man did you hear me?! This is fruitless and I have no time for games if that's what this is."

Olofi rounded on him quickly and time stopped for everyone but the two of them. At first Oluso froze in fear thinking something had hold of him only to feel that he was merely being slowed. The others were stock still unable to move at all. Chagrined that he had not detected the use of magic before it happened Oluso asked "What…is…this?" With a twinkle in his eyes Olofi said "Ah…now that's the respect one ought to have for their elders. Time is frozen for a bit but they will have no memory of this. It's just you and I for now. This portal will open because I will it to. You have been correct in your assumption that there's more to me than meets the eye, but who I am exactly is not important right now. Now what you need to be more concerned with is who you…truly are."

With that Lofin turned away and began to walk anew. Whatever spell he casted was lifted and the group resumed with no one being the wiser that anything untoward had happened. Only Oluso was aware. Max seemed disappointed that no argument followed the mystical inquisitors berating of the old man. They all noticed Oluso seemed a bit flummoxed suddenly. Even Daniel noticed it and was about to comment on it when the spire of the portal loomed heavy in their view against the dark horizon. Max mumbled "I don't know what that place is, but every vid I've seen where something looks vaguely like that, the results are never good."

"Shut up Max." Sparks commented. Soon they were all standing before the spire marveling at its construction even in its long dormant state. Downtrodden and crumbling, it was still a large work of art. Argos and the others walked around to see it from every angle, but Oluso kept his eyes locked on the old man. "I told you; it serves its purpose no longer." He muttered. The usual twinkle in Lofin's eyes turned briefly into a white blaze but the others were distracted by the architecture. Soon there was a low thrum, and the dull chipped façade where the weather and time had worn away the bright colors of the inner walls between the pillars began to glow.

For seemingly no reason at all the wind kicked up as an illuminated portal materialized but they could not see clearly whatever was on the other side. They all were a bit hesitant understandably as Lofin stood near it with a satisfied grin on his face now that he looked like a regular mortal again. Oluso was the only one that actually witnessed him open it. The others gathered near the threshold but none wanted to be the first to go through. Eron casually walked over to Daniel, and when he got close enough, he tossed the young man into the glowing abyss as he screamed. After a moment his hand came back through seemingly unharmed.

Then he stuck his head out so they could see he was alive and well. To Eron he said, "That wasn't very nice!" Max was muttering as he went through "The last time we did this I couldn't breathe for a bit." They watched him disappear into the portal. Eron felt guilty from the looks he was getting so he was next to go through claiming "He wouldn't have gone had I not thrown him. I saved us some time." Argos, Sparks and the twins all walked through together. Only Olofi and Oluso were left. To Oluso the disguised god said, "Your mother was a guardian of one such portal you say?" Silent the mystical inquisitor shook his head positively.

Olofi continued "Did you ever traverse through her portal?" Weighing that thought Oluso shook his head negatively. "Well, what are you waiting for" Lofin said as he disappeared through the glowing portal. After a moment Oluso took a breath and strode into the light.

Chapter Twelve

In Kemet, they did not begin the proceedings immediately but delayed the tribunal to begin the next day. It was being hailed as a "draconian tribunal" as three elder dragons would preside while witnesses came forth to give voice to their grievances resulting from the rogue magus's actions. Motu himself would be given an opportunity to defend himself, admit guilt or choose to stay silent. It was unclear how a final decision would be made. The previous residents of Inciniba were virtually the ruling class prior to the real fire forged retaking the citadel for their own having proved their predecessors to be frauds.

The city shields were just keepers of the peace for the most part. The elder dragons had no real jurisdiction there except for the fact that they were vastly more powerful than anyone present. They would not in fact be present themselves if Motu had not disturbed the world as he did. The truth was that their decision was the least likely to get backlash resulting in more fighting. If the Pantu tribesmen, Djaemon, City shield commander or representative from Tanji tried to have final say, it would likely be countered by one of the others citing their claim was more valid. The fact was that all of their claims were valid so there should be no competing, and arguing with elder dragons would be futile.

There would still be dissention if some disagreed with the elder dragon's final decision, but in reality, nothing could be done about it. Motu sat in a special cell below the city shield barracks. Recently a mystical inquisitor helped augment this particular cell with hidden devices that dampened anyone's ability to tap into their unesiphiwo while incarcerated here. Masindi was in a small cage of his own where the magus could see him through the bars of his cell. The still growing dragonling remained silent but stared intensely at Motu. The cage like the cell was similarly equipped but the magic inhibiting devices were also well hidden.

Motu wanted very much to meet this mystical inquisitor who set all this up as a favor for some misunderstanding with the city shield commander. Masindi simply sat and hissed while staring daggers at the one he blamed for being locked up. The dragon wasn't wrong. Motu plucked him from the magical ether long before he was to be reborn using a tainted conduit. Once free of the cell and small cage it was likely the young dragon could escape the city shields and anyone else wanting to pursue him, but the elder dragons were another matter. Especially Kibo.

Not being fully matured or having access to all of the memories from his previous incarnations has him at a vast disadvantage against full grown dragons. An actualized elder dragon evolved through specially made conduits was a level Masindi could only dream of achieving at present so he would have to be content with sulking and biding his time for an opportunity. Heavy thuds announced the approach of city shields coming to get this farce of a trial started. The weighty door slowly slid noisily to the side as an armored woman stepped into the cell. Tall and sturdily built, Motu looked her over trying to assess whether she was as stout as she looked or if it was the armor that made her seem that way.

Placing a strange set of thin manacles on his wrists she introduces herself "I am Zaniah, commander of the city shields here in Kemet. I trust you will be on your best behavior. I would hate to have to cleave you in half, but I also wouldn't mind saving us all the time. The choice is yours." Something within the manacles was hindering his connection with his unesiphiwo. It wasn't exactly painful but the feeling was uncomfortable to say the least. Looking down at them Motu commented "Another gift from your mystical inquisitor benefactor? You already know who I am."

Roughly pulling him to his feet Zaniah says "Yes, Oluso claims this cell and those bindings would keep you from using your…talents. The angry look on your face tells me he was telling the truth for once." Motu thought that was very interesting. To himself as they walked up the stairs he thought "When I see this Oluso, I shall skin him alive for this!". Forgetting the mental link, he and Masindi shared spooked him when the dragon rasped in his mind "Where was all this bravado last night when you were falling to the ground in an attempt to gain sympathy?"

Motu had abruptly changed demeanor and looked back at the city shields carrying Masindi's cage behind him. Zaniah instinctively drew her tetsuo blade not so gently swatting the bound magus in the back. "Keep moving! I can just as easily claim that the inquisitors' gadgets failed and we had to kill you to avert more disaster. Nobody would bat an eye." She stated coolly. Motu nodded and proceeded to the top of the stairs into the main hall. Having spent the night in the stockade below the city shield barracks where it was purposefully dark, Motu squinted to get his eyes to adjust once they stepped out into the city proper.

The streets leading out of the city and into the citadel were lined on all sides with citizens waiting for this very moment. As soon as he appeared to the public the jeers went up again with renewed energy. While letting the public express their displeasure the city shields were out in force to ensure they didn't get too enthusiastic in their expression possibly delaying the proceedings. Nothing was thrown, but they let the magus and his dragon hear it the entire lengthy walk. The manacles were now making his transplanted limb from the shadow realm creature throb incessantly.

Bowing his head under the auditory onslaught, Motu trudged to Inciniba with his city shield escorts and Masindi in tow. Perhaps one of the gods above in Izulu was aware of the proceedings as the thruster that served as this worlds sun was beaming more intensely than it had in a long while. It wasn't even the summer season yet. The heat seemed to weigh on the magus with each step. The throbbing in his arm wouldn't stop and Masindi had taken to telekinetically berating him. Since no one else could hear he tried his best to ignore it instead of verbally arguing back. Of course, he could wage the verbal war telekinetically as well but he was conserving all the energies he could muster.

The faces and bodies scrolling by as they marched him to the pinnacle of the citadel became a blur. Just to be sure Motu decided to try and access his unesiphiwo, and instantly regretted it. Luckily, he had refused the meals the guards offered at the stockade. A wave of nausea reverberated through his body causing him to dry heave. His knees buckled forcing the two city shields at his sides to grab him keeping him on his feet. His body spasmed again and he was glad there was nothing to be expelled from his bowels or there would have been further embarrassment.

Standing he thought "Yes, I will definitely have to eviscerate this Oluso character when I meet him." A mix of hissing chuckles could be heard behind him. At least Masindi was entertained. They made their way to the roof, and on three of the giant rungs sat the three elder dragons Kibo shimmering iridescent black, with Shira the silver and Mawenzi the gold. All three balefully watch them approach.

"Motu the necromancer as you have been so ineloquently dubbed stand accused of a myriad of crimes against the realm. Using unesiphiwo for your own twisted purposes creating abominations of life here which lead to corrupting of multiple lands and water supplies. Your preponderance for leaping from realm to realm has thinned the veils between them making way for all kinds of strange incursions. All of this is of course enough to call for your death, but you also sought to pervert my personal magic conduit for purposes I care not to know. If we didn't have this mess to unravel, I would simply have my sisters freeze and then roast you and be done with it." Kibo growled.

Mawenzi cocked her golden head to the side with bits of green algae hanging from her strong jawline and looked to the young dragon saying, "And this one has to be considered just as guilty." Masindi tried to placate them whining "I am just a young one! How can you hold me responsible? This magus plucked me from the ether well before my time!" Shira shook her silver head and lowered her face before the cage in which Masindi was sitting stating "You are a dragon!" The other two echoed dragon loudly as she continued. "Even when pulled from the ether before your time, and without your full host of memories or knowledge, you have access to more than what this magus will ever hope to know in five lifetimes! There's no excuse for being an accomplice to his madness."

Masindi wanted to argue but knew it was pointless. Like the magus he would sit back and listen to these childish complaints and wait for an opportunity to escape. G'Orn and his sister, two Djaemon revenants that were partially turned by Motu were brought before the assembly. There were hisses of disapproval from the Djaemon contingent in the back. G'Orn and his sisters normally vibrant red skin was now a muted grey and aside from scars they had received in battle and on hunting expeditions there were no ritual scars to speak of. That they were tainted by Motu wasn't the worst of it to the Djaemon present. It was quite obvious that even while enjoying normal life, they were not followers of Serat.

K'Ain, T'Ome, D'Na and the rest of the Djaemon there started a commotion when they moved to exit the citadel after the last display. Yasuke who stood at the head of the fire forged shouted "K'Ain! You do not wish to see justice done? Was the red desert not affected?" Turning K'Ain grunted something intelligible to most and continued on his way along with T'Ome and the rest. D'Na translated "Yasuke, you and your people fought bravely. You spilled blood and had yours spilled as proper tribute to Serat, but this is nothing more than politics. These Djaemon are not only abominations but it appears they were nonbelievers in life. We will head back to our Gcina Okubomvu to make sure our clan will be safe there. He will send someone to get word if you find a method to purify our waters." With that D'Na turned to follow the others to the city shield barracks to reclaim their arms.

Another round of commotion could be heard as the Djaemon moved citizens slow to get out of their way now that a crowd had formed in the streets. They eventually got the hint and the city shields themselves did not have to moderate the situation. Most seemed relieved but there were a few who disregarded the Djaemon reputation for ferocity. Not all of the city shields wielded tetsuo blades, and those that did knew better than to test the Djaemon unnecessarily. The ones with the legendary weapons on their backs had also passed rigorous mental and moral screening to get them.

The Djaemon were soon out of the city. They would wait until there was a clear line of sight to sandcast when they reached the edge of the desert. Before they got to that point they would have to walk. With them gone and the noise dying down the proceedings above in the citadel continued. "Yasuke, you have the list?" Kibo bellowed. Yasuke stepped forward with a large scroll and began going over the incredibly long list of complaints. Looking up at the elder dragons he asked, "Are we seriously going to have everyone listed here give an account of the wrongs done to them or their lands?"

Bristling at the idea Kibo shakes his head negatively replying "No, just read through them and find the most egregious offenses." Motu could stand it no longer. "Oh, please spare me this farce! Just kill me and get it over with! If you're all hoping for me to beg for mercy or make some other ridiculous plea, then you are all very sadly mistaken! I did what I did to bring my love back to me, and would do it all again tenfold if it were a success! Dear dragon, Master Kibo if you would be so kind as to end this all as beautifully as you described when I was brought before you earlier!" he exclaimed.

There was a moment of silence as all waited to see if the gathering of elder dragons would oblige. There was a morbid fascination amongst some of the witnesses that desperately wanted to see both the magus and young dragon instantly flash frozen and then immediately incinerated before their eyes. Thinking on her lost daughter, slain by revenants created by this magus, Kanaa wanted nothing more in the world than that very sight of Motu's frozen corpse burned to dust in front of them all.

Mael saw the look on her face and flinched before recovering as she turned to look at him. Jamaal tried to place an arm around her to give comfort but she shrugged it off. She needed to hold this rage, and would not let her husband or the boy they were taking in deny her that. Before he got any ideas about dampening the flames of her anger, she shot a glare at Simon, another magus in her eyes to let him know she would have none of it. As far as she was concerned all magi were to blame for her daughter's death. Too many people dealing with forces and power they have no idea how to control for their own selfish reasons.

Good people always paid a price for it. Kanaa knew in that moment that if this tribunal would not put Motu to death, she would do so herself. It would take planning and time to devise a way to get to him unnoticed. This Kibo sounded as if they were trying to find some sort of penance for Motu to pay. No recompense that they could come up with would bring their baby girl back to them. Motu lost his love, and Kanaa understood that, but his loss did not give him the right to visit the kinds of terrors that had now been unleashed upon the world. She looked down to where her leg quiver sat empty on her hip, then to Jamaal's back where his tetsuo blade would be slung.

Without a word, Jamaal knew what she was thinking. He started to shake his head negatively to say that was the wrong way to go about things but the tears in her eyes stopped all thoughts of admonishment. His wife was hurting and right or wrong, he would ride with her. Simon and Mael could of course go on their way. They were owed nothing, but Kanaa seemed to need this. Silently Jamaal prayed the elder dragons would simply carry out the execution so this path could be avoided. Up front Yasuke began reading off names, and a que began to form.

Mael watched the silent exchange and although he did not understand all of it, he did understand some of it as he was there when Zaria was taken from them at the hands of revenants. He looked to

Simon for any guidance but the older man simply signaled for him to hold off on any questions until later. While everyone was listening to the names being called, Kanaa began scanning to see who still had weapons available on their person. Simultaneously Mael, Simon and Jamaal moved closer to her. She tensed to break free of them crowding her until Jamaal bent down to whisper "I know you want to avenge her my love. If they plan to string this fool along, I will go to the end of the abyss with you to ensure his head is separated from his shoulders."

Kanaa wasn't satisfied, and never would be while Motu drew breath, but she did relax. Wiping tears from Jamaal's cheek see asked "What if I would rather place a bolt between his eyes?" Grabbing her hand to kiss it he replied, "Then I shall find some birds with pretty feathers so you have appropriate fletching on them." Smiling through more tears she says, "You always say the most romantic things." Simon seeing that things at least for the moment have been diffused comments "You two are quite a pair." They were about to respond when they heard their names called. "Jamaal and Kanaa." Yasuke announced looking to see if anyone came forward.

Awkwardly Jamaal stepped out from the audience followed by a shocked and now irate Kanaa. Grasping his wrist harshly she whispered loudly "You put us on the list?" Mumbling as they made their way to a spot in the que Jamaal said "They asked for witnesses or victims of his crimes. I didn't know we would be asked to come forth. I just thought they were cataloguing his misdeeds."

Mael and Simon sort of silently chuckled, both hoped this would perhaps dissuade Kanaa from attempting any revenge plot seeing as everyone would hear their story. If something were to happen to Motu then the city shields would have a pretty obvious motive. That was logically thinking though. Simon knew full well neither of them were thinking logically right now. He couldn't imagine the loss they felt, but hoped after some time and reflection they could rise above it.

Looking at the boy he could see that he had been swept up in all of this. Strangely he felt a deep duty to the kid despite him not being his own. They had grown quite a bit closer over their brief time together, and after seeing where he came from, learning a little more about his unceremonious departure and loss of his mother, Simon wanted to protect him from what inevitably was about to become an explosive situation. The problem was that the boy had also become close with his old friends. It was going to be a challenge getting him to leave this sacrificial mission to them to handle on their own.

Mael was becoming more powerful day by day. That would eventually make him feel invincible. Looking at his own missing arm was a daily reminder, and one that he did not wish this young one to experience if it could be avoided. He decided they would have to talk this through later. For now, they watched and listened to the witnesses that were coming forward, and waited on their friends to get their say. The least they could do was support them as they publicly expressed their greatest loss.

Chapter Thirteen

Kenzo waited for the forge to get to the desired temperature. Itsimbi was a very dense ore. Sakanoye was the shike here at the Tetsuo monastery located in the northern area of the red desert. Kenzo had his almond shaped eyes shut tight in concentration as sweat beaded on his forehead. Sakanoye was proud if this young acolyte. He had been patient, and paid close attention to the instructions given him. Today he was forging his first blade. It would be his own. Each of the tetsuo monks carried blades but they were not the oversized yet elegant cleavers the sworn protectors of the realm carried.

This blade would not be as heavy as those yet would still have enough folded ore in it that no one but the person it was blessed and attuned for could carry it. Most that saw the weapons these monks carried would not be intimidated and that's by design. They were also protectors and practitioners of their crafts in addition to martial arts, but not known to be aggressors. They were taught not to lead with their blades, and were in charge of deciding who was worthy of carrying the most legendary weapons in all the lands. Those that assumed that just because their blades weren't as overstated as what they forged for others, would be in for a rude awakening should they test their mastery in swordsmanship.

With more common ore and metals the forger could wait until the ore was heated to a yellow color, but with itsimbi it had to be nearly white hot before you could begin to shape it. Not all tetsuo monks had a large portion of unesiphiwo. Some that had any at all would be in consideration to become a magus, but those who wished to become master testuo smiths to forge for the next generation of guardians had to have at least some talent. Kenzo had proven to have a fair bit. The tricky part would come when the ukutshaya smoke began to mildly warp his consciousness.

The boy was not used to smoking it, and today Sakanoye was his sherpa into another world. He had been taught the rituals of blessings from a theoretical standpoint, but today he would be putting those lessons into practice. Ajit, the naga who had given the boy his first morality test was there as well with his snake lower half curled beneath him as he used his arms to pump large bellows increasing the heat of the forge. Sakanoye was pleased to see the boy had cleared his mind properly, and he could tell from the way the rest of his body began to relax that the ukutshaya was taking hold. "Good." The Shike whispered.

He continued to instruct him "When you feel to be on the brink of losing yourself to this meditative state, and no longer feel the heat, take up the hammer. Do not immediately strike the ore. Reach deep within yourself to find the source of your unesiphiwo. With that done, I want you to envision the shape of your blade before you begin to craft it. It will be an extension of you when training, in battle if it comes to that, and in life. You will be bound to the blade and no other hand not even my own will ever have the strength to lift it."

As if to illustrate the point six older monks came in carrying a small load of pure itsimbi ore to add. The amount didn't seem large enough to warrant that many people to carry. Painstakingly it was added to the casting mold in small chunks which began to sizzle and melt down immediately. The monks carrying it were not under the influence and therefore could not stand the heat and filed out as quickly as they could bowing to Sakanoye as they left. Kenzo took a deep breath and a vision within him formed in his mind's eye.

He was alone in a thick forest. The lush foliage made it very dark and to some it would have been foreboding, but to Kenzo it was welcoming. At the center he could see a bright source of light. This was not the Luhlaza woodlands where the Elinanye resided, nor was it any he recognized. This was a manifestation within him, and the light must be where the key to his unesiphiwo was sourced. Cautiously he walked toward it. Keeping his eyes closed he said, "I have found the source of my font master." Sakanoye was also now in a deep meditative state.

Without opening his eyes, he continued to instruct "When you embrace the source, your journey will begin. Feel yourself melding into the experience as the ukutshaya takes a stronger hold of you. Remember to control your breathing. Can you feel the heat?" Inside of his vision Kenzo stepped into the pool of light and began to feel weightless. He replied, "I no longer feel the heat." Opening his eyes Sakanoye nodded approvingly saying "Good, I will help you with this initial blessing. Diomae, come help us pour the final cast."

Balancing between the feeling of lucidity and intense euphoria Kenzo opened his eyes to see Diomae enter the forge. She was dressed as she always was wrapped nearly head to toe, her eyes and mouth exposed. He could see only a slight sheen of sweat above her brow seeping slightly into her headwrap. Together she and Sakanoye took hold of the large crucible bubbling with molten itsimbi using oversized tongs meant for multiple hands. Sakanoye nods for Kenzo to join them. Blearily he walks over to them and grabs two of the six handles. Sakanoye and Diomae begin to chant. The words weave their way into Kenzo's mind and spirit.

Soon he is reciting along with them without remembering if he had ever practiced the chant before, but the meaning was becoming more and more clear to him. Instinctively he knew to insert his name at the right time. The Shike and other monks echoed his name accordingly cementing the blessing to Kenzo. Finally, they coordinated the pouring of the remaining ore into the cast. Sakanoye and Diomae stepped back as Kenzo took up the hammer and began to shape the blade as he had envisioned it in his mind. With each strike a strange power reverberated through his body as the blade began to take shape. It was now solidified enough to pry out if the cast.

The blade and hilt were cast as one solid piece. Turning it onto the side that remained in the cast, Kenao began to strike it into shape as he did the other side. He was surprised he was able to lift it so easily after needing help initially and the other monks making a display of how heavy the ore was. As a result of using a smaller amount it did not need to be folded as many times as an oversized traditional blade had to be. The density of the ore itself meant no one but the person linked to the blade could wield it, but with help a group could carry the burden similarly to how Sakanoye's ceremonial blade was passed to him before lessons or sparring.

Stylistically Kenzo was shaping this weapon to be a hybrid between a katana and a saber. Looking down at his work Kenzo saw how crude it seemed. Chuckling Sakanoye said "Fear not we shall refine it for you. This is your first attempt after all. If you would please hold it steady on the anvil while we smooth the design out for you?" Kenzo was simply amazed at how in sync Diomae and Sakanoye were as they came together using various tools, heat, and techniques he did not yet understand to smooth out edges to make his blade look less amateur.

They applied what looked like a great amount of effort while he barely held it still. He soon remembered why. All their pushing and grinding would barely nudge the newly forged weapon. Having Kenzo hold it was a mere formality as it was good practice to either have someone hold it steady or do so with a device. A strange and beautiful dance began as they began to work in tandem as Kenzo could see and feel which imperfections they were trying to smooth out. He began to take the lead as he could work the ore more easily with less effort as it was attuned to him. Ajit watched, entranced by the entire production until at last, the blade was finished.

Sakanoye pointed to a tub with a special liquid for Kenzo to drop the new weapon into so it would be cooled and given a special coating simultaneously. Putting on gloves Kenzo retrieved his new blade. When it was cool enough to touch, Diomae brought over some tools to polish and sharpen the weapon. Kenzo admired their work as he made it battle ready. Sakanoye advised "Before we leave you will need to practice your stances, get a feel for your new blade. Learn how it handles and feels when it clashes with other blades. Become mindful of facing tetsuo and non-tetsuo blades. A skilled swordsmen will be able to use your assumed advantages against you."

With confusion written all over his face Kenzo asks "Why would I have to clash blades with a tetsuo sword master?" Chuckling softly Sakanoye replies "You are thinking that since the monks have always vetted warriors before attuning and forging blades for them, that we would never come into conflict with them. That for the most part is true, but sadly people change, and not always for the best. Aside from other guardians bestowed the legendary blades, who do you think is sent to deal with someone who has strayed from their path of protection to pursue a life of tyranny?"

The smoke of the ukutshaya leaves was wearing off letting Kenzo think more clearly now that they were done with the forging process, and what the Shike was telling him made more sense now. If the tetsuo monks made the mistake of giving a blade to someone that proved to be unworthy later, they may be the best option to either take it from them or render them unable to wield it since it would technically be their fault. It was best to vet them properly beforehand but no one had absolute perfect judgement and some people are very good at hiding their true nature in order to get what they desire.

Seeing that it seemed the boy was beginning to understand the responsibility of both vetting and forging the blades, Sakanoye instructed "Get something to eat, and practice your forms and stances after. Tomorrow you can spar with Diomae in the morning before we set off for Kemet." Bowing graciously Kenzo wrapped his new blade and went off to find a meal in the refectory. Ajit slithered his way over to Sakanoye who was grinning seeing the boy's exuberance as he did as he was told. "That smile of his will fade when Diomae gets a hold of him tomorrow." Ajit says.

Chuckling Sakanoye thinks on how Diomae will handle Kenzo's first lesson with an actual tetsuo blade. To date he had only just learned common swordplay practicing kata with other monks during morning exercises. When wielding or facing a fighter wielding a tetsuo blade very different tactics were needed. Kenzo was not fully grown but that could work in his favor, especially learning from a fighter that was slight of build herself. If done properly Kenzo may get the benefit of having skill to lean on rather than depending on a size or strength advantage, and if he grew to be a large man, it would only compliment those skills.

Kenzo barely slept a wink. So excited was he to begin his training. The boy literally cradled his new blade all night. There were plenty of jealous stares from the other novices who had yet to forge their first blades. A deep sense of pride and accomplishment reverberated through him as he realized he need not fear someone taking his new prized possession. None but he could lift it alone, much less wield it. The morning sun was either quick to rise or Kenzo had lost track of time overnight as it passed. Before he knew it the bells were tolling signaling it was time for early morning repast.

Rushing he got up to take the early meal option so he could get to the training courtyards before the others arrived. It was highly possible the boy tasted nothing from his plate as he inhaled the meal before sprinting to the courtyard. His shoulders dropped a bit and his confidence faltered as he saw Diomae was already there awaiting him. She wasted no time instructing "Set the blade down. We shall begin with stretching and breathing exercises as usual before we get to sword work." Reluctantly Kenzo placed his tetsuo blade down and joined her in a routine that was as familiar to him as the back of his hand.

Others soon joined them. Word spread fast and many knew he would be sparring with Diomae today. Kenzo struggled to keep calm and contain his excitement. He felt as if he could feel the others watching him. Diomae could tell he was in rare form, and understandably so. Still, she felt the need to caution him "Today and yesterday were days of great note as well as what should be joyful. Be mindful though that this also means you now have great responsibility. Most may not know or assume that what you wield is not simply another blade made of common materials. However, if they find out, it may make you a target."

Kenzo continued to stretch and perform breathing exercises as he nodded yet something about that confused him. "If they find out, then they know they can't use my blade. It's attuned to me." Diomae stays in her flow state but replies "They will not try to take the blade, but may figure you are presumed to be a worthy opponent. Defeating you could lift their reputation in the eyes of other warriors. Others may be jealous or were turned down when they applied for blades of their own. Not everyone likes that we decide who gets the weapons and who doesn't. Your death would symbolize payback for an assumed wrongful judgement. Either way you need to be wary. We give ourselves normal looking unassuming blades on purpose."

It was obvious from the look of surprise on his face, Kenzo had never thought of that possibility. With the stretching done, Diomae turns to the other novices and bows, they bow in return before either going about their chores or staying to spectate this session. They formed a wide circle around them. Diomae walked over to the weapons rack and selected a sword with a long-curved blade and told Kenzo "When you feel you are ready, retrieve your new shiny blade, and come at me." Taking up his new weapon he asked, "No katas or forms today?"

With a negative shake of her head Diomae makes sure her head wrap is secured before replying "Today is the first day you take swings with that thing and trust me, the movements you are used to are pretty much useless until you get a feel for wielding a tetsuo blade. Assuming it will be like it was before could get you killed. Now stop stalling and come at me!"

The iron in her voice compelled Kenzo to come full tilt at her swinging wildly. She moved as if to cross blades with him, but merely deflected the blow minutely and let the force of his swing carry him forward. Kenzo found himself sprawled on the ground; his new blade stuck in the dirt. He got up quickly dusting himself off. Barely stifled snickers were heard all around. "Ignore that." Diomae advised, then she continued "There's no way I could have clashed blades with you. Had I tried, it could have possibly shattered this one and then your secret would be out. You need to be in total control. You don't need to muscle the weapon. Most times you'll need to do the opposite in fact. The other thing is if you make that mistake outside of these walls, you would have been easily skewered, and that new blade of yours would just be a small monument to your death."

Walking back over to the weapons rack, Diomae bent down to pick up two blades with exotic looking guards above the hilts both sporting nasty hooks at the ends. "Now these…" she explains "Are my personal tetsuo blades, and we can clash with these. Hold nothing back but stay balanced. Relax and be strong when necessary. Fluid movement is the best. This will be a dance that can have many painful lessons. What comes next is not a punishment but to make you aware of what can happen." The giggles begin anew from the small crowd. "Pay them no mind." She adds, "Their time will come."

Circling her as he studied her beautifully crafted weapons Kenzo comments "What happened to unassuming?" After a couple flourishes with both blades Diomae says "I was mainly talking about size. I never said you couldn't have any style. Your weapon looks very nice after we smoothed out your initial design. Should we have left it to look like it came from a Djaemon forge?" At that remark Kenzo lunged forward lightly testing her guard.

"Absolutely not!" he exclaimed. Kenzo rushed in but more cautiously this time. Their blades clashed with a resounding clang. The collision reverberated through his arms and he backed away to regain steadiness in his legs. At the look of confusion on his face, Diomae had to work hard not to laugh herself. She quickly recovered explaining "It's the weight of my blades which have a higher amount of raw itsimbi ore than your one blade. You are correct that you are attuned to handle your weapon, but since you are not attuned to my weapons you feel more of the weight when clashing blades with other tetsuo blades masters. I would advise choosing a variety of partners so you get used to both eventualities."

It had been a long time since anyone had to confiscate a tetsuo blade but it was good to be prepared just in case. They tested each other's guards for the next few moments. Soon they fell into a strangely familiar rhythm despite not sparring often or at all before now. Kenzo had been limited to his specific instructors and the other novices in his class. When she felt it was time, Diomae broke from the patterns of strikes and parries he had become used to and went on a flurry of offensive moves. It was too much for Kenzo to bear and he yielded quickly.

Panting, the boy looked up with resignation. Yet he was hopeful. His arms felt lead laden as if he had finished the most rigorous training routine in his life. Kenzo told her so and she replied "It's likely that you have. I know it doesn't seem so but this can be more strenuous than doing strength training, and most assume otherwise because of the deceitful look of our tetsuo blades. Now you know how the Shike wears out four or five monks in one session. His blade has more ore in it than both of my blades together. When he slings it around easily, it slams into our blades like the dead weight of two bedrahin!"

Rubbing his arms and legs Kenzo believed it. As if they had spoken the man into appearing Sakanoye came into the courtyard. The shike was satisfied that some of the bright-eyed excitement had been knocked out of Kenzo but there still remained a fire within to be stoked. Patting the boy on the head he said "Rest up and pack. We head to Kemet at sundown. Hopefully we can witness some of this tribunal. Tomorrow, you spar with me." Kenzo looked over to Diomae who now wore a wicked grin. He simply bowed and sluggishly went to get his things for the trip.

Chapter Fourteen

The Djaemon had to wait until they were at the edge of the red desert before they could sandcast, speeding their travel through the hot sands in a matter of a couple days in comparison to most who could only walk in what would most likely take a couple weeks. They marched north from Kemet to avoid climbing the Mulanje mountain ranges, then turned south towards the dead marshes where there had been a lot of both revenant and shadow incursion activity recently. A strange howl went up as they were setting camp to rest for the night of their first leg back home.

D'Na volunteered to take the first watch but K'Ain would have none of it. He wanted first watch of the night. T'Ome looked as if he was going to attempt taking it but quickly made his way to a comfortable spot to sleep when he witnessed the look and response from their king. This was a rare opportunity for him. K'Ain hardly left their desert fortress since assuming the mantle. Instead of being out on hunts or raiding parties, his life was mostly oversight and delegating responsibilities to lesser clan members.

That howl they heard earlier came from somewhere northwest of them, and from the screams that followed it sounded as if whatever the cause, it was coming closer. K'Ain wanted first rights. Kneeling by the fire he took out a small dagger. There was a small amount of their home brew left in his drinking skin. After downing the remnants, he took the dagger, and made two small slashes just beneath his collar bones. Closing his eyes, he prayed that Serat would accept his small offering, and give him the strength to pledge a lot more from whatever beasts were coming their way.

D'Na found a nice bed of moss to lay on knowing it was likely that none of them would get much sleep. Her, T'Ome and the others would merely pretend to sleep until first blood was drawn. Their king had claimed first rights which was his prerogative, and once that was done, they would all be free to seek out their own offerings. Each hoped they would find an opponent worthy of contributing something to Serat themselves by spilling Djaemon blood. This was one of the most dangerous things about fighting Djaemon. They didn't fear injury or maiming, in fact they welcomed it which heavily influenced their tactics. As long as they were the last ones standing when the encounter was over, they would be praised by their comrades.

This also gave them a freedom of movement in battle most other warriors lacked. They rarely flinched or avoided contact from weapons. Most combatants whether Elinanye, Bayaka, nor the craziest that man had to offer willingly traded in melee weapon battles. The Djaemon did so often and with smiles on their faces when they knew someone's blade was about to bite deep into their flesh. When that happened often the opponent freezes or slows the momentum of their own swing as they seek to maneuver away from the blow the Djaemon is about to deliver.

That hesitation can soften their strike while the red skinned warrior follows through with reckless abandon screaming maniacally as they're cut open reveling in the fact that they are fulfilling what they see as their duties to their blood god. If one is not prepared for this kind of fervor in battle, they won't last long. Someone or something was about to find out that the shadow realm was not the only home for vicious unrelenting fighters.

There was a rush of thrashing noises as something moved through the surrounding foliage at high velocity. K'Ain stood with his favorite black blade in hand, a broad grin shone bright through his scarred red lips. Whatever was coming was quite large. The Djaemon king would have it no other way. Looking down at his blade he mumbled in their guttural language and pretended not to be paying attention. The noise that was sort of vague now became clearer. Twigs were being snapped; low foliage trampled. Something bipedal was running headlong in their direction.

In his periphery K'Ain could see bouncing lights creeping through bog of the dead marshes atop large silhouettes, and there were now multiple sets of what sounded like huge padded footsteps thudding like a stampede of wild bedrahin. Brandishing his weapon, he screamed "Ueka!". The charade was over as the gathered Djaemon nearly in unison answered "Aooooo!" before jumping up with an assortment of black blades at the ready. Just as one of the seemingly flame haired creatures from the shadow realm erupted from the surrounding tree line, K'Ain turned and threw his sword sending it flying end over end until it was embedded into the attacker's skull taking it clean off of its feet in the process.

As it landed with a heavy thud, K'Ain ran to retrieve his weapon before the body slumped to the side interrupting it slightly as he dislodged the blade wedged in cracked bone. Another shadow beast ran up to get punched square in the jaw. The meaty thud sent teeth flying and before the Djaemon king could follow up a black blade broke through its chest nearly catching K'Ain as well.

He deftly stepped aside in time to see D'Na kick the beast in the back to take her blade out of that body to quickly insert it into another that was fast approaching. A clawed hand slashed her shoulder sending speckles of her black blood flying into her king's face. Together they disemboweled the beast. All around the air was alive with a cacophony of blood curdling screams, slashes and sickening thuds as the Djaemon tore through the group of incoming shadow creatures with glowing blue or orange hair.

Seeing that they had not chosen to use weaponry of any kind T'Ome had decided to meet them on their terms. The oversized Djaemon was pummeling them at random. Stopping occasionally to pick one up nearly the same size as he was to swing them into nearby trees at the edge of the swampland, snapping their back in the process. After a collection of bodies lay strewn around him, he began giddily stomping them to death as they writhed in pain. Soon none were left alive and the Djaemon were reveling in their blood lust. A few Iigbin had come out from their subterranean homes beneath where the base of the Mulanje mountain ranges give way to the dead marshes.

Hearing the commotion, some of them were curious about the skirmish. Often after random battles there would be loot to plunder from the fallen on both sides. The bluish green skinned, goblin like creatures were smart enough not to reveal themselves, and were certainly not foolhardy enough to approach the Djaemon when their senses were probably the most heightened looking for someone else, anyone else to cut down in pursuit of their praise giving to Serat. Not wanting to volunteer to be additional blood sacrifices, they quickly went back down to their homes. Scavenging would have to happen when this Djaemon clan moved on. Avarice would have to give way to survival.

K'Ain, T'Ome, D'Na and the other Djaemon cleaned their weapons and admired some of their new scars and it was pretty apparent none of them could sleep after such an exhilarating experience. K'Ain nodded to D'Na and it was silently understood they would take advantage of this unexpected energy boost and push forward hoping to at least make it through the dead marshes. That was the roughest trek of land they had to traverse, and once they reached the Pantu grasslands, they should have safe passage through. Given recent events and the awkward cooperation between the Pantu and Djaemon, at least a temporary accord had been established.

Some of them wouldn't mind a tussle with the Pantu and their legendary dire panther mounts, but it was more important for the Djaemon to get back to Gcina Okubomvu to ensure the rest of the clan was thriving. They made it through the dead marshes without incident through the night, and bedded down during the day with sentries posted as they slept in shifts. Disappointedly to some of Djaemon the only thing that happened while they rested were awkward greetings from the Pantu patrols that occasionally came by as they made their rounds ensuring no threats to their herds were afoot.

K'Ain had no problems sleeping through most of the day, letting his most trusted clan members D'Na and T'Ome oversee the watches through the day. T'Ome nudged the king roughly with a foot at nightfall. K'Ain was angry at first until the pain hit him where T'Ome had scuffed him irritating the scar along his side. A fresh coat of their special ink was setting in to accentuate the new wound. The growl that started turned into a deep laugh as the Djaemon king was reminded of the previous nights' activities. Serat had to be pleased, he thought.

A monstrous punch to T'Ome's jaw from K'Ain startled the nearby Pantu tribesmen and their mounts who had paused fearing a fight was about to break out. There was a seemingly uncomfortable pause before the two large Djaemon broke out in laughter before embracing briefly as the rest of their raiding party gathered themselves in preparation to make their way through the rest of the grasslands. The Pantu tribesmen calmed down once they saw they would not have to intervene.

The herd was down for the night and a battle at this time could spook them making it necessary to corral a potential stampede. The night had started off pretty quietly and with some of their contingent off in Kemet witnessing the tribunal, the tribesmen here wanted to keep it that way. Nervously a small boy ran up to K'Ain holding a small parcel of some kind. The king looked inquisitively to D'Na who then asked, "What do you bring child?" The boy's shyness melted when he heard one of them spoke the common tongue.

Beaming he replied, "This is the best bedrahin jerky you will ever taste in all of Nyumbani!" D'Na translated and before K'Ain could take a bite, T'Ome quickly snatched the cured meat from his hand and chomped down on it. Everyone was speechless as T'Ome chewed and seemed to sputter a bit before exclaiming something to them all. D'Na turned to the boy saying, "He says it is indeed very good and has quite some spice to it." K'Ain could see that T'Ome was beginning to sniffle a bit and there were now tears streaming down his face.

At that the king tore off a larger chunk and ate it with gusto, also praising the snack. The boy frowned up at D'Na saying "Did that one think I was trying to poison the other?" Shaking her head, she replied "That one is T'Ome, the king's closest friend, and he is very cautious. He meant no offense; besides I think you may have sparked a strange new rivalry between the two. You're very brave to approach us so brazenly. We thank you for the gift." She stifled a laugh at how demonstrative the little boy's face became.

"Why do you think me brave?" he asked. "Surely you have heard of the ferocious Djaemon, and yet you walked right up to us." Turning serious the boy says "I grew up with those. They're likely three or four times as heavy as a full grown Djaemon, but they have claws and very sharp teeth. I'm going to ride one someday." Thinking about it from that perspective, she guessed he was right. The Pantu tribesmen lived among large predators. Being face to face with those everyday scaled others perceived dangers differently for them.

The boy ran off waiving which prompted other Pantu tribesmen to come over so the entire group of Djaemon could have some jerky for the excursion across the grasslands. The word had obviously been passed to the Pantu tribesmen that hostilities between them and the Djaemon were at a halt, but K'Ain had not expected outright hospitality in any form. It was an unexpected pleasant surprise. The Djaemon and Pantu tribesmen said their mutually misunderstood goodbyes that some realized through circumstantial context what the other must have been attempting to communicate.

As annoying as it was out of newfound respect for the Pantu tribesmen, the Djaemon waded their way through the grasslands without using their blades. Trailblazing with their weapons would have cut down and wasted a vital food source for the herds of bedrahin the tribesmen watched over. D'Na respected the fact that K'Ain had ordered them to disregard how they would have traditionally come through these lands. She wondered if it was the truce under the unusual circumstances that had brought the two peoples together, or was it a small act of kindness when strife was often more common.

She would have to remember to ask him once they reached home territory. For now, they had to be mindful of anything that could potentially be hiding amongst the tall grasses that was not a tamed dire panther or stray bedrahin grazing lazily. Again, any Djaemon warrior spoiling for a fight in hopes of gaining more glory were sorely disappointed throughout this leg of their journey. Soon they could see the expanse of the dune seas that made up the red desert. They were almost home and the air was becoming more arid the closer they approached.

Looking to the northeast they could just barely make out the tall spire of the long-abandoned portal near the tetsuo monastery, and to the southeast they could make out the black structure of Gcina Okubomvu jutting out of the sands as if in physical protestation of its surroundings. Pointing T'Ome made an observation to K'Ain and the others. Something wasn't right. The night sky in the desert was always a huge contrast to how it and the land looked under the burning suns heat. The great blue expanse overhead turned into an inky black dotted with pinpricks of light.

The seemingly infinite ripples in the sand became even more washed out under the pale lighting giving the place an ethereal quality. What T'Ome immediately saw was that there should be strong stacks of smoke rising from the various guard shack locations, and a large column in the center of their red keep where the home fire was located so the clan could gather around to keep the night chill off of them through the cool night.

As they finally broke through the last vestiges of the grasslands the terrain gradually changed as foliage of any kind became more and more sparce. Soon they were standing with their toes firmly atop of tiny ridges in the sands of their home created by the winds over time. K'Ain and the others could more plainly see that what should have been thick stacks of smoke were merely thin whisps as if the fires had been put out recently. It was time to see what had happened in their absence.

Without commanding anyone else to do so, K'Ain sandcasted turning himself into a miniature sandstorm. Seeing this the others quickly followed suit glad to finally be using a faster mode of travel unique to their people and only to those trained to do so. This technique was limited to desert areas. There were rumors of a rare Djaemon having the ability to do this over water but none of them had ever witnessed it themselves. The Djaemon gathered to glide swiftly over the sand dunes stirring up hails of swirling granulated dirt as they went.

K'Ain, D'Na, T'Ome and the rest of their group stopped just before the towering statues surrounding the desert keep. The giant effigy of Serat the blood god loomed heavy perpetually looking down in seeming disapproval. Today K'Ain believed the look was most appropriate. In case an attack had taken the clan members left behind, they went about entering as stealthily as possible. There were no sentries to speak of in the shacks on the outskirts which was just as unusual as there being no fire going at the home hearth. No signs of forced entry at the gates, and no bodies strewn about as they approached.

Confused by all of this K'Ain was tired of being light footed and quite angry that things had not been handled here as they should have. Someone was going to pay. Forcefully kicking in the front gate, the Djaemon stepped into the keep followed by D'Na, T'Ome and the others that came along for the raiding party to see hosts of sleeping Djaemon all huddled together for warmth. The most infuriating thing was there was a familiar looking slovenly Djaemon slumped on his throne fast asleep with an empty crude looking flagon sitting at his feet. An array of female Djaemon were similarly passed out around him just below the dais.

D'Na walked up behind K'Ain to ask, "Is that who I think it is?" Kicking bodies as he made his way to the dais in a rush K'Ain replied "Yes, I think it is! It's been a long-time brother. Do tell us how you come to return, relieve the sentries of their duties to protect our land, and put the fires out so that Gcina Okubomvu is no longer a beacon in the desert night?" When he reached the dais, he kicked the Djaemon sitting on his throne in the chest upending him and the throne.

In addition to the Djaemon rudely awakened by the kings' kicks in route to the throne the rest of the clan was quickly roused when the throne thudded loudly as it crashed to the ground. Sputtering the portly Djaemon tried to get to his feet raising his hands placatingly he begged "Dear brother forgive me! It was rumored you had died hunting an elder dragon or made some ill-advised deal with the Pantu. I only came in as you have no heir so logically, I would be next in line for the throne."

K'Ain went in pummeling him further as he spoke "You are a horrible liar brother! Which is it, was I supposed to be dead or dealing with old enemies? J'Ure you have but a few breaths left to tell me how you came to be here and why I shouldn't simply skewer you here as a very unfit sacrifice to Serat!"

Chapter Fifteen

Olofi, and Oluso were used to travelling through a variety of portals, but the others were having a bit of a time adjusting. This was very different for Max, Sparks and Argos when they stepped into the portal which brought them to Nyumbani. Argos was just an infant when he was thrown into their home dimension and so had no memory of his first traversal. Max and Sparks barely held on to their composure gritting their teeth the entire time as it felt as if their reality was being stretched. Argos stoically floated along.

Eron the silver-tongued savage from the Isles of Esikrwada laughed maniacally as Daniel the Lesser lived up to the new moniker by squealing the entire time. Akil, and Rahil travelled silently as was their nature. Soon the light surrounding them began to fade and they found their feet once again on solid ground. They all wait a bit to get their legs solidly beneath them before moving forward. There's a thick wall of smoke around them slowly dissipating and when it does, they can see a large structure behind them similar to the one they stepped through initially but the landscape was vastly different as was the climate.

Oluso pulls his great coat out of a satchel that looks much too small to hold a garment of that size, and wraps himself to fend off the chill. The wind is biting cold and there's a winter wonderland spread before them draped in fresh snow. Lofin looks around as Daniel the

Lesser shivers in his new armor producing a clinking sound. A small distance away they can see a high rising spire which usually signifies a place for worship or higher learning. Max mutters "Dude either we travelled a really far distance away where the seasons are total opposite of where we just came from, or perhaps we have switched realms…you know the veils, and all."

From the look the disguised god gave him, it was clear Olofi was not a fan of the mocking tone. Eron walked up to Daniel and placed his hands on his shoulders sternly trying to stop him from shaking saying "We should get this one some heat before he gives away our location with this racket." Something was glinting catching Spark's attention but when she turns towards Oluso it is gone. She could have sworn one of his eyes lit up briefly. Right before she was about to ask about it Lofin says "I am afraid someone is already aware of our arrival. Can't say I am surprised. This is after all nigh the legendary Al-Karaouine, one of the oldest schools where they teach those blessed with unesiphiwo how to use it."

Instantly they were surrounded by a host of robed figures some with gem topped staves, others with strangely intricate jewelry on their hands and wrists. The obvious leader in front of the gathering was dark skinned woman with no staff or accoutrement, but she had the most stunning golden eyes any of the mortals in this travelling party had ever seen. The leader also looked surprisingly young for a leader of magi but the voice that boomed out of her denoted a seeming endless source of wisdom was within her. Akil and Rahil swiftly pulled their tetsuo blades from their backs. Eron, and Argos followed suit.

Max and Sparks were unsure but for some odd reason Lofin didn't so much as twitch. Strangely Oluso was also rather nonchalant given the circumstances, and he also refrained from drawing any weapons from beneath his great coat. "Protectors, and enforcers of the law you may be back in Kemet, but here you have no authority. It would be wise for you to sheath your blades. We may not be able to wield them but with a word, I can make it so you cannot either." The striking woman stated coolly.

Lofin waved to them with a subtle hand gesture that they should lower their weapons, and to Oluso's surprise they all did so without hesitation. The mystery of who Lofin truly was ate at the mystical inquisitor and he was sure that he should know this already somehow. Being surrounded by a group of powerful magi correlated with his senses for magic or the use of it ringing loudly within his being, but there was definitely more to this woman as well, and from the look on Lofin's face, he knew it too. Lofin and the leader stepped towards each other and whispered briefly but the others were hard pressed to hear the subject.

With her golden eyes boring deeply into Oluso, the woman asks "The righteous warrior, hunter…seeker of justice. Does he know?" Confusion and a bit of angry indignation flashes across Oluso's face as he realizes he is who she is inquiring about but the descriptors are not familiar to him. Angrily he blurts "Do I know what?" with all eyes squarely on him now. Lofin chuckles before replying "Sadly I believe he has no idea, but that is for another time. We have need of your help, or more specifically one of you that possibly still remains…I am Lofin, this is Oluso a mystical inquisitor, Akil, and Rahil of the city shields in Kemet, Eron the silver-tongued savage, Max, Sparks and Argos, a recently returned Djaemon, and that is Daniel the Lesser."

With a skeptical look on her face, the golden eyed woman replies "Lofin…is it? I am Mila. Those you see here are the magi that have remained here to teach and preserve the knowledge necessary to train any who have unesiphiwo. We also keep that knowledge from those who would use it for nefarious purposes. Our portal has been dormant for untold seasons. So, it was quite alarming when it suddenly came back to life without the mother opening it. We suspected your arrival was a prelude to an attack, or an attempted theft at the very least."

With the subtlest of nods, she ordered the gathered magi to leave, and they begrudgingly did so silently, but some kept eyes sternly on Oluso as they left. Max sidled up to the mystical inquisitor and whispered "I don't think they're fans bro." The look Oluso gave him forced the man to give him some space. Sparks stifled her laughter shaking her head. "You just don't learn no matter what dimension you're in." she added. The look on Argos's face said he agreed with her. Mila turned and walked signaling for them to follow. As they moved to catch up to her Lofin stated "My apologies for the unannounced visit, and I assure you that we are not here to attack or pilfer knowledge, but I was hoping you or someone here would be able to help strengthen the veils without getting too much attention."

Oluso was straining to look casual as he followed and listened as closely as possible without being too obvious about it. The others were slightly less curious but were also amused by the whole spectacle. It was clear that Lofin and their new acquaintance knew something about Oluso that he himself had little knowledge of. Max, Sparks, and Argos were understandably lost in all this but even the two city shields, Daniel the Lesser and Eron had a hard time connecting the dots here. Max and Sparks were just grateful to be along for the ride without being exiled to islands they were unfamiliar with. Until they either figured out what their place would be here or found a way back home this would have to be enough.

Sparks was unsure but felt as soon as Argos found his proper place here in Nyumbani their next steps would be to find a way back home. It was likely they would not be accepted among the exiles that Eron was apparently descended from as they truly had no familial ties to despite appearances. Once Argos was settled it was assumed that whatever debt Max likely owed would be paid in full at that point. They followed Mila through a snow laden but well-maintained courtyard while her and Lofin spoke in nearly hushed tones.

The others were pretty certain this was done purposefully to annoy Oluso who was adamantly trying to listen in without them knowing. The attempt was futile and Sparks wondered why he even bothered with the pretense. They were led to what appeared to be a small, almost chapel like building off to the side of the main campus. Mila waved a hand and the double doors swung open to admit the group inside. Once they broke the threshold of the front entrance the interior appeared to be much too large in comparison to what they saw of the exterior. They were all flabbergasted, except Lofin.

Oluso's senses were tingling like he had never felt before. This place didn't simply have a few magic devices or special traps strewn about. The entire structure exuded a formidable power. The mystical inquisitor had some knowledge of this school but nothing hinted at anything of this magnitude existing here. Mentally he filed this information away to share with a few of his colleagues he actually trusted. "If any of you feel a hum, it's the dampeners this sanctuary of mine is equipped with to tune out as well as protect from any of the unesiphiwo testing done here. It also helps me keep things from being seen by prying eyes, or ears." Mila commented. At the last she was staring directly at Oluso, who would have blushed had he been light enough to do so of embarrassment.

"Please be seated." Mila offered and what was initially the foyer quickly became a cozy sitting room. Chairs to accommodate each one of them according to size appeared conveniently behind them. Max mumbled "Ok, this is trippy, but I'm not mad at it." Somewhat reluctantly they all took their seats. Lofin chuckled asking "Does anyone know you've stolen this bit of Izulu from on high?" Pointedly she ignores the question and asks "Can we do away with this absurd pretense, and what do you want to inquire of our portal guardian? I assume that's who you would like to specifically ask."

"Yes Orunmila, we can do away with pretenses here. No doubt you have seen and felt that the veils have been thinning as a result apparently of a rogue magus. Motu, I believe is his name. Now you and I could likely do so ourselves but you know too much interference would cause an uproar. The mothers of darkness, the traditional portal guardians are powerful in their own right but still mortal. Proven by the fact that there are not many left. The other reason I wish to speak with her should be quite obvious given present company." Lofin explains.

A glint comes to her golden eyes as she replies "Oh, dear Olofi you are funny, as are your other aspects no doubt grilling the others in Izulu as we speak trying to find out who interfered. The truth is we all do from time to time. It's only to be expected. The truth is we all have at one time or another but as a result of these silly restrictions, it's kept hidden for the most part. I'll play along and send for her to see what she can do." Looking over Oluso Mila then asks, "You don't think this one is hers, do you?"

Oluso was about to respond when Lofin cuts him off "No, but she may know of the circumstances that brought him to be." Angrily Oluso blurts "I am sitting right here!" The picture finally crystalizes for him and he says, "You are gods, aren't you?" Staring incredulously Mila states "Oh you're a dim one…you are as well child. At least partially." Now it was Max, Sparks, Argos, and the twins turns to blatantly scrutinize Oluso who refused to crumple under their uncomfortable gazes.

Max raised a finger as if to gently touch his great coat in response Oluso calmly says "Absolutely not. Proceed and I will unleash an untold number of spirits into your suits…loquacious ones." At that Max slowly put his hand down. To Sparks and Argos he whispered "You hear that? We're hangin with gods now. Best vacation idea ever buddy." Sparks could only shake her head as Max lightly punched

Argos in the arm who simply looked at him blankly. The twins were confused, and Daniel is simply happy to have his feet on solid ground. Mila suggests "Enjoy some refreshment and I will return shortly. Touch nothing but the light fare before you."

Daniel tried to object commenting "but there isn't any…" before he could finish the thought there appeared a circular table around which their seats were now arranged with drinks and hand foods to snack on. Eron was ready to dive into the refreshments but was pointedly skeptical. Daniel and Max were also enthusiastic but noticed the large blonde man carefully watching Lofin to see if anything happened when he took a sip or bite. Lofin went in with gusto and Eron soon followed suit. Gradually the others joined in once it seemed less likely they were being poisoned.

The twins were the last to partake. As they were taking off the partial masks that hid the lower part of their faces Mila returned followed by a taller woman with nearly alabaster skin, orange curly hair, and magenta eyes. She was just as striking as Mila but for very different reasons. "Lofin and company, this is the last guardian of our long dormant portal. At least it was so until you reopened it." Mila offered as a brief introduction. Looking them all over the newcomer exuded power and silently demanded respect.

Her wandering gaze stopped when it landed on Oluso. She clucked her tongue as if confirming something before nodding deferentially to Lofin. "Sidibene kakule Olofi. I am Orana, one of the last of the Mothers of Darkness formerly tasked with keeping the pathways safe. Orunmila says you now request my aid." Max's entire face froze at her entrance and it took a less than subtle rib shot from Sparks to snap him out of his trance as Olofi replied to her "Orana, Sidibene kakule child! Yes, we did come to seek you out. For your help if possible and also for information. You are aware of the incursions from the shadow realm, and no doubt, other realms?" Orana nodded that she was indeed aware of the incidents being reported along with a surprising number of casualties that resulted from some of them.

She added "I am not sure what you think I can do to prevent this from happening, but I am curious as to why you don't strengthen the veils yourself? You an Orunmila together surely have the power to do so. This is also a rather motley crew you've gathered into your service, or are these new disciples?" Oluso looked mildly offended when he said "I am no disciple. I am just seeking answers to a problem effecting many of our lands. Those three are my responsibility so they had to come. He can correct me if I am wrong, but Eron asked to come along, and the twins are here to keep an eye on me, I suspect to report what I do with the presumed exiles. Daniel here I guess is Lofi…I mean Olofi's pet project while he graces us with his presence."

Orunmila chimes in "Olofi would like to try and rectify things through mortal means so as not to upset his…aspects who reside in Izulu above this place. In other words, divine hands will not remedy this most recent calamity if he can help it." That did not sit well with Oluso who asked, "What if it was divine hands that influenced our current state?" The two Orishas thought on that before Olofi replied "Then I assume there may be at least a reckoning for the deity responsible." Oluso was not very confident in that happening. Surely there was a hierarchy with these higher beings, but he wasn't sure anything would really be done to the offender other than giving them a stern talking to.

Orana interjected "So you wish for me to attempt to fortify the veils between realms. My power only extends to the formerly dormant portal that you have temporarily reactivated, and the other portals it was connected to. What you ask for is another thing entirely. The scope is beyond what me and my sisters could dream of controlling as a group, and now there are but a few of us left. The purge took a great toll on our numbers. When the portals went dead there was no reason to seek out others to maintain and guard them."

Shaking his head Olofi says "You mortals often think so limitedly. The portals are just that, open pathways that were created to have predetermined points of entry and exits. A magical means to expedite travel without the individuals or groups needing to have access or talent with respect to unesiphiwo. Magic tethers them but the planes through which the individual portals go through are like main roads. If you can access the portals then it's possible for you to have access to…unmapped roads, or at the least strengthen the membrane that cocoons this realm making entry less likely."

Max, Sparks, Argos, Eron, the twins and Daniel could not make heads or tails of anything that was being discussed. Eron leaned in trying to look as if he grasped the concepts but failed miserably. Daniel was in a perpetual state of awe while Max and Sparks displayed varying states of confusion. The twins had long since ignored the conversation but kept a keen eye on all of them while they continued to enjoy the provided refreshments. Oluso followed along with the conversation while simultaneously weighing and calculating things in his mind. He may not have known there was divine blood coursing through his veins, but there was an obvious affinity for all things supernatural within him. He was dumbfounded as to how that had not helped him reach the status of magus.

Part of him refused to believe what Olofi and Orunmila previously hinted at, but for now he would focus on the problem at hand for the sake of the realm. Personal curiosities would have to be satisfied later. Olofi and Orunmila went through some exercises with Orana showing her how to reach out with her powers beyond the specific lanes provided by the portals her and the order of portal guardians known as the Mothers of Darkness were tasked with safeguarding long ago. For the others it simply looked as if she was in deep meditation, sweat beginning to bead down her pale brows.

Within her mind she could see a nearly infinite web of tendrils that looked like a cosmic representation of veins, and capillaries within a body. "This is an amazing sight, but I cannot hope to reinforce a network like this on my own. I will need help and even if we find the others who remain, I am not sure we are up to the task. Politics of deities and other like you aside, I think this is something you should handle. I think the creator will understand. Especially if these breaches that cause the incursions become more dangerous." Orana advised.

Shaking his head Olofi says "My aspects can be many things. Brash, loving cautious, and even hypocritical, but understanding when certain rules are broken is not among them." While watching this unfold Sparks was deep in thought wondering if she and Max would ever make it back to their home dimension. The way things were headed there it would not surprise her if it had imploded given the strife happening when they followed Argos through the strange portal that landed them here. Somehow it didn't seem to matter where she tried to make a life. It would all crumble to dust in the end either way.

Chapter Sixteen

Simba Kivuli the exiled magus returned from the shadow realm and his companion dire lion Lasekunene were well rested, and had taken the opportunity to hunt. They were careful to target bedrahin that had strayed too far from the main herds. Simba had no intention of taking on a group of Pantu tribesmen and trained dire panthers who were at full strength while he and his companion were still recovering. Now that his belly was full and he had gotten his bearings, it was time to find Lasekholo, Lasekunene's brother and Simba's long-time companion. Early during his initial time in the shadow realm, they were found as cubs.

Raising them up had proven to be a worthy investment in time and effort. Either lost or abandoned by their pride they would have become food for animals higher up in the food chain. Unprotected young did not last long. That trend was common in most realms. Simba was still relatively young at the time of his banishment so in some ways they grew up together. They would have to go back towards the Elinanye Luhlaza woodlands in order to find out what became of Lasekholo. Simba believed he would have felt it if the resulting conflict was fatal. Their bonds were strong and he did sense when Lasekunene was in pain.

It was more likely the dire lion from the shadow realm was simply confined somehow. That would explain why what he could feel from him felt hazy or hindered in some way. Simba hoped the clarity would improve as they got closer. The skills learned in the shadow realm would prove valuable now. As an aspiring magus stealth was not a necessary practice most of the time, but that changed once he was stripped of access to his unesiphiwo. It took time for the dire lions to mature, so they learned to sneak as a group.

Even after the lions had grown to their adult sizes, there were some creatures much larger and dangerous that roamed the grey expanse of lands. Simba was smart enough to avoid them unless it was absolutely necessary to engage them. It was true that the number of beasts here in Nyumbani were not as great as the variety in the shadow realm, but for now caution was still merited. At least until Lasekunene was closer to full strength and they had been reunited with Lasekholo. Dire panthers, dragons, drakes, and a myriad of other beasts could cause them serious damage in their current states.

The skirmish with the group of Iigbin was apparently more of a risky engagement than Simba had initially thought which was proven by the nicks and scars that was evidence that some of their crude attacks made it through his defenses. Taking a moment to plan out their route to the Luhlaza woodlands, the magus applied some of the potent smelling salve he had mixed to his various wounds. Catching a whiff Lasekunene growled. "You have more of the stuff on you than I, and you should be feeling better for it." The magus stated. He wasn't sure but for a moment he could have sworn the behemoth of a lion rolled its eyes.

"Ingrate." The man mumbled as he slowly got to his feet. All things considered, he felt better than he had in a long time. The great lion stood as well guessing it was time to move. Their movement was slow and methodical. The magus was mindful to simultaneously stick to some of the high grasses and areas with heavier foliage to give them cover while also avoiding Pantu tribesmen on patrol. The senses of the dire panthers would be most difficult to evade. A quick change of winds could carry their scent alerting the tribesmen of the unwanted trespassers.

Listening for the bellows and other noises herds of bedrahin made, Simba and Lasekunene tried to stay as far away in order to keep from running into the rolling patrol patterns of the tribesmen and their dire panther mounts on the outskirts of the grasslands protecting their source of food and commerce. There were a few close calls but they managed to get close to the border of the Pantu tribesmen grasslands just before it melded into the approaching pass leading into the Luhlaza woodlands.

There was now an odd demarcation between the two territories. Most of the grasslands were cut low by grazing groups of bedrahin, and the Pantu tribesmen were very particular about rotating the herds to varying patches of grass but there was a sizable patch between the Pantu, and the Elinanye that had become most unruly. As they approached this unofficial barrier it was easy to see why this area had become so unkempt. Simba's eyes began to tear up as the fumes assaulted them forcing him to dawn his leonine helm and his lungs tightened. The smell was putrid. Lasekunene began growling between sneezes.

The helm had magic properties that protected the magus from more than melee attacks. Soon he was able to breath and see comfortably. The lion did not have anything to help him cope. With his head clear Simba could see the dire lion protesting, and feared they would attract unwanted attention. Trying to mollify the beast he said "Let's just get through this nasty field as quickly as possible! Hopefully your brother is somewhere on the other side." The magus ran headlong into the field towards the famed woodlands hoping Lasekunene followed. He was not disappointed.

Despite struggling to breathe and see, the lion lumbered through the noxious field until they finally cleared it. They stopped as Simba gave his companion a chance to catch his breath when he spotted an out of place large clump of dirt and soil oddly shaped sitting just outside of the Elinanye border. The tree line and the entire Luhlaza woodlands was encased in a perfectly shaped dome of dirt and surrounding natural materials. The magus could feel the energy crackling off of the magically raised border, but noticed something else about the big clump of dirt they found.

Kneeling down to inspect the dirt he could see there were bits of the corrupted and desiccated grass in it. It had lost its potency but there were also traces of something else familiar to him and Lasekunene. Long gray strands and a not so fresh trail of blood was all they needed. Simba pointed it out to Lasekunene. Soon they were in tracking mode not caring if they drew attention or not. The lion could sense his brother was close and a sense of urgency was in his movements as they thrashed forward following the trail of trampled foliage and dried blood.

Soon they came to another large tuft of unkempt grasses, but this one seemed healthy unmarred by the sickness in the patch between Pantu and Elinanye territories. It was also an area that had not been grazed upon in some time. The rust-colored trail lead into it. As they approached a familiar low growl was heard as the tall grasses swayed slowly with movement. Lasekunene answers with a growl of his own and the swaying motion stops. Hesitantly Lasekholo limps out of the cover the grasses provided and slumps down on the ground.

The magus and brother cautiously approach looking the injured Ingonyama Enkulu over. There are a myriad of arrow shafts sticking out of his hide as well as some scrapes, scratches and bite wounds to his hind quarters. Simba was happy to be reunited with his closest companions and went to work applying his collection of ointments to help begin the healing process. Taking off his helm the magus took a closer look at the arrows still embedded. Mainly to himself he commented "Hopefully the skill with crafting the arrowheads is at a higher level for the Elinanye. If so retrieving them should prove less painful, and faster. I don't wish to be bludgeoned as I was by your brother's large paw."

Unlike Lasekunene, Lasekholo was too exhausted to put up much of a fight. It was hard to tell but that may have been because he had suffered his injuries well before his brother had. In any case the beast made no fuss at the magus applying the salves and barely winced when the arrow shafts and bolt heads were removed. As a precaution the magus had mixed a preparatory ointment meant to slightly numb the areas before going to work on them. This strategy slipped his mind when he began working on the first of the brothers. He wasn't sure but in his mind the look in Lasekunene's eyes seemed accusatory as the beast patiently watched him work on mending the other animal's wounds.

At the suspicious glance the magus couldn't help but apologize despite being sure the animal had no idea what he was saying. "I am sorry you had to suffer as a result of my forgetfulness Lasekunene. Many things are coming back to me. I shall do better. I need you both healthy. The enemies of the shadow realm were many, but they for the most part lacked the sophistication we shall have to contend with here. Get into the cover of the grasses with your brother. I shall look for a meal for you two. No doubt we will have to move on before daylight."

With that the magus stepped off silently to look for either a young bedrahin or perhaps a stray far enough from the herd for him to pick off with no one noticing. Unconsciously slipping into his unesiphiwo that got him exiled, Simba dawns his leonine helm and begins to crawl on all fours. In his mind he is Simba Kivuli and his movement now signify that the shadow lion is on the hunt for his brothers. Stalking, he finds a young bedrahin that has somehow strayed from the rest of the main herd. The nub of a horn is newly formed and there's not much meat to the young calf. It would have to do. Not knowing when they last fed, Simba was sure some food would go a long way towards expediting the healing process for both of the dire shadow lions.

Once they were closer to full strength they could of course go hunt for larger, more filling game. Moving slowly so as not to disturb the tall grasses too much alerting the calf, Simba creeps toward his prey. An untimely noise is made when his armor brushes into a patch of grass that is more ridged than the rest nearly spooking the calf. He freezes waiting for the animal to calm down and go back to grazing. Before he could pull his blade and pounce, there's a flurry of loud sounds that instantly send the calf into a panic. It bolts. Suddenly Simba is rudely upended as something crashes into him.

The break in his concentration forces him out of his transformation. With his prey gone the magus shakes his head to recover his wits looking around for the culprit. When his blurry vision cleared the gathering around him briefly confused him. He was surrounded by dark ebon-skinned beings from the shadow realm. He recognized the blue and orange flame-like hair. Drawing his swords Simba turns to look each of them in the eyes. "If you thought you found an easy mark. I can assure you; you are gravely mistaken." The magus growls.

Brandishing improvised or crude weapons they begin to crowd in. Simba noticed an especially tall warrior who stood back watching this unfold. He was horribly scarred. Looking the others over he noticed they too were scarred and recently by the look of things. One of the shadow creatures lunged in to stab him. Simba easily batted the thrust aside with one sword while smacking him hard with his other blade turning it horizontally. The wind rushed out of the shadow creatures' lungs swiftly as it was flung into several others. When it looked as if the remaining assailants were about to rush in as a group, Simba sheathed one of his blades, gathered a ball of energy into his palm and held it aloft threateningly.

From their recoil at this motion, it was apparent that magic had been used against them. "Ah, so someone here has used their unesiphiwo against you, have they? I am guessing it did not go so well for you. I too have a grudge against some of the magi of this realm. Together, perhaps we can crush them, or you can choose to make your feeble attempt at defeating me and you can die for naught. There's more meat on your bones collectively than what was on that bedrahin calf. At least Lasekunene and Lasekholo will have full bellies this day." He was unsure if any of them understood a word he spoke.

Back in the shadow realm he rarely had the chance to make an attempt at communication with any of the beings there. Communication in that realm was swift and often physical in nature beyond growls or aggressive screeching. Even while observing from a distance Simba could not recall ever hearing what might have been construed as a language from these anthropomorphic beings. Almost as one the creatures turned to look at the tall one watching.

Simba gathered that at least in part they understood, and looked to this larger one to make a decision. "You must be the leader." Simba stated flatly. The creature nodded. Good, Simba thought, that was progress. He continued "You seem to understand me. Can you also speak in my tongue?" The wispy glowing orange tendrils of hair flickered back and forth like flames as it opened its mouth. What came out was a combination of hissing that took place in an echo chamber. Disappointed Simba said "Charming, but I can't understand that."

The fiery haired creature threw its weapon and pointed roughly towards his sword. "You want me to lay down my arms?" Again, it nodded. Another wild series of gesticulations, and after a few moments, Simba was able to guess at the meaning. "I think I get what you're trying to convey now. You want to fight. No weapons and no magic are the rules of engagement. I assume if you win, you'll do what you wish with me, but if I win you and your group will join me. Together we will strike out at whomever gave you those wicked scars, and then you will help me get revenge against Kemet as well as the pompous magi that exiled me all those long seasons ago. Agreed?"

The creature nodded and briefly smacked his clenched fists together grinning evilly. Simba sheathed his swords before removing the belt that held them. As the belt and blades clattered to the ground, he returned the gesture before rushing in. Aggression was key to fighting these creatures. During the early days of his exile Simba had taken plenty of beatings at the hands of some shadow creatures before honing his close combat skills. Growing up as a talented potential magus in Nymbani, pugilism was not seen as necessary.

Being robbed of his access to his unesiphiwo forced him to learn, and that education had to be swift in order to survive. Here it would have been simple to just augment his physical might without them knowing. Pride would not allow him to fraudulently defeat this creature despite desperately needing allies. When a nasty haymaker came flying for his head, Simba deftly ducked under it countering with an upcut to its jaw nearly lifting him off his feet. There was a raspy exhort from the shadow creatures gathered around that sounded roughly like "ooooh."

It was a nice blow but Simba knew physically the creature had an advantage so giving it a chance to recover could prove fatal. Angrily the shadow creature lashed out sporadically. Nimbly Simba ducked and dodged a wild flurry of strikes which surely would have sat him down hard had any of them connected. When the final part of the most recent missing combination was over, the magus went back on the offensive starting with a kick to the shins, then midsection.

Its orange eyes nearly bucked out of his head as the air left his lungs. As he gasped Simba quickly stomped on his foot. The raspy squeal that followed was nearly ear shattering as the creature doubled over while trying to simultaneously grab at his aching foot. It was time to end this, Simba thought. The shadow beast had obviously underestimated the magus. Unable to collect its thoughts the orange haired shadow being looked up just in time to catch a clenched fist wrapped in an armored gauntlet hurtling swiftly towards his face before everything went dark.

Even with the gauntlet on it had somehow still managed to sting a bit. Simba stood over the leader lightly shaking feeling back into his hand as the creature was coming back to consciousness. It quickly got up shaking its head as it backed away. It saw that Simba had retrieved his sword belt and the other shadow beings were all confused and sort of cowering. For a moment Simba thought the creature would lunge at him so he reminded them all "I won on your terms. If you go back on our agreement, I am no longer bound to them. I will have no qualms about obliterating you. There will be others I can turn to my cause. It would be more fruitful for us to simply join forces."

Back on his feet the shadow creature seemed to be thinking things over now that he had his feet solidly under him again, rocking back and forth deciding what to do. When it seemed as if the creature and its fellow shadow realm denizens were about to make the wrong decision Simba gathered an orb of energy into his hands. Closing his eyes in concentration he began growing it larger and larger. Seeing this the shadow realmers began to stand down. When the leader saw that if he made that leap it would be on his own, he finally capitulated and got down on one knee before the magus.

Seeing this Simba expelled the energy without channeling it into anyone or anything and it dissipated. "Good, that was the wisest choice you could have made for yourself, and those that follow you. Here among the people magi, dragons, drakes, and other beasts of this realm, you will find me to be an ally worth having. Do right by me, and I will reward your efforts."

The magus was unsure that they understood everything but they were not attacking him. For now, that was all that mattered. A show of strength was all that was likely necessary to keep them in line, and power was the form of communication they understood best. Now he would see if perhaps they could help in getting that meal for his companions. Once Lasekunene and Lasekholo were firmly back on their feet, these shadow realm creatures would not dare try him, magic or no. Back in the shadow realm he was sure his two dire lions had a long-standing reputation that would have spread to some in this group.

Through a strange combination of him talking and a made-up sign language, Simba was able to communicate what he wanted. After some painstaking trial and error, they finally rustled up some bedrahin meat without incurring the wrath of the surrounding Pantu tribes. Instructing them to wait Simba brought the meat back to his dire lions who were grateful for the meal. Slowly some of the healing incantations were coming back to him and he expedited the healing process in them.

When he returned with them, the reaction was just as he had hoped. The creatures from the shadow realm cowered in fear, and were in awe that they were under his control. Not even the leader would dare stand up to him now. This was just one piece. More would be needed if he hoped to challenge another group of magi.

Chapter Seventeen

J'Ure could only take so much punishment before he eventually tried to give some back as K'Ain mercilessly struck him again and again. The Djaemon that were slumbering in the red keep woke up to a sound drubbing. Many were surprised to see that their king and the clanmates that accompanied him to Kemet had in fact survived after going to the dead marshes to aid in capturing the rogue magus there who had dared to invade the lair of an elder dragon. The man was also supposedly the cause of spreading corruption throughout the lands and more importantly to the Djaemon some of their water sources. A most precious commodity to those living in the deserts.

Most of this tale sounded too farfetched to the Djaemon left behind to protect Gcina Okubomvu. So, it was not too difficult for the king's brother to convince them K'Ain and the rest had fallen in service of the Pantu tribesmen while challenging an elder dragon no less. Shunned long ago for being too cunning in battle, manipulative, and for generally straying too far from the ways of the Djaemon, J'Ure took his brothers absence as an opportunity to lay claim to what he felt should be rightfully his. With all the variables involved in going to the dead marshes as well as following a hunch into a tentative alliance with the Pantu tribesmen, J'Ure calculated that those of the red desert clan pursuing this were doing so to their collective deaths.

His face and body were lamenting that grave miscalculation currently. Mustering up the courage J'Ure is able to block a few blows before returning some of his own. K'Ain is caught off guard by a flurry of meaty punches to his midsection. An uppercut forces him to lean back briefly. Blood gushes in his mouth as his cheek was forcefully pinched between fist and teeth. Spitting it out the Djaemon King exclaims "Serat be praised! There is still some of us left in you, brother."

A large boot to the chest sends J'Ure sailing back once again to crumple in the sand. Through eyes that are nearly swollen shut J'Ure peers up at his brother lumbering towards him. "I will always be Djaemon, just not a foolish one!" Getting up J'Ure rushes forward and attempts to use his weight to his advantage tackling the king. Laughing K'Ain uses his momentum against him, steps to the side at the last moment and slings him roughly to the ground once more. "Yield brother, you have no rights to my throne, and even if you did, T'Ome or D'Na would challenge you. You would lose to them just as badly or worse because they would cut you down instead of simply beating you. You lack the skill to best them either way, and the clan would not follow you just because of our blood ties." K'Ain said waiting.

J'Ure wanted to get up and fight back but there wasn't much more he could do and he knew he would not defeat K'Ain. "Are you so sure, they would not follow me brother? It did not take much to convince them this time after all, but I do yield. To fight further would be pointless." He replied. The truth in that angered K'Ain but he understood how this all happened. Reaching down to roughly stand his brother up K'Ain said "Your ploy only worked because you lied and told them we were no more. Our blood ties got you back into Gcina Okubomvu, and comfortably on my throne briefly, but would you have been able to spill enough to keep it?"

Turning to the Djaemon present inside the keep the king asked, "Would you have allowed my brother to remain here while the rest of you languished under his feeble rule?" After a moment there was a resounding chorus of "Nooooooo!" that rang out in the desert night. "You see brother? They were only waiting for confirmation that I was indeed in the grave. Once they had that it was only a short matter of time before they would have killed you and cast you aside." K'Ain said through gritted teeth before kicking J'Ure roughly one last time for good measure.

As he retook his rightful place on the throne on the crude dais, D'Na, and T'Ome went about setting things right with their desert keep. The rest of the Djaemon quickly went about placing sentries in the sandy guard shacks all along the perimeter. J'Ure simply cowered mumbling under his breath while the home fire was hastily relit. K'Ain sat there reflecting for a bit, disappointed that anyone from his clan would even briefly trust the words of his brother who had a bad reputation amongst the most devout clans of the Djaemon.

K'Ain went about berating them, scolding them and when he had vented his frustrations, he finally told them about what actually transpired when they set out to find out what was ailing the lands and poisoning their water supplies. With the home fire lit as it was supposed to be, there was only a matter of brief moments until one of the sentries called out an alarm. Without being asked D'Na hastily went out to see what the fuss was about. Looking over to J'Ure, K'Ain grumbled "If this is another part of your farce, I will flay you alive. It may be the only way Serat would accept you as a blood sacrifice."

J'Ure said nothing and simply sat there pouting like a large red petulant child. K'Ain waited for word to come back to him. When D'Na comes back she explains "Someone approaches from the north my King, A few monks I believe. One might be their Shike." K'Ain was a bit suspicious of that. While their relationship with the tetsuo monks was not as colored by a violent history as with the Pantu Tribesmen, they were not exactly friendly either. A more accurate description would be to say they tolerated each other since both groups inhabited these desert lands. Other clans in regions closer to a different monastery may seek to challenge the strange order but K'Ain thought it more practical to poke that Ibhere only if absolutely necessary.

He was quite aware that the monks distributed legendary magical weapons of some great renown, and if his clan targeted them for raiding parties, it would only be a matter of time for those armed with tetsuo blades would come to avenge them. One or two of these warriors were sure to be a challenge and a great sacrifice to Serat to any Djaemon successful in defeating such a foe. Wiping out a monastery would bring a host of them. He would never say it out loud but a move like that would likely decimate his clan into nonexistence.

K'Ain and D'Na walk out of the main keep to watch as three rather diminutive forms make their way towards them. Two of them are wearing what could be the robes of the tetsuo monks. The third looks to be a dark skinned, bald man, his robes a pristine white. The other two look to have hoods drawn, and as they get closer, the Djaemon watching can tell that one of them is actually wearing a head wrapping above her robes, denoting that her origins likely lie far to the west of this desert land. As they draw nearer K'Ain can make out more details and they confirm that it is indeed Sakanoye, Shike or zen master and leader of the tetsuo monastery north of Gcina Okubomvu.

As they approached the outer perimeter, the sentries were unsure of how to respond but K'Ain sent word to them that they were to be permitted without incident. A portable version of his throne was brought out so the king of the Djaemon could greet them properly. It was set just beneath the great statue of Serat. The other Djaemon arrayed themselves around him leaving a path for the visitors to come through. As usual D'Na took the lead to act as translator. T'Ome wanted to see how this visit would go but felt the need to keep an eye on the king's conniving brother to ensure nothing embarrassing came to pass while everyone's attention was elsewhere.

They could tell now that one of them must be an acolyte or understudy, but was confidently carrying a weapon on his hip. The shike was ever the embodiment of wisdom and self-assuredness, but the woman was blatantly anxious. The head wrapping covered everything but her eyes which were alert, ever watchful and blazingly tense. The knuckles on both hands were stark white as her fists clenched tightly to the hilts of the undoubtably beautifully crafted weapons sheathed at her lower back. She looked ready to draw them at a moment's notice.

D'Na noticed her posture and looked back at K'Ain for a signal for how to handle this. He nodded slowly letting her know he saw it as well. A subtle hand gesture from the king signaled that she should be watchful but if anything were to happen the monks had to draw first blood. Once that happened it was out of his hands. They would start no quarrel with any of the tetsuo monks, but if they decided to strike, then all praise due to Serat the spillage in homage to the sanguine order would be returned. Consequences to follow be damned.

Once they were close enough to speak, the Shike greeted K'Ain. He noticed Diomae and tried to nonverbally calm her. Kenzo pulled down his hood to reveal his young face, bright almond shaped eyes, pensively ogling the huge Djaemon statues as Sakanoye spoke. "Sidibene kakule great K'Ain ruler of the Djaemon in the red desert! I am Sakanoye of the Tetsuo monastery not far from here, this is Diomae, and Kenzo monks of our order." Kenzo also noticed Diomae's change in bearing but took his cue from their leader.

D'Na returned the slight bow Sakanoye gave to the Djaemon gathered and their king. K'Ain reverted to their native tongue which upon hearing it Kenzo was sure sounded hostile. D'Na's translation was surprisingly tame. "King K'Ain welcomes you to Gcina Okubomvu, the great red keep in the desert! A blessed tetsuo blade would make for a wonderful gift for the king." Sakanoye seems to consider that responding "Apologies great king but we are only passing through on our way to Kemet. I had hoped you could give us some insight as to the veracity of the report the magus captured is indeed the cause for the recent strange occurrences."

Sakanoye was about to graciously try to rebuff the request for a tetsuo blade when J'Ure came bursting out of the keep closely followed by T'Ome. "I told you!" J'Ure blurted. D'Na was about to take out her black blade and silence him for good when the king waived her off letting his brother continue. K'Ain roughly screamed something and once again D'Na translated "What are you speaking of?" J'Ure raised his eyebrows at this farce. K'Ain could speak the common tongue simply refused to around non Djaemon.

J'Ure continued "I told you; your king had been consorting with outsiders for his own gain, and now he is willing to trade the services of this once great clan for a magical trinket!" Surprisingly Sakanoye responded "The blessed blades are not for trade or barter! You are a fool to believe otherwise." The Djaemon were all caught off guard by the vehemence of the Shike's response. Kenzo and Diomae had never seen their master so much as lose his temper. J'Ure turned on the head monk replying "Oh that's right…you vet all recipients. I am guessing your choices throughout the seasons have been infallible?"

Smoothing down his robes Sakanoye regains his composure before replying "It is because the past choices were not without fault in their discernment that the vetting process was initiated, and we certainly would never dole out such a grave responsibility for any…services." J'Ure screamed something unintelligible which began a back and forth between he and the Djaemon king. The monks looked back and forth in confusion before D'Na let them in on what was being discussed. "J'Ure has issued a blood challenge to you for questioning his word, but the King maintains that he was cast out of the clan long ago. He therefore has no right to make such a challenge."

They were all aghast when Sakanoye stated "I accept." K'Ain yelled something else none of the monks understood and D'Na dutifully let the Shike know, "He has no rights here." Nodding Sakanoye says "I understand, but it matters not. This one has challenged the integrity of my order. As much as we for the most part stay out of the affairs of others, I think my brothers and sister will understand if I make an exception this one time." With that the old monk began stripping down to the waist.

J'Ure grunted something else and Kenzo noticed he too had begun to refrain from using the common tongue. D'Na relayed the message "He says magic blades are forbidden." Sakanoye looked to Diomae seeing if perhaps she had packed any of the practice weapons from the monastery. She shook her head negatively. D'Na who watched the nonverbal exchange figured out what was happening and quickly unsheathed a wicked black blade that was slung on her back tossing it to them. It stuck in the reddish sand hilt up waiting to be taken.

J'Ure yelled something and D'Na responded by screaming something at one of the nameless Djaemon who reluctantly threw his untested blade towards J'Ure in what Kenzo felt was surely in a disrespectful manner. It nearly hit him. Had it done so it certainly would have drawn blood. A small part of Kenzo wished it had and wondered if that would have at least partially earned the unblooded warrior his name. The curiosity would go unfulfilled. Sakanoye examined the blade D'Na had given him it was indeed very crude compared to anything he had forged aesthetically but it was definitely sturdy and should hold up well. He nodded his approval to her before flourishing with it and getting into a low stance in high guard.

At first it looked as if J'ure he would not accept the sword provided waiting for the blade of a true warrior of the sanguine order to offer theirs. When none was forthcoming, he reluctantly picked it up, weighed it in his hands to feel the balance and swiftly charged. Well, swiftly for someone of his girth could be realistically expected to move. Sakanoye deftly avoided a flurry of wild slashes only clashing blades every third or fourth swing. Choosing to dodge most of the blows. K'Ain respected the tactic of the much smaller warrior knowing he was without what would certainly have been an advantage had he been able to wield his own blade.

The gap in skill between the two was obvious and quite wide. Accentuated by the fact that Sakanoye refused to counter strike at various openings. Instead, he was allowing the bigger fighter to simply tire himself out after multiple missed swings. When he began to slow exaggeratedly, Sakanoye went on the offensive casually after a parry or repost. Instead of slicing him open, the Shike began whacking him on his back and backside with the flat of the blade. This was likely causing some bruising but drawing no blood. When J'Ure noticed what he was doing, the Djaemon became enraged at the insult redoubling his efforts to cut the old man down.

His rage did not help matters as his swings became less accurate and wilder. Not to mention his energy was already waning. Sakanoye took full advantage and soon both the Djaemon and monks gathered could not help but laugh making J'Ure even more angry. Throwing the blade down in frustration the Djaemon tried one last strategy charging hard in an attempt to engulf the monk in his monstrous grasp hoping to choke the life out of him.

As up in age as Sakanoye was, he was still much too fleet of foot for the larger warrior to catch. He kept dodging, and whacking at each fumbled attempt until finally J'Ure fell out of exhaustion, helped slightly by the Shike's foot tripping him on the last pass. He went down in a heap followed by a cloud of sand so hard was his collapse. Holding the dark blade to his ear Sakanoye says "Yield."

"Do it!" J'Ure screams through gritted teeth. Bending down Sakanoye whispers "According to your king, you are likely not worth the blood sacrifice and I certainly will not avail you that honor if your own would not give it to you." Standing up he weighs the blade in appreciation before flipping it back to D'Na who caught it and sheathed it. As he was walking away J'Ure suddenly found a reserve of energy and popped up hoping to catch Sakanoye unawares. Without thinking Kenzo unsheathed and slung his sword end over end into the air.

The weapon narrowly passed Sakanoye as he turned just in time to see it coming landing squarely in the middle of J'Ure's chest. The weight of the tetsuo blade upended him sending his feet splaying out wide as he went horizontal in midair before thudding thunderously in the sand. K'Ain and T'Ome quickly ran over to stand over the kings' brother staring blankly at the sky as his black blood pooled in the sands of his birthplace. Sakanoye began to apologize but the king quickly waived him of before he could finish.

T'Ome looked to be comforting the king as they huddled over J'Ure's inert body. K'Ain muttered something Sakanoye and Diomae couldn't hear. It was doubtful they would have understood had it been louder. Kenzo looked stricken. D'Na says "That was the kings' brother but he had brought nothing of worth to this clan but shame, and strange ideas we had no desire to explore. It's probably best none of us sacrificed him to Serat. It would not have made for a worthy tribute. Tell the young one he did us a favor and is now rightfully blooded under our laws."

Kenzo was still visibly shaken and only came out of his trance as he vaguely realized he was being addressed. Glad that the boy had not inadvertently started an incident between the tetsuo monks and the Djaemon while also realizing that could easily have been the result, Sakanoye comforted him as best he could. A fracas broke out as there was some confusion as none of the Djaemon were able to pull what looked like a normal sized blade from J'Ure's body.

K'Ain screamed for silence and Sakanoye nodded to Kenzo silently telling him to retrieve his weapon. The Djaemon parted to let him through watching him intently. His feet felt leaden as he walks up to the body before reaching down to pull the blade effortlessly from the corpse. The blood, the endless stare into nothingness and horror-stricken expression on J'Ure's face would haunt him. K'Ain muttered something at him and D'Na asked "The king wants to know your name."

This confused him as he was sure Sakanoye had given their names after his initial greeting, but perhaps the king had forgotten. Hesitantly he replies "Kenzo." Bowing slightly as he said it. Another guttural outburst from K'Ain prompts D'Na to tell them "You are to feast with us tonight and continue your journey to Kemet tomorrow when the sun sets." The king looks thoughtful as the other Djaemon are preparing to go in for the night. Suddenly it looks as if he had figured out what his thoughts were and he exclaims "K'Nzo!" Soon a chant goes up carrying on the Djaemonization of the boy's name.

Some of the tension has left Diomae but it's obvious she is still uneasy around this Djaemon clan. Cocking her head to the side she says to Kenzo "Looks like you have been accepted into the clan. I would advise not drinking anything that is not water. You may wake up ritually scarred." Together they all went in for a night of feasting.

Chapter Eighteen

Bablu Aye could tell that Esu was intrigued or at least that was what the trickster god exuded as the harbinger of disease and healing spun his tale of how they could both build a foundation for their empires that could one day rival the splendor they saw before them in Izulu. At long last Esu could stand it no longer and burst out in a fit of laughter to the point of tears. "You and I both know this is no more than ploy to raise yourself above your station amongst us. The sky god and creator will see through this for what it is. A plan to usurp more power and simultaneously duck the consequences of meddling too much in the affairs of mortals below. Had you let this Motu fall as he should have, he and his love would be in the embrace of death. Yewa will have her due. Now why would I ever insert myself into such a calamity?" Esu said when he calmed enough to speak.

Pondering Esu's query Bablu Aye responds "Is this not within your purview? Olofi was to be the bridge between deities and mortals but you were always the true mediator. Mischief has always been your lot. You love to foment chaos, and this would be a grand opportunity! Trickster god, tell me what manner of beings have you beguiled lately? Mortals are easy game. How about you set your sights a bit higher shall we? I've no doubt of your talent. What say you?" Esu chuckles at the combination of Babalu Aye attempting to praise him while simultaneously sowing seeds of doubt in order to challenge him to rise to the occasion.

Once again splintering into many images of himself, Esu returns the challenge. "Do you think partial platitudes and flattery is the way to goad me into this farce? What of you? You have listed why you think I would desire to be involved. A bit flimsy is your reasoning there, but I'll blame that on hubris. You are the god of pestilence and healing. That's a bit odd. Is it not? One would think that you would be one aspect or the other with another of us in the opposing aspect to serve as your foil or true measure of balance. To gain any true power I would think you would lean into a side and stay there. You could singlehandedly sow your own brand of chaos and rise in power, all without anyone's help."

Now it was Babalu Aye's turn to chuckle. "You almost had me there, but the fact is I do need your help brother. Denying part of myself to feel one aspect or the other is not the answer. You may get the chaos you desire were I to walk that path, but I would not like to be in either domains dominated by either pure malady or a utopia of perfect health. With access to both I can have a domain that I am at once the cause and cure while curating worshippers from both spectrums. I need you to ensure I am not implicated until it's too late to do anything about it." He stated.

Esu veered back into a singular form thinking this over replying "You have yet to tell me what boon I would be given for my participation. Surely you do not think I would risk life and limb for your campaign alone?" Stepping closer Babalu Aye says "You my brother get to return to your former glory in addition to pulling a ruse on the gods here on Izulu, once I am firmly ensconced below too potent to be bothered with the others, I will give you leave to influence all the conflict you desire down below. Olorun has sought to keep us at too much of a distance from the mortals here. Things can be as they were in the realms we have long since abandoned."

That sounded a bit too good to be true to Esu. Yet he was still tempted by the potential prospect. Aside from that he was also very cognizant of how disastrous a failure to properly execute this plan would be. The trickster god was fairly confident that in the event things went badly it would prove to be just as entertaining and he would be able to absolve himself for the most part with minimal backlash to adversely affect him in the end. When it came down to it, Babalu Aye would twist in the wind on his own. Of course, he didn't have to let him know. Only a fool would believe otherwise. "Very well Babalu. First order of business will be getting down there without anyone noticing, and know that should anything go awry, I will deny any involvement." Esu stated with raised eyebrows awaiting a response.

Shaking his head Bablu Aye replied "Had you stated otherwise I would not have believed you. Any way I accept. Have you not heard? Olorun has called a meeting. When it convenes there will be a great chance for us to slip down to the surface unnoticed until it's too late." Esu was still a bit unclear how growing Babalu Aye's power base below would help ensure he would be beyond reprisal attempts from the other orishas, but that was none of his concern. At this point whatever the result, it was sure to cure his boredom. In the end Babalu Aye himself would bear the full brunt of the consequences.

They could feel a large wellspring of power migrating from all areas of the floating city-ship as the gods answered the call Olorun put out for them to assemble. Carefully they made their way to the bottom most terrace overlooking the jewel in space that was Nyumbani below lit by the huge thruster flames. After the many planes of existence, they had witnessed, this was still a beautiful sight to behold from this vantage point. Those dwelling below had no idea what kind of havoc could be visited upon them when these two touched down. Their world was already on the verge of another disaster.

Bablu Aye slowly looked over the precipice before swinging one leg over the ledge. For a moment he just stood there after moving his other leg bracing with both hands on the railing staring down at the spinning globe glowing beneath them. As they could feel a majority of the host of deities had joined Olorun and the others far above them at the apex of Izulu a light came into Babalu Aye's eyes. Looking to Esu he said, "Join me brother!" leaping into the void of space falling to the surface of Nyumbani below. With a heavy sigh Esu leapt overboard in pursuit. Soon their bodies began to breach the atmosphere. As the friction of their bodies falling through the various layers began glowing as they hit the thermosphere. From below they looked like falling stars.

Slowing their descent, they began to manipulate the air around them once they reached the troposphere in order to guide themselves to landfall in a less populated area. It would not do to slam into an epicenter. They needed to quietly get the lay of the land first to see where it would be best to consolidate power from. At least that's what Bablu Aye had in mind. For now, Esu was simply tagging along. They steered themselves into a seemingly abandoned area. Babalu Aye figured it would be a day or two on foot for them to reach where he felt the presence of the magus he had initially tricked into his service. On their short journey he and the trickster god should be able to formulate a more solid strategy for what to do once they arrived.

That would take some doing as they were unaware of the trial going on. The two fallen deities look up briefly as if they could see the gathering that had begun in their absence far above them in Izulu. Had they been able to see the scene above unfold they would have witnessed Olorun striding confidently into a grand hall within the dome-like capsule atop the giant city-ship that had become the home for most of the orishas since relocating after creating this dimension.

There were still some stragglers finally making their way in. All of them wondering what was such an important issue that the creator would gather the majority of them together. Rumors, whispers and other murmurings bounced off the gold laden walls, ceilings and floors as Ogun stared daggers at Olorun as he took his place at the head of the large gathering. Shango, Oya, Ochosi, and Yewa were scattered about on the outskirts of the gathering listening to and observing some of the lesser deities mill about gossiping. The ripples of conversation stopped as it became clear the Olorun was going to address them.

"Brothers, sisters, and family beyond I know you must all be curious as to why I have asked for this audience. By now we can all see the slight changes that have gone on below spreading some kind of ailment across Nyumbani and it may continue. Now had this come as a result that the mortals below stumbled into something as they are wont to do, then I would simply sit back and observe as we have when similar things happened on other worlds. However, I have it on good authority that one, possibly more amongst us have willingly caused this calamity to come about. I now give you a chance to come forward so that the rest of us may go about our business. We know the agreed upon rules." Olorun waited to see if any would admit to the tampering.

Dead silence was the only response as they all looked around to see if anyone would step forward. No one did. This was expected and Olorun was prepared. "Very well, line up. Since no one will come forward we shall use true sight to reveal who is being untruthful about their involvement below." The sky god proclaimed. The announcement was met with a cacophony of denials and complaints about how unfair, unnecessary or literally unwarranted this line of spiritual interrogation was. Especially given that many of them would periodically venture below. As far as gauging how much interaction was too much, that would be a difficult thing to quantify.

The spread of a sickness infecting both large swaths of land and the magic of the world was worrisome but hardly reason to go through such measures. Tired of hearing the multifaceted arguments flitting about the great chamber, Oya and Shango were the first to simply approach Olorun to get things started. Their eyes glowed as they took each other's hands. Through this mutual touch they could get glimpses of recent events and experiences. Olorun could see nothing of consequence from either of them. Breaking the contact ended the brief communion and they were absolved of any wrongdoing or tampering.

Ochosi went next followed by Yewa, and Ogun. It was seen that they had indeed been down to the surface, but none so far were the cause of the mishaps negatively influencing this relatively new world. Ogun was the last to break the connection seeking to use the opportunity to view whether or not Olorun was in fact involved with the possible encroachment into his domain. Hypocrisy was not an uncommon thing even amongst the gods, but he could see that the creator had told the truth. In fact, there was no evidence that the strange technology had reached this dimension by other means. At least for now the Orisha were not involved.

Olorun was becoming frustrated that no discernment had been revealed. Orunmila was accounted for and Olofi had assured him that she was not involved via another brief message. Together they were exploring how to help mend the veils between realms that were thinning. Another residual effect of the recent incidents. Oshun, and Obatala volunteered next revealing more of the same. They too were innocent of inciting this calamity. Many others stopped complaining and just submitted to the testing despite their misgivings. Looking around Olorun noticed a couple conspicuous absences.

Yewa gave voice to his suspicions "Where is Babalu Aye...and Esu for that matter? I have not seen them recently. Did they not heed the call as the rest of us did?" They all looked around to see that in fact the two mentioned were missing from the assembly. Grumbling, they began to file out of the chamber. Oya, Shango, Yewa, and Ogun stayed behind. Flames of the eternal forge burned in Ogun's eyes and he stared balefully at Olorun as he said "I go now to tend to my duties down below. The age of engines will come when I deem this place ready."

He did not wait for a response but simply opened a portal and stepped through it disappearing they assumed to a land mass below that he fancied. The eyebrows of the three remaining with Olorun hinted at a curiosity for whatever the cause of Ogun's ire was. Olorun just stared blankly giving no indication that he would reveal the source of their current rift. Yewa stepped up to express her concerns "It's interesting that Babalu Aye, and Esu are missing. I had already spoken to Babalu but was going to get to Esu eventually although my missing chalices would be of little use to the trickster."

Oya and Shango said nothing but simply watched Olorun consider the possibilities. Olorun advises "It is more likely that Babalu Aye took the chalices. Esu has no need of them as you say since he can appear as he wishes. It is however also just as likely that Esu would be intrigued by the prospect of causing mischief. Them both being absent at the same time while we look for those responsible for what is happening below is…telling. It's true that others were missing but most are accounted for. I may need to visit Serat, but this does not look to have his prints upon it."

Yewa shakes her head in agreement before adding "Yes Serat would have left a longer trail of blood behind in his wake. For now, he has seemed happy to let his worshippers do it in his stead. If we find that either or both Esu and Bablu Aye are responsible for my missing chalices as well as the damage done below, what will the punishment be?"

When Olorun takes too long to render an answer, Yewa storms off saying "I may not be able to embrace them in death but I will be sure to spend ample time with them chained in my domain. To steal the use of my visage for their personal gain is sacrilege that I will not endure. Fix it Olorun, or I will!" Sheepish grins were spread across the faces of Shango and Oya now that the three of them were alone. Olorun didn't like it. "What are you two about now? You're usually going on about how one of you has wronged the other. I thought happiness was a power that escaped you." Eerily they shared a chuckle before Shango finally lets him in on the joke.

"You do realize that true sight goes both ways?" Olorun nodded in agreement. Oya adds "You were able to see that we had not been down to the surface, nor had we any influence in starting the disasters there. We know that you had no part in that either, but there was another interesting detail you failed to mention." Olorun feigned confusion over what they could be alluding to. Oya continued "Don't play coy! What was your decision on the talents we gave you to weigh?"

Shango joined in "Yes tell her the truth! Tell her the lightning she gave you was but a spark compared to mine." Oya jokingly elbowed him in the ribs as they both stepped closer to Olorun awaiting his answer. The creator gesticulated and rubbed his shorn head as if a recollection had just come to him exclaiming "Oh, those talents, of course! It was hard to gage really. So, I gifted them to a mortal just awakening to the world soon after we spoke back then."

The last was purposefully mumbled so as not to be easily understood, but Oya and Shango caught the gist of what he said. For a moment they looked on incredulously, not sure of how to respond. Soon they both burst out in laughter. Shango nearly had tears in his eyes responding "So you call a meeting to see who has been interfering below, only to reveal that you, yourself have been in fact interfering. I would ask if you jest, but I had seen the truth of some of what you say, but it being your perspective and a bit broken up needed some clarity to make sense of it."

Oya was waiting in the wings to pile on "Olorun please explain how what you did was not interfering in the affairs of the mortals below? Had you any idea of how this power could one day tip the scales in life for this young one you burdened?" With a guilty look Olorun replies "In truth I just wanted you two to stop bickering. When I held the talents, I just wanted to be rid of them. I did not want to aimlessly toss them, and was rather curious to see what the results would be. I do not often give in to these urges as I know the lot of you all do, and in much more direct manners might I add."

At the last Olorun had his eyes squarely set upon Shango who had been known to occasionally take liberties with mortals below. He and many of the other gods had taken their fair share of opportunities here on Nyumbani and within a myriad of other realms before they settled here. "Besides" Olorun continued "It's not as if I was the source of the current situation down below. That's why I called the meeting. Yewa may be on to something, but I cannot allow her to take things too far if it turns out those who did not answer the call both stole her chalice and caused the ills the mortals below are going through. I just want to mend things and let them evolve as they will. The minute meddling, I have done is but a drop of water flailing in one of your storms Oya. Nothing of consequence will come of it."

Shaking their heads. Oya and Shango were not so sure. Shango said "I am not so sure of that, but worse will come when one or more of the others recall the brief glimpses you unwittingly gave them during true sight. Most were likely too focused on what you were seeing so as not to be implicated, but eventually these visions will no doubt ruminate in their minds eye until they see what you have been up to. It may not be the source of the recent troubles below, but they will see that one who has been staunch in defending unnecessary rules has not been adhering to them himself."

Oya tuts in agreement as she strides confidently out of the chamber. Just before she has fully exited, she offers "Since they will not be able to seek any reprisals from you, they may seek to have their hand in adding their own spices to that cauldron brewing below. You sought to satisfy a curiosity. Do you think yourself the only one to have such potential queries?" Shango had nothing else to add so he simply left behind her. Olorun was left to think on the coming consequences. Serat was never one for pleasant conversation under the best of circumstances but the god would have to be questioned as well just to be sure.

Chapter Nineteen

Kenzo was still looking very stricken from the earlier events that took place outside of Gcina Okubomvu, the desert stronghold for the Djaemon in the area. The red skinned warriors were making an attempt at being gracious hosts to the Tetsuo monks that paid them a visit on their way to Kemet. In their eyes Kenzo was now blooded and a guest of honor as a result of his new status. Although the boy often dreamt of glorious battle, and was recently given the honor of forging his very own tetsuo blade with the help of the Shike of his monastery, the weight of taking a life felt to be more than his small shoulders could bear.

He ate the food the Djaemon offered, listened to their songs but had the sense to not partake in the special brew they distilled. It seemed that Diomae had given him sound advice. Surprisingly the Shike was either familiar, or had a history imbibing such strange drinks. Both Diomae and Kenzo were taken aback when the Shike took the offered tankard made from a large horn from some beast they were sure they had never seen. By the size of the horn, they likely would not want to. Kenzo's eyes nearly fell from his sockets as the old monk chugged the pungent brew down quickly resulting in roars of cheers from K'Ain and the rest of his clan.

Seeing his master jovially carousing with a group of dangerous warriors helped relieve some of the tension Kenzo had been feeling for a bit. Before he forgot the boy grabbed his tools for tending to his blade and went off to make sure it was properly cleaned. It wasn't likely to happen but he wanted to be sure that if they needed him to use it again on their journey it would not stick in the sheath when attempting to draw it. Diomae followed to keep an eye on him, and also because she was not in much of a drinking mood.

Kenzo noticed but uncharacteristically did not object. Truth was, he welcomed the company, and he was very aware that Diomae seemed very uncomfortable ever since it became clear they would be making a stop here before continuing on. He found a quiet spot near what looked like a makeshift well or place they deposited water from another source, sat down to clean his weapon. Diomae unsheathed her two curved blades and laid them on a cloth before bringing out a whet stone joining him. Kenzo watched her closely and tried to follow her but was not as prepared. He had a cloth which he dipped into a nearby bucket he filled prior and went about ensuring all ichor was gone from the blade and hilt.

Noticing he was missing a whet stone, Diomae offered him hers, and corrected his technique as he went. When he seemed relaxed enough, she asked "How are you feeling?". While continuing to sharpen his blade Kenzo answers "Better now. I can still see his eyes staring into oblivion. I don't think I will ever forget. I knew he was about to harm master, so I don't feel bad about taking action. It's just the results were…unexpected." Diomae nods her understanding as she sheaths her weapons but stays to listen in case, he had more to get off his chest.

It was good that he seemed to not only be processing but also able to communicate his feelings. Most would simply hold that on their own letting it destroy them from the inside. When he went to speak surprisingly it was not about his inner turmoil but hers "I noticed how you kind of shut down at the sight of this keep, and how you have seemed on edge ever since we came to be among the Djaemon. They seem to be a sore subject for you. With respect, I would like to know why? The Shike as well as the other monks have been aware as well but when we ask, they say it's not their tale to tell." He explained.

She nodded again, grateful that the monks and others at the monastery had chosen not to gossip about her to the novices. Sliding closer to him she began to untie some of the laces that kept her sleeves, upper garment and head wrapping bound tightly to her leaving only her face revealed. When Diomae saw Kenzo's eyes go wide briefly she chuckled "It's not what you think young one…I am from a small coastal city far from here near one of the many shipyards of the greymoors. Some of the Djaemon clans to the west of us would routinely conduct raids. During one of the last attacks when I was but seventeen seasons I was caught up in the fight. We do not have city shields so everyone who is able to fight is charged to do so. After a pretty sound defeat, I was captured. They believed I fought well, and these were their tokens of appreciation."

Sliding back her sleeves she exposed an intricate tapestry of scars they had given her that went from her wrists all the way up to her shoulders, and Kenzo assumed it included her neckline. In a way they were to his eyes a thing of beauty, but there was no way for him to comfortably say that without offending her given the source of their genesis. All he could muster was "I'm sorry. That had to hurt." Diomae began to retie her garments blinking back tears adding "You have no idea. They even darkened them with their ritual dye. Smelled something awful and felt like fire! They thought they were doing me a great honor."

Kenzo now understood her misgivings, and wondered how she came to be with the tetsuo monks, but that was a question for another time. She was handling things pretty well in his estimation. It was time to get some rest before heading out in the morning. A contingent of Djaemon would be travelling with them which may now complicate things more than they already were. They returned to the main part of the keep where the festivities had died down somewhat. Sakanoye was snoring contentedly on his bedroll near the home fire surrounded by Djaemon warriors drunkenly slumbering along with him.

It was an odd yet strangely satisfying sight for Kenzo and Diomae. The Shike was rumored to have had a very intriguing life prior to joining the monastery as well. Kenzo very much wished to hear his tale of how he lived before leading a life of meditation, forging and training novices. He was unsure whether Diomae would be able to offer any insight, but thinking on it, it was likely that he would get a similar response he was given when asking other monks about her. It was only right that Sakanoye be the one to tell him if and when he chose to do so. They found their bedrolls and laid down for the night.

Izulus' light blazed the horizon with a ferocity that was very familiar to those that chose the desert life. Many of the Djaemon that had partook in imbibing the night before were slow to wake, and predictably groggy. The Shike who had gone drink for drink with these red skinned warriors, most of which were two or three times his size was found not only awake at first light, but in high spirits with no signs of a monstrous hangover. Kenzo and Diomae who chose not to join in the previous nights' festivities were supremely surprised to find their master ready to begin their journey calmly sipping tea while the inert bodies around him were just now beginning to stir. A series of groans began to cascade throughout the entire main hall of the desert keep.

Kenzo wiped the crust from his eyes, went to find a place to more thoroughly clean himself up before their journey after packing up his supplies so he would be ready to shove off as soon as the others were ready. Diomae went in search for a place to do the same starting with her daily ablutions. They agreed to meet back up in the main hall near where Sakanoye was meditating after concluding his morning tea. As he went Kenzo observed the Djaemon going about their daily routines. Once he had himself together the boy found one of the less exotic looking rations the Djaemon offered and broke his fast saving the rations they had prepared at the monastery for the journey ahead.

D'Na, the tall female Djaemon chieftain noticed him and came to sit a comfortable distance from him as she checked her weapons. Looking around Kenzo remarked "Everyone here is assigned the same duties? I mean it looks as if the males and females have no division of tasks or specific roles." A chuckle escaped D'Na's lips before she replied "You would have me gathering herbs for medicine and meals? Preparing the food while the males hunt? There are only two castes here, the blooded and the un-blooded. What hangs between your legs or lack thereof does not matter. Serat only cares for our faith and sacrifices to him. The unnamed and un-blooded handle all of the menial tasks of the clan until they earn their names."

Kenzo took a moment to study all the Djaemon toiling away at what most would consider the mundane tasks necessary for the group's survival trying to see what differentiated them. When the realization became clear he felt silly for not noticing earlier. Trying to glance at D'Na without being too obvious he observed her hair, shaven on the sides with the top in a long black braid that became a thick loc at the bottom. She was scarred from nearly head to toe. Some were obviously in a specific pattern while others had to have been earned in battles. The natural scars were in great variety likely from blades, claws and teeth of some kind or another.

In contrast the Djaemon doing chores had the same crimson hue all over their bodies but it was unblemished. Kenzo assumed that this must also be a sign of youth but the lines in some of their faces were evidence that this theory would be easily refuted. D'Na laughed again softly seeming to divine what the young monk was thinking based on his expressions "Not all of us have the heart and faith to devote their minds and bodies to seeking glory in the name of Serat. Some are content to live here within the keep, remain nameless and un-blooded until they die. Some just lack the skill, and it would be pointless to send them out. Either way we can all contribute. Is this not true where you come from? Before the tetsuo monastery I mean."

The boy looked a bit confused before answering "I am not so sure about the village I came from because the monastery is all I know since I was left there at an early age, but other places I have had an opportunity to visit did not break up the tasks as you do here. I see nothing wrong with it as long as it works for you. I was just curious. I meant no offense." She replied with "None taken." Before going off to settle an argument that had broken out between some of the blooded and un-blooded near the home fire. Kenzo tried to follow what was happening but could not as he could not understand their native tongue. He went to sit with Diomae and Sakanoye who both looked packed and ready to go.

Together they made their way out of the keep to stand before the large statues and effigies that stood as a huge warning to any that approached this desert keep unbidden. Sakanoye asked as they began to walk towards the Djaemon formation "Are you expecting trouble?". Confusion was seen on both of their faces as they simultaneously replied "No." Jovially the Shike shook his head saying "Good, I heard you were both fastidiously cleaning your weapons last night. I thought perhaps you heard something I was unaware of. Travelling in the company of a prominent Djaemon clan, one would think most will steer clear of us. The sightings of creatures from the shadow realm have been sporadic at best from recent reports. Kenzo…how are you holding up? Or should I say K'Nzo?"

The Djaemon adaptation of his name nearly made him laugh but also reminded him of the gruesome nature in which he had earned it in the eyes of the clan around them. Kenzo nodded to signal he was alright or at least he would be. The fact that he seemed just shy of laughing at the jest meant he was headed in the right direction mentally. Diomae and Sakanoye were happy to see that. Sakanoye hoped some of the things they may see and witness on this journey would solidify the weight of responsibility Kenzo would soon bear when tasked with forging and blessing blades for others. Discernment of who is and who is not worthy will be integral to keeping things balanced.

A smaller gathering of Djaemon set out before the main group would step off. T'Ome and D'Na briefly spoke with them, and then came to join the tetsuo representatives they would be accompanying to Kemet. Kenzo's eye went wide in surprise as the advance detachment sandcasted, kicking up the desert sands in a wild formation of sandstorms rushing off to map their route. T'Ome roughly said something in their tongue and D'Na translated "If you shared our ability, we would make this journey much quicker. They have gone to scout ahead."

Kenzo was amazed at the size of T'Ome. Everything about him was remarkable. He was a walking red wall of scars and muscle. Trying not to smile Sakanoye chided him "Don't be rude boy. It's not polite to stare." Chuckling he added "I do understand though. The Djaemon can cut quite the image." Securing his belongings as they began their march Kenzo responded "Yes master. I believe you are right. Anyone willing to ambush us would have to have a death wish…even his paunch has muscle!" Diomae shushed him as they stepped off when she finally noticed K'Ain was absent from their entourage. To D'Na she asked, "Is your king not coming along?"

D'Na shook her head negatively replying "No, K'Ain is not much for what he considers politics but, he still wants to be aware of any new developments. Things here were mishandled while we were away so he will stay behind to ensure that doesn't happen again." Sakanoye and Diomae were unsure what was meant by that but they were almost certain it likely had to do with J'Ure. Kenzo was too busy gawking at the other Djaemon with them. Not realizing they suddenly stopped for some reason, he walked into Diomae's back. The other two noticed the Djaemon had stopped to look back at the entrance to their desert keep.

As one they began to chant in their guttural language with their heads slightly bowed. Both Sakanoye and Diomae mimicked the posture but said nothing. Kenzo followed suit. After a resounding cheer of some kind the Djaemon turned to resume the march. D'Na could see that the boy was dying to ask what was said but also wanted to be polite so she offered "We asked Serat to bless this journey. We have a few unnamed with us." Sakanoye could see that idea seemed to please the boy and did not have the heart to elaborate on how "brutal" a Djaemons version of a blessed journey could be.

Along with the rear guard Sakanoye, Diomae and Kenzo began their march east with D'Na, T'Ome and their contingent of Djaemon representatives. Kenzo paid keen attention to the "nameless" among the Djaemon troops. Since he had spent some time around these people it was easier to pick them out. The smooth, nearly unblemished red skin devoid of scarring was obvious but something else stood out to him. The weaponry of the un-blooded among them was not the traditional black hue as he saw slung over the backs of D'Na, T'Ome and some of the other Djaemon who looked to be fierce and well-seasoned warriors.

After a long day march, they were just reaching the outskirts of the Pantu grasslands. Sakanoye had heard the rumors of the tension between the Djaemon and the Pantu tribes had died down given recent events but this would be the first time he would witness for himself if they were true. Diomae seemed to be more relaxed but quite obviously still had her guard up. Kenzo and Sakanoye both understood. They too were wary but tried to outwardly give off the impression that they were not at all on edge. Low growls could soon be heard as dire panthers soon got wind of their group approaching. They were quickly quieted as they and their riders stepped out of the tall grasses.

Kenzo could see the collective shoulders of the nameless Djaemon drop when it was plain that no conflict would be forthcoming. Instead, there was a rather cordial chorus of greetings heaped upon them as they passed through. D'Na who had been paying attention to the young man's observations stated "Some of them have never left the confines of Gcina Okubomvu, and this will be their first opportunity to earn their names. During long periods of peace lasting many seasons we sometimes have to create an opportunity."

Sakanoye and Kenzo could see and almost feel Diomae's disposition shift as her back went rigid as they continued to walk. The moment of tension made things quite awkward as she added "That I am very aware of D'Na. What of those who do not wish to be a part of your people's rights of passage rituals?" D'Na could tell there was something there, and that likely the reason Diomae had been so standoffish while at their desert keep had to do with the tetsuo monk crossing paths with another Djaemon clan previously. Sensing the tension, T'Ome sidles closer to D'Na, a wicked grin rests on his craggy face.

D'Na continues to answer her question "Not all clans live the same. Not all of us devote to Serat, but most of us believe this way of life contributes to being prepared. The Pantu that thrive in these grasslands because they and their mounts are ever vigilant in keeping guard over their borders to protect both their people and the herds. From your reaction it feels like the Djaemon where ever you came from did more than test your borders. In the past we have done this to earn scars and give them but never to slaughter. Larger groups in need of initiation will seek out the lair of large beast known to be a danger to those living near them. Of course, that line of action is sometimes curbed by ever enthused Elinanye who revere all forms of wildlife."

In Diomae's mind none of that explanation justified what she and her people experienced but she also knew now was not the time or even the right group of Djaemon to address this issue with. They had reached the other side of the grasslands, and could see the large stone structures slightly north of the dead marshes where the tops of smoke stacks could be seen. The Djaemon formation was called to a sudden halt as news from the advance group filtered through the ranks.

Smartly Sakanoye, and Diomae took the opportunity to switch out to dry stockings beneath their boots. Kenzo followed their example as the Djaemon spoke quietly in their native tongue. They wait for D'Na to bring them the news. Whatever it was, the nameless seemed really excited about it. After conferring with T'Ome, D'Na came to them as the larger Djaemon went to give instructions to their group. "The encampment is not a group of Pantu tribesmen but seems to be a gathering of beings from the shadow realm lead by a magus with dire lions. We will camp here while still under the Pantu tribesmen's watch. I have ordered no fires so we do not alert the shadow realmers to our presence." She spoke.

Sakanoye nods his understanding as he and Kenzo prepare to lay down for the night. Diomae says "I'll take first watch. The Pantu may be under the impression that we are all allies but I'm not so sure." Neither Sakanoye nor Kenzo tried to refute what she said. They all wondered where the beings camped outside the dead marshes were headed. Kenzo doubted they were also going to Kemet to sue for peace, but it was an outside possibility. Perhaps they had found a magus that would speak for them. When he thought of voicing his musings to Sakanoye, he could see the Shike had a smirk on his face as if he already knew what the boy was thinking. Kenzo was content to lay down. He would think about bringing it up in the morning when they set off again.

Chapter Twenty

Once again Olorun stood near the bottom most balcony near the enormous thrusters beneath the city ship of Izulu giving heat to the surface of Nyumbani below. Having examined most of the deity hosts on Izulu, the creator was more than sure the culprit or culprits have been reasonably narrowed down. Just to be sure he would have to venture to the other satellite city within the orbit of Nyumbani where another prominent deity resides that has very close ties to at least one group of mortals below.

The lunar city ship was where Serat the blood god, patron deity to the Djaemon chose to reside. It was also where the souls of his worshippers came after their final sacrifice was made. Occasionally these scarlet souls would flood to the surface en masse creating the legendary "blood moon" for the denizens below to observe. Serat was not an Orisha. There were a few theories amongst the gods on when the blood god arrived here and why. Olorun was not interested in looking into that mystery now. All he wanted to know was whether or not Serat had chosen to go down to stir the pot a bit for unknown reasons ending in the malignant results cascading through the lands.

The creator leapt from the balcony to fall through the stars curving speedily around the celestial body that was Nyumbani following the swelling curve of it to the other side where the lunar ship hung in the night sky. This ship was not built to look like the modern technological marvel that Izulu was. This place was for better or worse an underworld of sorts. Along with some of the other lesser-known deities that made their home here, long lost souls came to rest here when not claimed in other domains. The most prominent of course was the aforementioned Serat.

If not for the light of Izulu's massive engines being reflected back, this place would be nearly as dreary as the shadow realm itself. Instead, because of its position relative to the city-ship acting as the sun here, the lunar body glowed with a muted yet ethereal quality that seemed very bright at times. Especially to the mortals below looking up. The Djaemon souls that came to rest here resided down below within the crust of this forsaken place. The surface was ashen, and looked like a white desert. The ground rumbled as Olorun touched down. The creator thought he had heard something akin to keening as his weight settled kicking up plumes of space dust.

Crenelations rise in the rock to form a large circle around Olorun as he stands there. To the back of the formation a dais raises from the ground with a familiar looking throne like rock formation materializing. It was huge sitting before Olorun who just smirked at the theatrics. Suddenly Serat appeared in all his horrifying glory. The sky god was not impressed because they could all manifest themselves in whatever size they desired. They were gods after all. He had to admire the attempt at intimidation though. Serat was gloriously massive and scarred settling onto the huge throne he had created for this unexpected audience.

"To what do I owe this rare pleasure creator?" Serat boomed in his grating sonorous voice that seemed to shake the stars. Olorun could not help but laugh as this was as close to pageantry the blood god of the Djaemon would ever get. "Dear Serat, I have come to ask if you had any knowledge or participation in some of the alarming deterioration of the lands below? You had to have seen the results from your vantage point here." Olorun inquires. It was Serat's turn to laugh. Had Olorun not been a god he was sure the sound of it would have been very unsettling.

"You do not come to ask if I only witnessed this, you came to ask if I had a hand in it. Tell me Olorun, sky god, creator and venerable face of the orisha here in the realm of Nyumbani, what would you do if you learned this was in fact my doing? Do you think I would submit to discipline handed down from you or any of your kind?" Serat asked. Shaking his bald head Olorun stated flatly "A simple yes or no would suffice. If you think us too weak to press the issue if it comes out that you have indeed overstepped, then there is no harm in admission." Serat's black eyes shot through with swirling red narrowed as he tried to discern whether or not that was a threat.

Again, the blood god's sinister laugh bubbled into space reverberating even in vacuum where sound should not travel. A crimson tide of souls began to boil out of the nearby crevices on the lunar city ship covered in cracks making it look like a nearly shattered moon held together by miracles and despair. The swarm of souls was nothing but another intimidation tactic that would not work on Olorun, nor any of his counterparts. He was sure the Djaemon below had to be in a frenzy as from the surface of Nyumbani this spectacle would look like the very moon itself was bleeding. Those that stood staunchly within the sanguine order would mark this as a sacred night.

"Enough!" Olorun shouted and his words turned to a wild wind quickly whisking away the spirit horde of Djaemon souls Serat had gathered unto himself. Olorun then grew to match the blood god in size, and they stood as titans ready to do battle. Serat was eager but when Olorun grasped his wrists it was not to attack but to execute true sight and they were instantly transported mentally into each other's recent history. With his suspicions confirmed that it indeed was not Serat who had caused the spreading malady below, Olorun released Serat and reverted back to his previous stature.

"I came here not to challenge or scold you, Serat. We of the Orisha respect you but also know the source of your genesis and font of your power. You seem to have forgotten what and who came before you. You are not a primordial power here. You are a manifestation of your worshipers who willed you into existence when they needed something to live for. Something larger than themselves to have faith in that could in turn empower them to reach for greater heights. As a people they somehow pooled their unesiphiwo to bring you into existence, and you have grown. A deity you may be, but we are not the same. We created and shaped this realm along with many others. You would be wise to observe the inhabitants below more closely. Never has the clay sought to overthrow the potter." Olorun added before leaping once again into space.

A scream of fury followed in his wake from Serat, but nothing more. No doubt the blood god did not relish being read as less than. Surely, he would work to prove Olorun and any of the other Orisha wrong if they shared the creator's opinion on the hierarchy of gods here in Nyumbani. Now it was Olorun's turn to disguise himself as a meteor falling through the atmosphere. Between this planetfall and Serat's earlier theatrics it was likely a few more religions were spawned this night, perhaps giving birth to more new deities.

Olorun certainly hoped that wasn't the case but with the world so full of potential through magical means and various powers constantly adding things to the mix, other gods running amok, nearly anything was possible. Weaving his way down to the surface he made sure to revert back to his most comfortable corporeal form but hid himself from the possible prying eyes that would take note of his arrival. He landed near where he felt his aspect Olofi had also made planetfall some time ago. Unlike his counterpart, Olorun would not take the guise of an elderly traveler but would instead simply tone down his normal appearance closing his third eye from view.

Even from a distance he could feel the corruption of the lands and twisting of magic. The evidence of fighting, the passage of revenants, and invaders from the shadow realms could be felt by the creator. His were the threads that had woven this plane of existence together. Alterations, even minor ones would have traces left behind. Loose threads only he could see or feel that may not be obvious to the other gods traced out a map that only Olorun could see. Painstakingly, he would trace those threads to their origins. Invisible, Olorun took to the skies, looking down to see where the trail lead. Listening, he could hear the story of the one the mortals held responsible for these conditions was on a trial of sorts.

That could wait. He would return after visiting the true scene of the crime as he saw it. The corruption had indeed run deep seeping much further below the surface than he thought. Flying by feel he made his way overland to where the blight had to have begun. Touching down once again, Olorun found himself standing on a cliffside quite a distance from where he initially came down. He wondered how a mortal could have swiftly traversed the planet spreading the ilk as far and wide as they had in such a short time. There was no doubt now that a god had to have been involved.

None of the mortals had ever been known to void walk without help. Even the portal guardians had the aid of Orunmila, and he could not feel a hint of her presence or power here. What he did feel was a specific mixture of sickness, a presence of the infirm nearly to the point of death, and the promise of the antidote or healing. Many had died here. Looking over the land the residue of bodies could be seen by those who could look into the spectral plane. Some of those that were slain here were caught between realms. Their bodies were still fighting on against their will yet the spirits were languishing here lost. No closure for them yet.

There was evidence that a rock face had been destroyed here during what must have been a battle between a group of magi, Djaemon priests, and another group Olorun was not familiar with. Going down to where some of the land mass had fallen, he could feel where the power remnants were most potent, and there was no doubt now who the guilty party was, Babalu Aye. Kneeling down to touch the ground, Olorun closes his two eyes and opens his third. Ghostly images of what happened in the not-so-distant past play out before him.

Leaving a piece of his energy to remain on the ground to keep a small connection, Olorun floats above to take in the entirety of what happened. Looking out a plethora of phantom battles ensue as groups of magi take out oncoming Djaemon troops swiftly advancing through the chaos of magical energy blasts, volleys of arrows and other projectiles. The ones lucky enough to make it through make those within their reach pay the price before reinforcements finish them off gruesomely. The lost spirits begin keening as the trauma that ended their collective lives was being replayed. Olorun shut them out, analyzing and rewinding portions of this battle to better understand what happened.

The group that he was not familiar with seemed to be wielding a measure of magic themselves but were obviously no match for the combined strength of the magi gathered. They put up a good fight but were summarily wiped as energy blasts were exchanged. The largest of these blasts is what destroyed the cliff face sending two of the magi tumbling below. Floating back down, Olorun let things play out so he would witness it more closely, ignoring how things above were playing out. He could feel that this was what he needed to see.

A woman magus had fallen into the rubble along with her partner but she had been fatally wounded during the fall. Both were buried.

The man was crawling out from under some of the rocks, wounded but not mortally so. The problem was that he would not survive the stone tomb he found himself in. As Olorun was thinking of that the moment he had been waiting for came. A portal opened and in strode an entity meant to look like the goddess of death, Yewa. The likeness was uncanny and would easily fool a mortal. Olorun however, could still feel the lingering power signature accurately identifying who this was.

Out of haste, desperation, and a desire to reclaim his lost love, this magus made a deal with the Yewa imposter. A portal was provided in addition to the gift of two very familiar looking basilisks. The magus along with the basilisk used the portal to escape the impromptu grave. Once above ground the magus turned a group of dead or dying Djaemon into abhorrent mindless slaves which would supposedly increase Yewa's power base. Shaking his head Olorun thought the magus had to be more than supremely distraught not to have thought this proposal through.

Yewa, the goddess of death does not need the help of mortals. She is given an untold number of souls daily with no effort from any other entity. It is simply the way of the universe. Olorun was not sure how she would react when the truth of her stolen chalices and how they were used was revealed, but it would not be good. Initially the creator thought this must be the work of Esu since this seemed like the kind of thing he would enjoy, but the power signature could not lie. Them both going missing when the subject of the world's corruption was being investigated was telling. The trickster god may not have been involved at this moment in time Olorun was viewing now but it was fairly likely he was choosing to be a part of it now.

For now, this was the only conclusive clue to be found. There was no doubt that if found out, Esu would let Babalu Aye twist in the wind, and without more than a suspicion or circumstantial evidence, the trickster would likely go unscathed as he tends to do. The sky god could not help but to chuckle at the slimy elusiveness the Esu had displayed over time. It would seem that Bablu Aye was trying to emulate some of his prowess to a lesser degree of efficacy. Olorun could feel that his aspect was working with others to remedy some of the damage done. Olofi knew his feelings on interference and over stepping, but at this point did it matter that much?

Things had already been skewed to the point of nearly needing intercession by the gods in order to set things right, but after all this time loudly advocating for not getting too involved, there would be backlash. Closing his third eye, the world here goes back to the drab collection of dust that was left behind in the aftermath of the battle devoid of spirits. They were still there of course, but Olorun was choosing not to see them. Yewa would of course have to be consulted on when they will be retrieved so they can find their proper resting places.

After the brief conversation with Ogun who thought someone had usurped his domain on Nyumbani, the creator did not relish having a similar talk with Yewa when it was actually true that someone had not only used a replication of her visage, made deals in her name, but also left souls that were rightfully hers to languish in a strange purgatory here. Esu may find the situation ironic and amusing whereas Yewa will find no humor in it. After all the turmoil they had been through elsewhere, Olorun and the orisha had enjoyed a long period of relative peace here on Nyumbani.

This farce could shatter that peace and descend the gods into chaos if things weren't handled delicately. Making himself hidden from mortal eyes once again, Olorun took to the skies following his connection to his aspect. Not long after he found himself floating over Al-Karaouine, and Olofi was not the only godly presence that could be felt. Orunmila was with him, and another. This third presence was not that of another orisha but there was definitely something similar and strangely familiar to the energy coming off of him.

Lightly touching down on the school grounds, Olorun kept himself invisible as he followed his senses towards his aspect. Observing the magi, and magi in training as he went along until he found what must have been Orunmila's private domicile on this campus. He approached the seemingly small chapel like structure and before he could knock the doors swung open to admit him. Walking into the main hall of the deceptively large building Olorun saw two beings that felt off somehow.

Both wearing armor that easily looked out of place. Most likely they were the unsanctioned insertion of technology Olofi mentioned. Another proud citizen from the Isles of Esikrwada not often seen in this part of the world was enthusiastically scarfing food and drink while a remarkably unscarred Djaemon looked on. Walking into the next chamber Olorun saw his aspect disguised as an elderly mortal,

Orunmila, three mothers of darkness with eyes closed in concentration, and another curious mortal with an oddly familiar aura.

The three female portal guardians' brows were furrowed with intense focus as sweat beaded their brows. Orunmila and Olofi were verbally guiding them as they pooled their strength as they went about trying to fortify the veils between realms to prevent future incursions. The gods silently greeted each other so as not to distract the mortals at work. Technically Olofi and Orunmila were not directly interfering by giving them guidance but this was definitely striding the line. Given the circumstances Olorun would not tarry over this when there was so much more to be concerned about. He would have to wait until this was done before he could tell them of his findings.

Looking over the brooding mortal in the corner watching it all, Olorun finally recognized the essence of familiarity emanating from him. In his mind the creator said "Ah…Ochosi. This one is the result of one of his carnal explorations. We will need to talk when I return to Izulu." The portal guardians began to strain as if bearing some incredible weight. Orunmila encouraged them "Don't give up, you're almost there. With as much tampering as there has been lately, we knew this would not be an easy task. Together you can fortify the breaches and lessen the chances more from the shadow realm come here."

The portal guardians began to glow with their efforts briefly for one last push then simultaneously collapsed. Oluso, and Orunmila ran to comfort them as they came to consciousness. The mortals in the other chamber rushed in to see how things developed and Olofi and Olorun greeted each other formally as both reverted to their ethereal appearances stunning the mortals in their presence. Orunmila did the same when she was sure the mothers of darkness were well on their way to recovery from the strenuous work.

Chapter Twenty-one

Sakanoye, Diomae, and Kenzo began their march towards Kemet from the border of the Pantu grasslands at first light. The smoke stacks they noticed the day before were gone meaning the shadow realm encroachers had moved early as well. There was no way of knowing where the other group was moving. They would have to wait for word from the advance group of Djaemon. D'Na was at the head of their formation while T'Ome helped bring up the rear watching their backs as they came out of cover of the grasslands.

North of where they exited the grasslands, they could see the tops of the stone formations that approached the dead marshes. The plan was to head due east in an attempt to skirt the dead marshes by not going through the heart of them. After that they would have to head north unless they wanted to ascend over mountainous terrain. The journey would take longer but it would also be less taxing. Thinking on that Sakanoye mused there was another positive aspect to taking the longer route. Once they rounded the mountains, it would put them closer to the citadel which was just north of Kemet proper. There was also all manner of beasts that made their homes in the mountains. With the shadow realm and others contributing to the variety of wildlife, it was likely best to steer clear of places that made good havens for them.

This leg of the trek was relatively incident free aside from a few scuffles that broke out amongst the nameless of the Djaemon who were eager to prove themselves, earn their first scars while doling out some damage in exchange to be recognized by the clan. Kenzo watched with great interest and seemed almost crestfallen when T'Ome and D'Na diffused each potential altercation. Not understanding their language, he assumed they were being informed that fights between their own like this would not gain them the respect they desired.

The peace was definitely about to be disturbed as the rear guard called out. Even at a significant distance when the group turned around to glance behind to see what was drawing the Djaemons attention, an eruption of dire panthers came screaming out of the dead marshes they had come out of some time ago. Most of them had riders, and they were yelling something but were too far to decipher what it was. They were pointing and gesticulating up ahead but Sakanoye, Diomae, and Kenzo could not see what the threat was. D'Na, T'Ome and the other Djaemon were at a loss as well. Some of the younger Djaemon thought perhaps this was who they would trade blows with and prepared for battle enthusiastically.

Low growls could be heard from the fast-approaching dire panthers, and Kenzo's heart began to race. When those growls were answered by something that sounded much larger, his heart sank to his stomach. Squinting some of the Djaemon seemed to be able to see something approaching from the opposite direction, and Sakanoye noticed movement above them. At first, he thought it was a rock slide.

As it got closer, he realized it was not an accumulation of dirt and rocks falling. "D'Na, can you see this?" the Shike asked. Unsheathing her black blades, the Djaemon chieftain nodded that she could. An order was roughly barked at the Djaemon and they responded with a blood curdling scream as they too brandished weapons.

Everyone froze as a veil of invisibility was uncast revealing two huge dire lions from the shadow realm, one with an armored figure sitting astride it, silver manes flowing. The armored figure with the leonine helm gazed up at the flow of detritus falling faster down the mountain side. As the rumbling became louder Sakanoye could now recognize the man shaped beings running headlong towards them with all manner of crude, improvised weapons. Kenzo was surprised as something else stood out about them. They were all ebon skinned with hair that looked like blue or orange flames.

Just as the denizens from the shadow realm flooded out of the mountain valley to where Sakanoye, Kenzo, Diomae and the Djaemon were, a rush of wind washed over them as the Pantu tribesmen on their mounts flew by to clash with Simba Kivuli and his shadow minions. Untraditionally the tribesmen were unabashedly using their long curved Khopesh. The Djaemon at the front of the formation joined them running into both the warriors running downward and the ones with the armored figure. More screams rang out as flesh was torn; limbs severed. Kenzo was frozen in horror briefly before Diomae snapped him out of it by yelling his name "Kenzo, to me!" she ordered while whipping out curved tetsuo blades of her own.

There was a strange flash of energy as one of the Pantu tribesmen was hit and thrown from his mount. The dire panther slowly limped towards its rider before huge grey jaws clamped down hard on its neck. The grey dire lion shook until the panther lay motionless. The other Pantu tribesmen fixated on the armored figure and his lions to keep them occupied. D'Na and T'Ome were both making quick work of any shadow realmer they ran into. They were the very definition of no quarter given. Seeing the occasional magic blast tear into a group of warriors made Sakanoye regret not having a traditionally sized tetsuo blade.

Sakanoye, Diomae and Kenzo all took their deceptive tetsuo blades out but stuck together as the Djaemon ran rampant decimating the shadow realm invaders. The groups that went to help the Pantu Tribesmen with the dire lions were having a less successful experience. The huge silver maned lions were not only batting Djaemon and dire panthers back with impunity, but the armored figure was blasting them all casting what had to be spells. Intermittent gouts of energy went spraying sporadically into the Djaemon and Pantu ranks. Curiously when one got close enough this mystery warrior produced black blades of his own, dispatching them quickly. It was obvious they were not only talented with unesiphiwo, but a skilled swordsman as well.

Pointing and yelling Sakanoye advised D'Na "They will need to be dealt with quickly!" D'Na nodded her agreement as she beheaded an onrushing glowing haired invader. T'Ome grunted something unintelligible as he cleaved through a four-man row of shadow realmers. As the Djaemon leaders ran to the front to help with what seemed to be the most dangerous of the shadow realm groups a number of the attackers coming down from the mountain side sprang over the Djaemon attempting to engage them, immediately striking out at the tetsuo contingent.

Sakanoye's deceptively small blade of forged itsimbi ore was a blur as it tore through blue and orange haired shadow realm invaders giving some of the attackers pause. Kenzo was thrown back when blocking a wild thrust. Awkward looking improvised weapons seemed to rush in on all sides. Diomae moved in concert with her Shike while also covering Kenzo as he recovered. She wasn't as quick or adept as Sakanoye, but she was dismantling bodies just as well. D'Na saw the monks caught by surprise just as she and T'Ome left to take on the shadow dire lions.

Just as the Djaemon chieftain was briefly thinking of returning to their sides to ensure they weren't swiftly overwhelmed; she saw the small but powerful tetsuo blades dismembering and drawing blood just as well as any of the other warriors here were. Serat would indeed be proud of the tetsuo monks. Smiling she thought by the looks of the old one he might prove a good convert when this was done. The vanguard and Pantu tribesmen were having trouble with the dire lions so she ran to focus her efforts there. T'Ome rushed to the front unleashing a war cry that stopped the giant beasts in their tracks, giving the Pantu a chance to regroup.

The magus in strange armor hurtled a blast of blue energy at T'Ome that he deflected with his large black blade. It luckily ricocheted into an incoming group of shadow realm attackers. They writhed and convulsed to the ground laying lifeless, blank eyes staring into the infinite void. The magus was frustrated yelling something but the leonine helm stifled his speech. He drew two elegant looking dark blades, jumped astride one of the silver maned dire lions and charged T'Ome. This gave the line that was breaking in the battle a chance to recover now that only one lion was there.

The Pantu tribesmen were able to better coordinate their attacks and feints to control the direction of the fight. They were beginning to turn the tide but more shadow realm attackers were incoming. It was obvious they were able to hold their own but that would not last. Eventually they would need to retreat into Kemet or get overrun. Sakanoye was surprised that the city shields had not come out to help. Someone had to have heard the commotion by now. They weren't right outside the city walls but the combination of fighting and roars of multiple dire beasts had to travel a bit.

The Shike decided he and his two acolytes from the monastery would be the best choice to get to the gates and alert them to what was happening. "Diomae, Kenzo, to me!" he ordered. The three of them dodged and sliced their way towards the front with the intention of breaking away when an opportunity presented itself. The boy looked to have taken some punishment but was holding strong. Diomae was an uncoiled ball of rage but still under control…barely. Sakanoye would have a talk with her when this was over. For now, her focused intensity was needed. He wasn't sure but at certain moments he thought he saw a smile developing on her face as she eviscerated shadow realm invaders as she and Kenzo followed him.

A massive paw swipe sent T'Ome flying. Black blood flew from him and he lay in a heap, his large black blade lay a short distance away. The lion with the magus riding it came in to ensure he did not rise when a huge black blur blazed past forcing the shadow lion to rear, sending the rider tumbling to the ground hard. D'Na looked up just in time to see that it was Baaqir, and Sheba who ran interference giving T'Ome time to get up. The red behemoth did so laughing heartily as he wiped blood on his chest. Shaking his head Baaqir tried to take advantage of knocking the shadow lion rider off. Before he could get within blade striking distance a bolt of energy forced him to change directions quickly.

With the fighting getting heavier all around, Sakanoye, Diomae and Kenzo disengage and begin sprinting for the city gates. By now the piles of bodies for both sides are beginning to build, and once again it's obvious there's no winning here as more shadow realm invaders are coming. Sakanoye wonders where they're all coming from. There doesn't seem to be a nearby rift through which more are spilling out of. T'Ome seems to have recovered enough to join them as D'Na and other Djaemon slowly disengage to give them an escort.

Kenzo was glad to see help was coming. The boy was able to hold his own but was not used to fighting this constantly. Any longer and he would have been overcome. He was confused as he heard no commands in the common tongue nor in the Djaemon language. It seemed even the Djaemon were able to reign in their bloodlust in order to disengage to fight another day. Amongst the chaos of battle, the procedure was almost organized despite the lack of verbal commands or signals between the Pantu tribesmen and Djaemon warriors. Each group looked to have intuited what the other was trying to achieve and acted accordingly to accommodate this improvised plan.

Running headlong for the city gates of Kemet which were closed at the moment, Sakanoye began yelling and waving his arms trying to get the attention of the city shields on sentry duty who were sitting atop the gates at the outlook post. Times must have changed indeed since the last time Sakanoye had visited. Normally the sentries would be stationed on the ground just outside the gates. "Hey!" he screamed frantically to get their attention. One of the city shields looked down in surprise seeing what was fast approaching their gates in addition to the fighting that had broken out some distance away.

The man nudged his partner who yelled down to open the gates. Alarm bells rang out, and the city shields within scrambled to open the gates while also preparing to be ready to shut them to avoid allowing a throng of shadow realm attackers in. Sakanoye thought he could see the outline of what must have been a larger traditional tetsuo blade slung on the back of the city shields men atop the gate outlook. If true the shike was disappointed at the lack of vigilance. They should have seen them sooner and certainly should have been looking out in the distance.

When this was over, he would make it a point to learn the identities of those on sentry duty and speak to their commander.

Sakanoye, Diomae, Kenzo, D'Na, T'Ome, and some of the Djaemon made it into the gates along with Baaqir astride Sheba. A few of the city shields wanted to protest as their rules usually forbade the tribesmen to bring their mounts within the city walls. An exception was made this time in light of the current circumstances. Running up to Baaqir, Kenzo asked "What will happen to the rest of your tribe out there?" Comforting Sheba after sliding off her back Baaqir replies "They will attempt to continue the fight and lead this shadow realm force away from the city with help from the Djaemon."

That made sense but Kenzo and the others were understandably pessimistic about that working successfully without either leading them into the grasslands or another area where others would be even more vulnerable to attacks. An unearthly screeching rang out forcing everyone to look skyward where the noise came from. A collective gasp went up as three elder dragons had taken to the skies upon hearing the alarm bells and the commotion from the battle. The tribunal would have to be delayed while this situation played out. Dark black, gold and silver wings spread placing the city in crawling shadows as they circled.

Everyone for a moment froze. There was a brief break in action below as the combatants looked up. Not being apprised of the presence of elder dragons, Simba Kivuli placed his leonine helm back on reaching out with his unesiphiwo to search for other presences that may prove to be threats or perhaps an ally. It didn't take him long to feel another magus near that was being held in the citadel as well as an additional dragon. Oddly the city shields and citizens that now came boiling out of the gates did not seem to fear the great flying reptilian beasts.

If the growing crowd of reinforcements would even the odds, then certainly having dragons swung the advantage back to Kemet. Things had changed more than he thought during his exile. Relations between man and dragons was basically nonexistent before he was tossed away to the shadow realm. Much as he hated to make this decision, it was best for him to retreat while he could before the dragons laid waste to them all. Sure, it was likely that if the dragons began to flame the battlefield now some of their own would be caught. Simba Kivuli did not know these dragons but from what he had learned of the past usually the beasts were not the most discerning when their ire had been raised.

Collateral damage was of little concern to creatures that thought of a majority of other life forms as inferior. The battle itself had gone on longer than he had expected, and the magus was rather taxed being so long out of practice. Using what energy, he had remaining he opened a portal to another region in this plane through which they could escape. A ragged cheer went up from the gathered Pantu tribesmen, Djaemon and Kemet city shields when they saw the shadow realm invaders seeking to escape along with the two silver dire lions who had laid many of them low. Before making his own escape Simba Kivuli mentally reached out to the magus he felt.

"I don't know who you are, but since you are not out here amongst the defenders of this place, I assume you are not in the citadel willingly. If I had to guess, I would also assume your fate will end up much like mine seasons ago. I am Simba Kivuli, the shadow lion. Perhaps we can be allies, or you can relegate yourself to their decisions of your fate." He did not wait for a reply but followed Lasekholo and Lasekunene into the portal he created. Motu was still sitting in his bonds with most of the people assembled for his tribunal looking on. He wondered if anyone else heard the magus telepathic speech but figured they hadn't.

The only ones there with any unesiphiwo to speak of were the fire forged and the one known as Yasuke had no reaction at all but everyone was more enthralled with whatever was happening outside of the walls. People were rushing around to take care of the commotion. Motu knew it had to be serious to have gotten the attention of the elder dragons. Another voice intruded into his thoughts, this time one he was familiar with. "Will you take him up on his offer? I would not put much faith in these people giving you any chance at redeeming yourself, and Kibo is certainly not likely to show you any mercy after abasing his lair with your unannounced intrusion." Motu looked over at the cage some distance from him to find Masindi staring intently at him.

The young dragon's tail was swishing back and forth. He looked to have grown significantly since their capture. Motu wondered why he didn't simply escape to fend for himself rather than share the fate of a man who these citizens had just testified had to be demon seed or worse. The respite from all the slanderous testimony was a relief. Aloud the magus replied, "If I throw my lot in with this newcomer, what will you do?"

The foundations of the citadel shook as Kibo, Mawenzi, and Shira swooped in to retake their positions on the dragon perches. Masindi looked as if he were trying to shrink in his cage. Smoke rising from his huge black nostrils Kibo leans down to ask, "And who might you be throwing your lot in with wayward magus?" Motu was content to stare back defiantly saying nothing. Kibo straightened up continuing "Very well. If this was an ill-conceived rescue attempt, trust that we shall be ready when this mystery conspirator returns. You will not escape justice, and if you can help repair some of the damage you've done…some redemption is not out of the question. Just know that for most of these people forgiveness is."

Chapter Twenty-Two

The elder dragons once again took their places on the huge iron perches atop the citadel. The fire forged, Djaemon, Pantu tribesmen that were in the city, citizens of Kemet and Tanji villagers who had come to give witness filed back in to reconvene Motu's tribunal. If anything, the events from yesterday's battle was even more damning. Many were still distracted by the recent events, but duty dictated that this proceeding continued. With more battles and disturbances likely on the horizon, it was integral to settle this and find some solutions quickly.

There were many who silently advocated for the immediate execution of the magus now becoming known as Motu the necromancer for him raising up revenants in the name of some god he claimed manipulated him into doing so, resulting in the conditions Nyumbani was experiencing. That testimony was scheduled to be heard today after the final witnesses against him provided their accounting of how his actions had adversely influenced their lives. Nervously Kanaa walks into the entrance to the citadel followed by Jamaal, Simon, and Mael. When they got to the roof where the tribunal was to reconvene, Yasuke and his fire forged were stoically awaiting the prisoner and young dragon found with him to be brought up.

There was quite a stir as the Djaemon contingent or at least some of it had returned to Kemet along with the Shike from the Tetsuo monastery north of their stronghold in the red desert. From the mumbles and whispers Kanaa, Jamaal Simon and Mael gathered his name was Sakanoye. Mael immediately noticed a young boy in his company along with a woman who was obviously with them but seemed uneasy being among the Djaemon they had entered the city and citadel with. Mael was very curious to see someone around his age travelling with a band of Djaemon and the Shike.

Kibo, Shira, and Mawenzi were getting restless and began shifting on their perches making the gathering crowd nervous. Once again, the Magus was brought up from the dungeons attached to the city shield barracks followed by the now mid-sized cage holding the young black dragon whose scales were striated with green throughout. A string of hisses went through the crowd until Yasuke himself demanded silence before nodding to Kibo to begin. Mael turned his attention to the gigantic black elder dragon. He wasn't quite sure but it appeared as if Kibo actually rolled his prismatic black eyes as he looked at the list Yasuke was holding.

"Kanaa of Kemet! You're on the ledger scheduled to be our final witness before we hear from the accused." The dragon proclaimed. With anxiety written on her face, Kanaa steps away from Jamaal and the group to stand before the draconic tribunal a short distance from where Motu stood, bound in strange shackles. "I'm Kanaa." She said nervously. "Proceed." Kibo boomed. Shira and Mawenzi echoed the command causing Kanaa to flinch briefly. Gathering her thoughts, she gives her account of what happened on their homestead "My husband and I have a nice property just outside of the city proper. I convinced

Jamaal to settle here twenty seasons ago when I became pregnant with our daughter. This mongrel took her from us with his sick campaign!" She began, pointing to Motu as she spoke.

As she continued, she gained confidence describing the wonder and beauty of their lives and what bringing their daughter into the world meant to them. Tears streamed down her face when she got to explaining the sudden reappearance of an old friend of Jamaal's who was also a retired magus. Expressing that she really wanted to blame the old friend until she heard about the other ramifications of what Motu had done. Raising revenants, tainting the lands which lead to these abominations coming to their home, attacking and eventually killing their daughter. Looking over to Simon who was listening intently along with most of those gathered, she mouthed "I'm sorry.", and went back to be embraced by Jamaal.

Murmurs went through the gathering until they grew to full blown boos and objects being thrown towards Motu. Everything came to a halt as Kibo bellowed "Enough! Calm yourselves so we can get on with this!" The noise died down to complete silence immediately. Motu stood as best he could. His robes were in tatters, he was dirty, and looked as if he had not eaten in some time. He had not. After the days upon days of testimony, none here had even a hint of sympathy for him, and he knew it. That did not matter to the magus as he inhaled to gather his thoughts looking down at his shackled wrists and unmatching arms.

Looking down sternly Kibo rumbled "Speak necromancer before we decide to simply turn you into crystalized ashes. I am sure some here would have no qualms about us doing so after the strife you've caused." Mawenzi and Shira made a show of preparing to inhale deeply as if they were about to simultaneously freeze and flame him on the spot. Kibo leaned back a little, purposefully expelling black smoke from his nostrils. Turning around to face the people and not the three elder dragons sitting threateningly on their perches, Motu raised his voice above the latest round of growing jeers. "I am Motu as most of you know by now. Many of you have lost much, and for that I am sorry. Forgiveness is too much to expect so I only ask…that you try to understand." A wave of groans went up until Yasuke finally stared the audience into submission.

Once all was quiet again Motu continued "If you could regain what you lost, what would any of you not do? I had lost the one thing that mattered most to me in life, and was propositioned by a god in return for having my lost love restored to me." The skepticism coming from all in attendance at the citadel was palpable. "That's your excuse? A god bartered for you to ruin this realm in return for you to get your love back?" Mawenzi sneered. "Eradicate these vermin and be done with it." Shira added. Many roared in approval of that sentiment before Kibo once again growled "Silence! We can dispose of him when he's finished if we are not satisfied with his paltry justification."

Motu resumed his testimony "Have any of you heard of the Igazi Eliphezulu?" Something that had to be a string of curse words screamed by an enormous Djaemon which startled many in the crowd. D'Na stepped out to translate "T'Ome, kin to the Djaemon king from Gcina Okubomvu says that clan is nothing but a myth. Any remnant of them was destroyed long ago. Igazi Eliphezulu is a nightmare given to your children to keep them from exploring into territories long held by roaming Djaemon clans." Motu could only shake his head. It seemed none of the others present were familiar with this Djaemon clan.

"I truly wish this were only some tales devised to scare children. They are a real clan, and they've come to an arrangement with some lesser-known people. A group of cast offs and rejects. Some of them had some measure of unesiphiwo, and no training to speak of. A dangerous combination. My cadre and I were sent to deal with one of the larger pairings out marauding with plans to keep going until they ruled as much of these lands as possible or death embraced them. In fact, had your clan in the desert not burned the bodies, you would have found a few members as evidence." Motu stated.

Someone in the crowd had heard enough and hurled a long blunt object flying end over end towards Motu. Before it could land a gout of flames spung from Yasuke's hands incinerating it midair dusting the shackled magus's face in hot ashes. Shaking his head while trying to blink away the dust as the bindings made it difficult for him to wipe his face, Motu silently nodded his thanks before continuing. Kibo interrupted asking "Can you name this god who manipulated you into raising revenants in their name in exchange for the revival of your love lost to a battle with a mythical clan of Djaemon? Forgive me if I find none of what you say the least bit compelling."

The grumbling started anew but Motu spoke up to get ahead of it "At first they appeared to me as Yewa, goddess of death, only to be revealed later as Bablu Aye." Before he could finish the explanation, the gathering erupted in boos. Many foreign objects came flying Motu's way. Too many for the fire forged lead by Yasuke to burn before they struck. Through the debris hitting him Motu closed his eyes and continued to give his account of what happened the day he was approached by a deity. He did not care if they believed him. He just wanted to get it off his chest.

Simon was unsure if the magus was somehow tapping into his unesiphiwo when Motu resumed speaking, but it was odd as his voice seemed amplified by some unnatural means forcing the crowd to listen, seemingly mesmerized. "It was a hard-fought battle. The Igazi Eliphezulu were fierce, brutal warriors. Each group had a magic user assigned to them augmenting their efficiency, and it was quite plain that they had an intense distaste for any magus with training from a facility with high regard. As raw as they were, their presence had the effect of mitigating some of the advantages my cadre would have enjoyed battling most combatants."

Motu looked around and could see that for the moment he had them. In the end they may not see things his way, and he would likely end up with his head on a pike, but he would at least have his say. Not everyone was under his spell though. Turning around he could almost see the hint of smirks on the elder dragons faces, and there was a one-armed man in the crowd staring at him strangely. He also appeared more lucid than the others. Closing his eyes, he resumed his tale "We had already lost two groups of magi, but were turning the tide somehow. There was one staunch group fighting with such ferocity and fervor that we knew we needed to contain immediately to avoid losing our slim advantage. Ubulhe was in a duel and went to press her opponent but did not see the magic user in time that came up to give their ally support. They had gone to a nearby cliff face where the magic user used their unesiphiwo to blast the area. I was behind and caught up to her too late. The blast took us both out of the fight, burying us in rubble."

This was the first time Motu had spoken about this to anyone. Masindi, the young dragon he had brought forth from a corrupted conduit, the only sentient being he had been around since his campaign began had not heard this story in full. This telling was certainly not going to move the dragon to sympathize with the magus that pulled him from the ether far too early. The dragon's memories were slowly coming back to him but he was still somewhat upset that he was not able to develop into a more mature state. Had he been allowed to do that; Masindi would not be as vulnerable as he was now.

The elder dragons had him at a huge disadvantage and they knew it. Loyalty to species was deeply engrained in most dragons, but that only came after they reached a certain level of maturity. As a result of these three in particular reaching the status of "elder" through use of a hibernation strategy rarely used amongst their kind, the tendency not to embrace others not included in their lineage was even stronger. For elder dragons specifically this aloofness pertained to dragonkin as well. In their eyes, everything was beneath them. Which was all the more surprising to Masindi when he noticed that even during these proceedings there was often a small curly haired, freckle faced girl that would unabashedly approach Kibo, and he tolerated it.

That fact slightly annoyed Masindi but he could not dwell on it and so he focused on Motu, as he told this previously unreceptive audience what happened from his perspective. The young dragon could not help but to respect the gall of the magus attempting to enchant his captors who were holding a trial based upon him misusing his talents with magic to corrupt the world as he raised a host of revenants in the name of a god most had never heard of. This would end gloriously of course, Masindi thought. As entertaining as this disastrous result was going to be, the dragon hoped he would come through relatively unscathed.

In the midst of Motu telling his tale, the elder dragons, Masindi and Simon who was a magus in his own right were not under sway of his enchantment. They were all frozen just the same as time stood still. The entire city of Kemet became a living diorama as Esu, and Babalu Aye approached it. Bablu Aye got wind of this tribunal and wanted to intervene without leaving any witnesses, and Esu became the facilitator in making that happen. Walking through what looked like a creepily accurate wax museum Babalu Aye asks "Will they remember us coming here?"

Chuckling and making a show of dusting off his finery, Esu says "Not to worry. None of these mortals will know of our presence except for the poor magus you have dragged into all of this. If we befall the wrath of the other gods, he will be implicated. Don't look so sour. This should be fun!" Esu plucked a ripe piece of fruit from a vendor frozen in the market square as they made their way through the city, and to the citadel. Bablu Aye could have sworn he saw the vendor's eyes move the moment the petty theft took place, but avoided saying anything. The city shields standing at the entrance to the citadel could have just been holding their bearing stoically as some sentries are taught.

Esu and Babalu Aye slid quickly by the frozen guards and made their way to the top where the tribunal was being held. "Oh, these are new. I like them. Kind of beautiful in a horrific way when you stare at them long enough." Esu commented looking at the elder dragons sitting on their perches. Two of them looked bored while the black one seemed simply disappointed. Esu turned to the downtrodden looking magus sporting shackles and an oddly grafted arm of a being from the shadow realm. Tapping him Esu added "This must be your boy."

At the trickster gods touch Motu was able to move. Confused as he was mid speech it took him a moment to register what was going on. When he saw Bablu Aye he screamed "You!" standing as if to confront the god but was once again stopped short held in an invisible grasp. Babalu Aye let him feel the weight of his power walking slowly to the magus saying, "You forget your place, and I could not risk you naming me." Barely able to breath a ragged chuckle began to bubble from Motu's lips. "You find this humorous, do you?" Babalu Aye growls.

Releasing the pressure enough for the magus to speak, the god of sickness and healing awaits his answer. "Too late for that I'm afraid. I told them who you were, as well as who you appeared to me as initially." Motu states before being wracked with pain as a strange energy coursed through his body. Falling to his knees the magus writhes in pain as the two gods look over the rest of the mortals gathered. Bending down Esu examines the dragonling in a small cage. Turning to Bablu Aye he says "We should leave soon. No doubt one of the others will feel what I do here and come looking. You don't want to be here when they come."

Babalu Aye knew that to be true. He released his hold on Motu and reached down to turn his shackles to dust with a touch. The magus did not look grateful but also knew there was no true choice in whatever the god had in mind to happen next. Esu opened a portal and stepped through followed by Babalu Aye. The latter stuck his head out asking "What are you waiting for? Would you rather I leave you to let them decide what to do with you?" Angrily Motu got to his feet and began to step through before turning around. "Where's the fool going?" Esu asked.

Motu struggled to blast the lock on the cage. The shackles must have been sapping some of his power somehow. Babalu Aye was growing impatient. "We don't have time for this, and when we leave, they all reanimate!" Pleading Motu replies "I brought him here before his time. I should take him with us. At the least I cannot leave him to face them." Rolling his eyes Babalu Aye blasts the lock and hastily goes back through the portal Esu created. Motu struggles under the weight of an inanimate Masindi, but makes it through. Just as the portal closes Esu snaps his fingers releasing time in Kemet.

The elder dragons, fire forged, city shields, Djaemon and citizens all come to life confused as if waking from some dream they were having a difficult time remembering. Kibo knew something was wrong but could not figure out specifically what it was until he noticed two of their most prominent prisoners were conspicuously missing. Roaring he took to the skies. Shira, and Mawenzi were quick to follow. Then the black elder dragon noticed something else. His connection to the magus was being interfered with and he could no longer track his whereabouts.

'Oh, you sly devil. You must have had help for this." He mumbled. Mentally communicating with the other elder dragons, Kibo expressed his suspicions. They spread out to search but could find no evidence of the magus. It was obvious to them he had not gone on foot or any conventional means of travel. They went back to the citadel where those gathered there were arguing and screaming for answers. "Enough!" Kibo roared. "The magus and young dragon have escaped, and I doubt they did so alone. The fact that there's a missing part of my recent memory tells me another powerful entity had to be involved. Our kind are usually not as susceptible to your spells and other magic augments, no matter how talented you are."

The city shields under the orders of Zaniah their commander, a search party was mobilizing in addition to groups of Djaemon, Pantu tribesmen and even some of the tribunal witnesses were gathering weapons and supplies to join them. Kibo knew it was all for naught. Nevertheless, the elder dragon would find a way to find the fugitive. Perhaps the next time he was captured judgment would not wait.

Chapter Twenty-Three

Back at Al-Karaouine Eron was still enthusiastically stuffing his face while Orana was recovering after her fellow portal guardians left. Orunmila was helping her through it as Olofi and Olorun were reaching out with their godly senses to feel the renewed strength of the veils between realms. They seemed satisfied with the efforts of the reunited mothers of darkness. Things should hold, at least until there came another disturbance strong enough to test them. Oluso impatiently paced which was beginning to unnerve Sparks. Only Max and Argos seemed unbothered by things. Akil and Rahil, the two Kemet city shields sent to shadow them sat and watched in silence. Given that they were mute, nothing was unusual about this.

Most of the group that made the journey to this school of magic were very surprised when Olorun offered to give them the ability to speak, and they declined. Max sort of understood having lived for so long with his prosthetic leg. He thought it was possible they had lived their entire lives as they were. Any change to their existence may inherently diminish who they were as well as the bond they created through their shared experiences. The sky god simply shrugged and accepted their refusal. Eron thought it was a foolish decision, and was disappointed when no offer to improve him was offered.

Suddenly all three deities came out of various chambers simultaneously. The mortals in their presence were a bit taken aback as their eyes were all glowing. Max was the first to notice "Um, what's going on? You guys about to start Armageddon or Ragnarok or something?" he asked. Olorun, Olofi, and Orunmila ignored him. Olorun was clearly only addressing the fellow gods when he said "I assume you felt that." Simultaneously Olofi and Orunmila shook their heads affirmatively. "Someone briefly froze the time continuum but it was localized. I felt it being slowed a little while ago before Olofi came here." Orunmila added.

Looking around at the other Olofi admits "That was me. Had to show one of our parties that they needed to be wary of how they were talking." Olorun and Orunmila were curious but figured it would hold for later. Orunmila said "This time it had to be another god as well. This was no spell from a magus, and it came from Kemet. Do we agree on that much?" Olorun and Olofi gestured that they did. Oluso who had been quietly listening stated "The tribunal is being held there for the magus supposedly responsible for all the mishaps here. We should return." Daniel the lesser walked in and saw the befuddled looks on the other mortals while determination was etched on the gods present. "What did I miss?" he blurted.

"Ah, Daniel the lesser! It seems that someone has been playing with the time continuum back in Kemet. Olorun has his suspicions as to who it is, and we must head back there to investigate." Olofi explains. Oluso, Eron, Sparks, and max begin gathering their belongings. The twins of the Kemet city shields look on stoically as Daniel still seems befuddled by it all. Olorun and Orunmila begin changing forms as if trying to decide which disguise fits best. Olofi asks "Is that necessary now?" Before they could answer Orana came in inquiring "Should me and my sisters come along?" Olofi was quick to negate the idea, shaking his head and saying "No, you should continue to rest and gather your strength in case we have need of you again. There may be other things within this realm the culprits have tampered with."

Turning to Olorun, he awaited the answer to his previous question. The sky god grumbled in the midst of another transformation that made him seem younger than the other forms he had tried and stated "I am not sure. Part of me wants to keep the pretense alive but I am unsure if Babalu Aye and Esu have even bothered to if it is indeed them. If so, they've gone far beyond minutely tampering in addition to the previous transgressions that started all of this. You wish to go in as our true selves?" Olofi nodded his approval at the latest transformation before replying "I'm not sure it matters much anymore. Before you were suspecting manipulation by deities, and that has proven to be true. Now we must confront them, and the more mortals that witness us may further influence this place more than you would like. Even if we continue to tip toe our presences will be heavily felt. The elder dragons can sense us as more than we appear to be."

Oluso chimed in "Not to mention you three have revealed yourselves to us. Will the city of Kemet matter that much more?" Olorun offered "I could simply erase your memories of us if you think that would help." The mystical inquisitor got quiet and went back to packing. Max stifled his giggling at seeing the man humbled. Sparks and Argos both shook their heads. Finally, the three deities in attendance settled on which appearances they would exhibit. Olofi reverted to his elderly man disguise. While Olorun had chosen to remain in his natural state, his third eye prominently featured as Orunmila also chose to revert to her professorial form she had come to use while at this academic setting for students blessed with unesiphiwo, and those who just seek knowledge of such things.

Nervously Daniel the lesser hastily pulled on the armor Olofi had made for him. Soon, the others were gathered along with their gear. Max's mechanical leg glowed slightly where Oluso had installed the strange power source which had him and Sparks a bit apprehensive. Her armor was powered by the same thing. Argos still a bit self-conscious about his ostentatious blade placed it in its sheath and waited as the twins joined them with their oversized tetsuo blades. Seeing everyone gathered and ready, the deities went to exit this very special domicile.

No doubt Olorun noticed some of the accouterments that had to have been taken from Izulu. However, he refrained from mentioning it, surprising Olofi. As ordered Orana stayed behind with her sisters to rest. Together the group that had traveled from Kemet made their way to the portal with two more orisha in tow for the return trip. Once more Olofi activated the portal much to the dismay of the students and staff of Al-Karaouine. They would be long gone by the time anyone reached the portal. Eron commented, "I'm surprised they had not stationed anyone to guard this place after our earlier intrusion."

As if remembering something or more like the remark reminded her Orunmila conjured a globe of energy and tossed it high in the sky. Before anyone asked, she explained "They will see this as a sign from me and know it is not more interlopers." A bluish-purple light once again ignited as the portal opened. One by one they stepped through into the magic gateway. Daniel stayed as far as he could from Eron remembering his last experience with this mode of travel. Going in after the large barbarian warrior had already entered. A hint of amusement lit Olofin's eyes as he looked on. He and Olorun stepped into the portal together last.

Having been through this before the short journey was not as harrowing as the first for the mortals. They step out of the portal they entered a short distance from Kemet when they began to search out a portal guardian. When Olorun and Oluso step out it once again goes dormant. It is immediately evident that not all of the shadow realm invaders were with the main group that was seen north of the dead marshes. What they found were also not the garden variety. There were a group of shadow harbingers.

They were larger than the other humanoid beings more commonly seen. Sparce strands of glowing hair were atop the heads, their vocalizations were even more unintelligible. Their footfalls shook the ground as they walked and the brief flash of light from the portal while it was activated had attracted their attention. Max and Sparks began charging their weapons as Argos, the twins, Eron and Oluso pulled their blades out. There was now nearly a stampede of these gargantuan creatures barreling towards them. Before Max and Sparks could open fire Olofi stepped in front of them ordering "Stand down!"

Orunmila took flight and began instantaneously transporting the beasts back to the shadow realm. Olorun joined her. After it seemed like the wave of the shadow harbingers were growing and some would likely get by them, Olofi began working in tandem with the other two gods. Eron, Daniel, Argos, the twins, Max and Sparks stood watching mouths agape as these beings herded these terrifying creatures back to their dimension. The seamlessness was just as amazing as the spectacle of what was happening. When they were done, the group was speechless.

When they were able to gather their thoughts, Max unsurprisingly was the first to inquire "If you three alone can do all of that, why not just fix things yourselves and go back to wherever you came from?" As Olorun glided softly back to the ground he replied "We do not wish to interfere too much if we can help it. That's why we tend to watch from afar for the most part. There are some of us who stay groundside and have duties to tend to here. Some unfortunately are more involved than they should be. Often that leads to situations such as this. Whole realms have been destroyed from deities being too meddlesome. Habits like that lead to it matriculating down to the mortals that inhabit them. Your own realm is a prime example. The devices you have introduced to this one is an afront to Ogun. If you meet, I would be wary."

Instead of the clarification he had hoped for, Max was even more confused now. Sparks looked to him with the question they were both internally wondering. What could have possibly happened back home that lead to its destruction. The twins were now looking at them suspiciously as Sparks asked "Is our home destroyed?" Olorun had a look of pity in his glowing eyes as he answered "No child, but it will be soon. It was in turmoil when you left was it not?" Her and Max nodded affirmatively. "Until we know more, let us assume less conspicuous appearances for now." Olofi advised. The three Orisha transformed into their mortal disguises. Olorun looked the part of a younger magus, Orunmila the middle-aged professor, and Olofi the wizened old geezer.

The twins and Oluso were signing back and forth furiously for a brief moment before Eron asked "What game are you three playing at?" Oluso replied "The esteemed escort of the Kemet City shields are upset that their suspicions were wrong and I was right all along. These two are not in fact from the Isles of Esikwrada." Looking back at Max and Sparks Eron said "Ah not my kin after all? Their commander will no doubt be disappointed. I think she fancied the idea of deporting you." Seeing as the deities in their various guises had begun to step off in the direction of Kemet, the others hurried to catch up. Daniel the lesser tried to remain as close to Olofi as possible.

Eron, Oluso, and the twins put their blades back in their sheathes when it seemed no shadow realm or revenant ambushes were afoot as they trekked on. Relatively speaking the return journey was uneventful. That was until they reached the city gates. From a distance it seemed there was an unusual haze surrounding the city. Oluso stopped just short of the entrance. They could see the sentries who were moving but extremely slow. Max who had been keeping a close watch on the mystical inquisitor saw a slight glow come to one of his eyes as he was about to reach into what must have been some invisible boundary hinting at something enveloping the city.

Anyone curious about what was about to happen were disappointed when Olofi snapped his fingers dissipating the suspended animation of the city. The city shields at the gates nearly fell forward as if coming out of some trance. They were just about to challenge the group when they noticed Akil and Rahil. The twins saluted with their tetsuo blades and had the gesture returned as the rest entered the city uncontested. All around the city seemed to be waking up from a stupor. As they walk through everyone looked as if they were disorientated and just realizing where they were.

Murmuring rippled throughout the city as people were coming to their senses. The three deities in disguise along with Eron, Max, Sparks, Oluso, Daniel the lesser and the twin city shields that had accompanied them walked through the awakening city until they came out the opposite end headed towards the citadel. They were quite the motley crew and normally would have drawn the eyes of many as they passed by, but everyone seemed to be in a daze and paid them little attention.

"What happened here?" Sparks asked. Looking around Olofi said "If the sky gods' suspicions are correct, I'd wager the renegades among our kind came here and did not want anyone present to witness and remember them coming and going." Olorun added "That would work if it were only mortals coming to investigate. For those of us with higher power senses, the happenings here will not remain hidden." They wanted to ask more but the pace with which the three gods were moving didn't lend itself to further conversation.

Argos noticed Oluso was having less difficulty keeping up as the gods seemed to be walking yet the others were nearly sprinting. Daniel the lesser was the furthest behind panting loudly when they came to a halt at the base entrance to Inciniba. The fire forged serving as sentries here barely took notice of them as with the citizenry so they entered making their way up to where the tribunal should have been taking place. "Can you feel it?" Olorun asked. Olofi nodded that he could. Orunmila chimed in "The suspension is strongest here, and the mortals are coming around slower. This is the epicenter. You should be able to divine exactly what took place once we reach the apex of this place." The three elder dragons were just retaking their perches atop the citadel.

It was slower than what they saw in the city but the people here were indeed beginning to come out of their involuntary stasis. The elder dragons were the first to notice them once they reached the roof. Kibo growls groggily "Lofin, I see you brought some friends." All three of the huge creatures shake their heads and blink as Yasuke finally notices their captives are conspicuously missing. "Raise the alarm and find them now!" the leader of the fire forged yells. Grumbling ripples throughout the crowd as Lofin waives at him dismissing the need. The god in disguise explains, "It's too late for all that. Besides the magus had help. The kind well out of your…range of abilities to combat." Despite that proclamation the fire forged that were the slowest to recover went to help those that were already searching in vain for the escapees.

Those gathered for the tribunal did not like the sound of that and some even recognized Lofin from his last appearance as well as the twins, Argos, Max, Sparks and of course Eron who had become a staple within the city. A few remembered seeing Oluso but the other two were unfamiliar garnering whispers. In an attempt to explain the new arrivals Lofin briefly introduced them "These are my siblings Lorun, and Mila. They had also hoped to find answers at this tribunal." Pulling Yasuke closer to Kibo so only they could hear Olofi explains "We will need to clear this area so that we can divine who took them without cause too much of a stir."

Yasuke didn't seem convinced "After all that has happened, do you think it matters if you're revealed? Does the right to know what happened only extend to the few?" Olorun thought that over as Yasuke went about relaying orders that they would have to delay the proceedings obviously with the accused not in attendance. Others were even slower to come out of the fog the brief time stasis caused. Soon there were only Yasuke, the gods, and elder dragons present on the roof of the citadel. Reluctantly Oluso, Eron, Argos, Max, Sparks, Akil and Rahil were asked to wait a level below them. Only Daniel the lesser refused and in protest he petulantly stood in the middle of the stairwell between the level below and the roof.

The others were just as curious and listened intently but could hear none of what was transpiring. Olorun's eyes began to glow as he walked the roof while Kibo, Shira and Mawenzi watched. Closing his eyes, he felt for the imprints left behind by two of his kind. When he reached a certain spot, the sky god bent down to touch the ground. As before a ghostly image of what had been done played out before him. When it confirmed his suspicions once again, he made noises confusing the elder dragons and Yasuke as they could not see what he was envisioning. Noticing their confusion Olofi walked over to Yasuke and placed a hand on his shoulder.

"As this is supposed to be one of my purposes, I guess it's appropriate for me to be the bridge between mortals and the gods. For but a moment I shall lend you my sight so that you too can know what we know." Olofi said as he nodded for Olorun to begin the process anew. Yasuke didn't quite know why he did it but he reached out to place his hand on Kibo. The elder dragon then instinctively stretched his wings out towards the other two. They did not know what was happening but a gold and silver wing from Mawenzi and Shira reached out to slightly touch Kibo's.

Suddenly they were all privy to the phantom replay of what transpired while they were all frozen in time. For some reason Yasuke was horrified as he watched Babalu Aye and Esu walk through them casually stopping only to examine a few that took their fancy until finally coming to Motu and his young dragon. They all watched as a rift was opened and the rogue gods and magus stepped through it along with Masindi. When the scene concluded Olofi took his hand off of Yasuke and it all went away. Yasuke and the dragons shook their heads as if clearing it somehow. "Ah, now that clarifies things. I knew

Motu couldn't have escaped without the aid of someone vastly powerful. How should we proceed?" Kibo asked.

Yasuke was confused by the question and answered with one of his own "What do you mean we? These are deities we are dealing with now. Not just a magus gone rogue. I think this is a problem for Master Lofin and his friends to solve." Yasuke and the elder dragons all turned to Lofin who was looking a bit sheepish as he turned to Olorun and Olrunmila for guidance with his hands splayed.

Chapter Twenty-Four

Simba Kivuli and his silver dire lions from the shadow realm took refuge north of the Luhlaza woodlands. They could not go into the Elinanye protected land as it was still encased in a dome of magically erected dirt and sediment pulled from the grounds below and around it. The exile felt that they should be relatively hidden so long as they did not attempt to gain entry into the woodlands alerting the elves of their presence. This was a time for them to regroup, lick their wounds and to strategize on how to circumvent the elder dragons. They were variables he had not planned to deal with.

He could tell the shadow realm beings he had unofficially conscripted were not very happy. For the most part they were dealing with their wounded and scowling at him. There was nothing they could do to him really. After he had adapted to life in the shadow realm this was true, but now back in his home realm with his powers restored they would be foolish to attack him. The dire lions at his side were even more of a deterrent. The use of his unesiphiwo was something that not all of the shadow realm beings had seen but the lions were all too familiar to them. Best of all they needed no translation. They would remain at his side no matter what and conveyed to all who saw them that Simba was indeed in control. At least on the ground. The giant flying beasts from the shadow realm might have been useful against dragons here, but elder dragons may be another matter.

Looking at Laskholo and Lasekunene, Simba muttered "It is a fools' dream, eh? Controlling one of the huge flying beasts from your home. Luckily, I didn't have to enchant you two. My power was useless there, and never had a chance to find an egg from one of them. Chances are if we did, I would have cooked it. My cubs were hungry!" Their large silver eyes just stared blankly in reply. The exiled magus rubbed their manes and patted them roughly before walking off a bit to think things over.

The anxious beings from the shadow realm looked to be getting ready to approach him when another portal opened up. What makeshift weapons they had were instantly at the ready for whomever stepped out of it. The shadow lions were up instantly. Simba Kivuli quickly dawned his leonine helm and gathered some of his unesiphiwo in case he had to hurl a spell at the newcomers. A dashing figure dressed from head to toe in black and gold stepped out of the lit portal followed by another not as well dressed but still dapper man. Finally, a man in tattered magus robes holding what looked to be a black dragonling with green striations sprawled throughout his dark scales.

Oddly none of them seemed the least bit concerned with the danger they had just walked into. The confidence both intrigued and worried Simba Kivuli a bit until he felt a familiar sense from one of them. Looking over the man holding the young dragon Simba noticed one of his arms was extremely dark in comparison to the other. He had recently seen limbs of a similar hue and when the recollection hit him, he turned to see the beings from the shadow realm was where he had seen them. Turning back to the new arrivals he remembered where he had felt this man's presence. "You were who they held at the top of the citadel. I am Simba Kivuli. I was able to reach out to you but heard no reply. I assume these two are your benefactors. Have you come to bind me as well?" the exiled magus asked.

Esu casually walks around Simba Kivuli sizing him up. "We have no need to bind you, but it looks like we have two of a kind. Two erstwhile magi caught up in their passions leading them into trouble. Dare I say, you need us more than we need either of you." The trickster god opines. Simba looks incredulous after removing his helm. "Who might you be and why would I have need for any of you? I have escaped my exile to the shadow realm and can bide my time exacting revenge. I have two dire lions and a good number of minions. More will come. You look like fancily dressed magi yourselves. With my power slowly rising back to normal, the ones that decided to banish me will rue that day soon enough." He offered.

Motu was stewing and remained silent as he held Masindi who was just regaining consciousness. When Babalu Aye did not immediately respond Esu continued "I guess you're leaving it up to me to tell him. Very well. I am Esu, and my esteemed colleague here is Babalu Aye. We are not mere magi but gods. Respect it. The surly one there is a magus, Motu if I am not mistaken. Inadvertently he is responsible for your newfound freedom back in the lands from which you came. His mess became the tool that brought you back. Sounds to me like you owe us."

Simba looked them over skeptically and did not seem convinced. The shadow realm invaders were getting anxious but seemed to feel the power coming off the orisha and were satisfied to keeping their distance while still keeping an eye on them. Simba Kivuli asks a bit too sarcastically "Esu, is it? What are you the god of?" Light comes to the Esu's eyes as he strides closer to the magus questioning him. Simba takes a small step back as the god seemed to grow in stature as he got closer. Figuring it for an illusion or some other trick Simba held his ground. Esu proclaimed "I am the trickster, but back where we come from, I was one of many bridges between the deities and the mortals. I can also be a bridge between mortals themselves by way of language. However, when I am bored which is often, I dabble in sowing discontent. The conflicts you find yourself in are not of my making. Nonetheless I am here to…spice things up a bit."

To emphasize his point Esu walked over to the denizens from the shadow realm changing his appearance instantly to look like one of them. They flinched as he reached out towards them. Simba was about to laugh when it appeared nothing happened until he noticed they were no longer speaking in gibberish. With a wave of his hand Esu made it so the beings from the shadow realm spoke a tongue that Simba could understand. Babalu Aye stepped forward stating "I am the god of pestilence and healing. Since coming here, I have felt my powers waning a bit and hoped to get that old feeling back by building a resurgence with the help of Motu here. Things took a bit of a nasty turn when some of the other Orisha did not like the results of him raising a somewhat necrotic army for me here. By association you are now implicated regardless. Esu here did you a favor. It should be much easier to coordinate and fight more efficiently now that you and the shadow realmers can understand each other."

Simba watched amazed as Esu went through a slew of transformations and even replicating himself before going back to the original appearance he had when stepping out of the portal finally adding "He's right you know? Whoever banished you will be coming when they learn of your return, the city shields of Kemet and the elder dragons will come as they likely think you're a part of this mess started by Babalu Aye and this poor fool who looks to have lost a limb and borrowed another from your new shadow militia. Lastly, other Orisha are definitely going to investigate what happened here. They are sticklers for absurd rules and all."

Motu and Simba both look up simultaneously asking "What rules?" Babalu Aye explains "Olorun, the sky god and creator doesn't like for us to be too hands on. My influence here goes against that policy. We have all been here since the inception of this place, but he turns a blind eye for the most part when deities come down from Izulu. Ogun, I believe with a few others reside here more than in our palatial city ship above. Giving you some of my powers was bound to have collateral results, but I did not know how much." At that Esu began laughing uncontrollably.

Tears streaming down his face Esu tries to compose himself as Babalu Aye, Motu, Simba Kivuli and the wary group of shadow realm beings look on. Waving at them he lamely apologizes "I'm sorry, but that is absolutely precious! You had no idea that giving a desperate magus some of your powers of pestilence would have adverse effects in this world? Oh, we may suffer, but the trip to Esihogweni will be glorious!" No one else seemed to get the humor in the situation. Least of all Babalu Aye who asked through clenched teeth "This is not the time for levity! The others will have been alerted to what we did back at Kemet. You're supposed to be helping to mask all this!"

Turning away from the stunned magi and shadow realm beings Esu addresses Babalu Aye directly "That was the deal, but it was also before I knew how much of a mess you made of things. We are here now so we shall have to deal with it. The good news is that we now have more minds, hopefully more equipped minds to come up with some actually clever solutions. So, what do you say? Care to outwit the gods with the help of an old trickster? "Motu and Simba Kivuli knew the last part was intended more for them. Babalu Aye was already committed to this and by way of association and inclusion in the initial scheme, Motu had previously thrown in with this lot already. The real question was would Simba Kivuli cooperate with them.

To think on it, he went to sit with his shadow lions. Esu and Babalu Aye let him have his space content with sitting with Motu. Masindi was finally coming around. Groggily the young dragon looked around. Not recognizing where he was, he roughly jumped out of Motu's grasp seeking to get his bearing and equilibrium. Seeing Babalu Aye he comments "Ah, fitting that the deity that got you into this sordid business is the one who plucked you from the proverbial jaws of despair." Shaking his head Esu left them to go see what Simba's decision would be.

Although the formerly exiled magus was looking a bit pensive, while amongst his two large companions his confidence began to build. It made him question the validity of Esu's claim to godhood. He asks "How do I know you are what you say you are? You could be a powerful magus for all we know, playing at a game that went well beyond your means. Now you need our help to climb your way out. What's to stop us from tearing you apart and going on our way?" Esu made a show of dusting his shoulders off as a glint came to his eyes. Simba Kivuli was not impressed. His tone and change in posture alerted the huge shadow lions at his side.

They went from sitting at his side relaxing to standing with bared teeth growling menacingly as if awaiting the signal to pounce. "You can't be this stupid." Esu replies. The god looks from Simba to his companions and back before continuing "I am the trickster god, but illusion is not my only power. Though it can be quite useful." As if to emphasize the point Esu transformed himself into a spitting image of the formerly exiled magus, right down to the leonine helm and armor. The trick caught the dire lions off guard who began pacing in confusion.

Simba Kivuli was speechless. Esu took the silence as an opportunity to continue "It is unwise to take my pleasant demeanor as a sign of weakness. As easily as I made it so you and your host of shadow realm compatriots can communicate, I can take that away. We can simply leave you to foolishly plan your revenge on those who cast you out long ago. I would think you would value having not one but two gods aiding you in your efforts. You now threaten to tear me apart with your pets? How will they know which of us to attack?" Esu or more accurately the image of the god in disguise as the magus in shadow realm regalia multiplied the illusion.

In response the lions went into a frenzy of roaring before dashing through some of them which disappeared only to be replaced seconds later. Finally, they all vanished leaving only the trickster god standing close to Simba Kivuli. Seeing a foe to focus on Lasekunene pounced. Just before a silver clawed paw looked to be about to slash into the trickster gods face and finery, Esu whispered "Sleep.", and the beast went limp in midair falling in a heap to the ground. Lasekholo saw what happened to his brother and refrained from even attempting, but stayed close to his master growling low by way of protest. "Smart boy." Esu commented.

Simba put on a good face but was shook, and everyone knew it. He looked over at Motu who was standing next to the young dragon. The fellow magi looked at each other with a shared resignation in their eyes. It seemed at least for the moment their collective destinies were tied through however these strange conflicts would be resolved. Perhaps Motu was thinking he should have just accepted the loss of Ubulhe, his love. The mangled, decrepit remains of her physical shell were either in Kemet or back in the now destroyed underground lair he had built in the dead marshes, never to be restored. Even if it were possible to do so, he now was not so sure she would have wanted that.

Surprisingly Simba Kivuli pondered if he should have come out of his exile. Survival was tough in the shadow realm, but he had eked out a life and niche there no one could have expected. Once it was discovered he had returned, there was no telling what the reaction would be. Certainly, being mixed up with these two deities, if that's indeed what they were would likely not end well. Something told him the kind of scrapes they got themselves into would definitely be fatal to mortals caught in the storm of their making. At a short distance and without words, the two magi knew they were having the same pessimistic thoughts. Masindi sat in silence looking as calculating as ever.

Babalu Aye was about to say something when an ominous crimson light could be seen growing on the moon hanging in the pale night sky. Strangely the atmosphere itself seemed to change as a deep rumbling within the ground began. They all stared skyward as the light seemed to stretch towards Nyumbani a great distance away. Shaking his head Babalu Aye says "We don't need this." Esu did not agree replying "Perhaps this is exactly what we need. A good distraction at the least. Someone else worrisome enough to draw the attention of others from Izulu who are on the way or likely already here."

While the others were staring in awe, Masindi finally spoke up "What does this mean?" Esu turned to the young dragon and answered his query "This means that Serat, the blood god who has never set foot in this place is attempting to do so now. There's no telling what him throwing his proverbial hat into the ring will mean, but the other gods will have to be wary of the effects. This may embolden the Djaemon and all other blood spawn here throwing the balance off more than it already was. I doubt he is a real threat to the Orisha but you never know. This will give us time. Babalu Aye, if you wish to carve out a place here in which you can have dominion, let us hope Serat doesn't burn it all in service to his sacrifices."

The corruption of magic and lands, disturbance of hibernating elder dragons, and now a gradual gathering of deities who would not have previously made planetfall had Motu not made the deal with a disguised Babalu Aye not too long ago. Guilt was beginning to mount within him. Somehow Simba Kivuli could sense that as well. Walking over while the others attention was on the spectacle happening in the skies the magus whispers "I don't know what brought you to be wrapped up with these two, but it cannot be good and it doesn't matter now. What matters is that we survive to do our own bidding. I for one do not wish to be bound to beings I cannot trust. Something tells me these may be the dregs of the deities and they're trying to use us to raise themselves above their stations."

He wanted to say more but felt the eyes of Esu on him. Slowly turning he found the trickster god watching them with a smirk etched on his face. Simba desperately wanted to wipe that smug look away but wouldn't risk using his unesiphiwo in what would likely be a feeble attempt. Nodding to Motu, he hoped to convey that he would bide his time, play their game for as long as was necessary, but when the time was right, he would take his leave of them. Hopefully Motu and the dragon would combine their efforts and do the same when that time came. In silence they all watched a host of crimson rays streak to the surface. Somewhere off in the distance, Serat had arrived.

How he made his official introduction to the world would only complicate things further.

Chapter Twenty-Five

The city shields had come back into Kemet empty handed with no clue as to where Motu and the dragon had escaped to and no idea who the magus with the dire lions had gone with the collection of forces seemingly comprised of shadow realm invaders. Zaniah, the commander of the city shields watched as Akil and Rahil gave their report. She was unhappy about Motu's escape. Not everyone knew about who had helped him and Yasuke along with the elder dragons thought it would be wise not to spread the word on that without more information. People were already in a panic. The involvement of gods would only heighten the sense of dread that was growing.

Oluso took what were basically his wards back to Salim's. Max, Sparks and Argos didn't seem to mind. The place had good food and drink. They as outsiders had become sort of minor celebrities. The proprietor Akachi was happy for the additional business with the influx of customers from the small villages and other established communities outside of the city. More and more people were seeking the presumed extra protection they would get from being within the walls Kemet provided. Reluctantly the Djaemon were more accepted than usual. They added to the feeling of security as their numbers bolstered the protection provided by the city shields. There was no telling when the invaders would be back. There was no question amongst the population that they would indeed be back.

No one had a clue as to the identity of the magus running amok with dire lions. That was worrisome and it caused a lot of speculation. Inside Salim's Mael enjoyed a meal with Simon, Jamaal, and Kanaa. He couldn't help but notice someone nearly his age sitting with what looked to be a monk, a young woman and a huge Djaemon warrior. Simon could not help but notice how mesmerized Mael seemed. "Intrigued by another boy your age? Introduce yourself. Friends are good to have." He advised.

Hesitantly Mael got up and walked over to where they were sitting amazed that the other boy didn't seem in any way intimidated by the rather large Djaemon. He was far larger than any of the other Djaemon Mael had seen thus far, heavily scarred. He was also maniacally tossing back huge tankards of dragon's piss with what should have been an unhealthy enthusiasm. The boy sitting calmly next to him was simply eating his food unbothered by it all. Nervously Mael approached, with his experiences of trying to make new friends still fresh in his mind from when he was in Tanji.

At first no one noticed then the young monk looked up from his dish. Sakanoye also saw the young man approaching and decided to watch to see what his younger counterpart would do. Mael saw the young man kick a stool out offering him a place to sit. He did so still wary of the Djaemon nearby steadily guzzling as everyone looked on. The young monk stated between bites "My name is Kenzo, what's yours?" Relieved that the conversation didn't begin with a rude comment Mael answers "Ishmael, but everyone calls me Mael. Sidibene Kakulhe." Kenzo returned the greeting and then introduced the others sitting with him "This is Sakanoye, our Shike and master forger, and this is Diomae." Each nodded in greeting.

With poorly hidden smirks on their faces, they turn partially away to let their youngers have their own conversation. Kenzo asks "Is there always this much going on here? I've only lived in a small village and the tetsuo monastery in the red desert." Shaking his head Mael replies "Not really. I have been here a handful of seasons and this is the most I have seen such…mixed company in this city. I too am from a small village not far from here. You mentioned the red desert, is it common for you to be amongst the Djaemon?"

Kenzo smiled at the bit of common ground the two youngsters found immediately before explaining "No, our association with our southern neighbors in the red desert is a recent development. We mainly stay to our monastery, and the Djaemon do whatever it is they do at Gcina Okubomvu. From what I understand they still practice small raiding parties into other territories so they can earn their scars and names but tend to avoid the tetsuo monasteries. We passed their keep on the way here, and let them know where we were headed and why. The corruption caused by the escaped magus has had a wide reach."

Mael could feel Kenzo looking at the changes in his skin pigment on his face and where his arms were exposed but he had the decency not to ask. He was grateful for that. For a few moments they just sat there watching everyone in the tavern, taking in the camaraderie of warriors gathered after surviving battle. There was indeed a lot going on. Simon walked over to introduce himself to Kenzo's master. "Sidibene Kakulhe, my name is Simon. Is that your acolyte?" the magus asked. Looking at the two boys conversing Sakanoye returns the greeting "Sidibene Kakulhe Simon, I am Sakanoye, and young Kenzo there is indeed one of my understudies at the monastery. I assume the young one there speaking with him is under your tutelage?"

Simon nods his head affirmatively and adds "Yes, Mael is learning to harness and control his unesiphiwo under my guidance. We have no official binding or sanctions though. I just wanted to keep him from getting himself in trouble. Gods know he was well on his way when we happened upon each other when we met here not too long ago. He's a good boy. Life has been tough on him early." Sakanoye nods his agreement and understanding. Diomae went to refill her tankard and grabbed the Shike's as well. Simon nodded to her before asking "Is she another?"

Watching her walk to the bar to ask for the refills, Sakanoye replies "In a manner of speaking yes. She came to us some time ago, battered but unbroken despite a very harrowing experience that left many in her village slain, scattered to the winds by a notorious Djaemon clan. It's a wonder she can remain in their presence in any capacity without blindly lashing out with her tetsuo blades at anyone with a hint of crimson in their skin. Through meditation we were able to make her more stable mentally while honing an inner strength she already possessed. Once I saw that she could see through the pain, I knew she was deserving of a blade of her own to protect herself and others. She chose to stay on with us. Learning to be a master forger has been good for her, and she has been invaluable in weapons training for the neophytes and guardians new to wielding the powerful weapons we provide."

Looking on as the revelers begin to liven up even more with the potent smoke and drink flowing so freely through them Simon asks "What do you think happens now?" chuckling as he accepts the tankard from Diomae, Sakanoye says "This is but the calm before the storm good magus. The renegade and the mystery warrior with the shadow realm seemingly at his or her back will either return or start trouble elsewhere. Some of us will have to at least attempt to thwart them. The disturbance of the elder dragons can be nearly catastrophic, and we are lucky to have some with even a touch of discernment to their disposition. They are a rarity and waking them before they wish to be roused often results in swaths of lands reduced to smoldering embers." It was rumored one of the small isles Max and Sparks were suspected of being from had already found out how catastrophic it could be. Except they were flash frozen instead of being immolated.

At the thought of such an event they all took heavy pulls from their respective tankards as they watched T'Ome in a bit of a drinking contest with Eron as others gathered around to cheer them on. "If he keeps at it, he won't be long for this world. The appetites of the Djaemon are nothing to trifle with." Simon commented. With the noise level steadily raising, Kenzo and Mael took their conversation outside. Mael briefly looked to Simon for approval but the magus waved him off. Sakanoye nodded silently letting Kenzo know that he was fine with them leaving. At first the two mentors were simultaneously thinking the two boys would be eager to show off their weapons and powers. They shared a laugh as they guessed what the other was thinking.

It was probably best to let them be. They would soon have more harrowing things to worry about. Oluso walked into the tavern with Lofin and two other new arrivals. Simon thought he saw them when they returned to the citadel but could not be sure as he was recovering from the group enchantment that everyone was still talking about. All were up in arms at Motu's escape and likely return. There had been less incursions from the shadow realm but there were still large remnants causing havoc in other areas. The recent attackers were no doubt only regrouping. There was no telling how long the elder dragons would remain. Many felt that if they had not been there to preside over the tribunal, Kemet might have fallen under the onslaught lead by a magus and two dire lions.

Not all of the city shields had tetsuo blades and not all of the fire forged were trained to use their unesiphiwo in battle. Elder dragons certainly turned the tide forcing them to retreat. The gods in disguise simply found a quiet corner in Salim's to observe it all. Nervously Daniel the lesser tagged along as Lofin's valet. Feeling more comfortable in his armor, the man walked with more confidence but made sure not to open his mouth. Boasting had done him very little good and for once he was keeping as low a profile as he could. Akachi, and K'mbo were flitting about serving customers happy that business was taking a turn for the better. K'mbo was noticeably avoiding the Djaemon customers.

Jamaal and Kanaa found a small table away from the commotion. They were sharing a meal and Jamaal was deep in his cups. Still in mourning she didn't bother to scold him about it. Despite the jovial atmosphere most of the patrons were very worried about what may be coming, and things that had not been remedied from recent incidents. Kanaa most of all was not satisfied. Jamaal was in shock as she quickly snatched the tankard from him before taking a big gulp. He couldn't help but chuckle, and was repaid with the best gift he could be given. Through tears she smiled as she had not since they lost their daughter.

Wiping the tears, she took another swig and mumbled "You big oaf." Kanaa punched him roughly in the shoulder. She continued "How about you go get that obnoxiously large blade of yours and we go hunting?" The request seemed to instantly sober him up a bit. "You wish to go after the magus ourselves? We have no idea where he went or how he got there." He stated. The look in her eyes told him she was deadly serious. Nodding her head, she added "All true, but the city shields, fire forged, and elder dragons of this territory that none of us knew existed could bring him to justice. I simply cannot let this stand husband. Perhaps your one-armed magus friend can use some of that foolhardiness that I know is still within him to help us track and kill Motu the necromancer. With or without you I am going."

The steel in her voice affirmed what he thought and for him there really was no choice in this matter. Jamaal finished his drink and stood to go outside to retrieve his weapon before coming back to see if

Simon would join them. His friend looked to be in some engaging conversation with the Shike from the monastery in the red desert. Zaniah, the commander of the city shields along with her two silent lieutenants seemed to be waiting for things to get out of hand. It would seem to Jamaal that he and his group were no longer of great interest to the law enforcement of Kemet. For this he was grateful. Nodding to Simon, he went outside to check on where his blade was stowed.

There really was nothing to worry about, but it was more of a habitual thing. If the blade wasn't attuned to you, you simply had no chance of lifting it much less wielding it for unsavory purposes. As he suspected, it was safely embedded in the ground next to a line of tetsuo blades of a few city shields men. Looking over some of the craftsmanship on the hilts, Jamaal tried to guess at where they were forged. Two of them were nearly identical. "Probably for the silent twins, and by the look of some of these etchings, I'd wager they were forged near the greymoor woodlands. Those boys are far from home. Perhaps they fled the life on the high seas." He observed.

Before he could move on to look at what had to be the commanders ornately gilded tetsuo blade, there was a flash of bright red light streaking across the night sky. For a moment the entire cityscape was shrouded crimson. There was a chorus of gasps as everyone outside was surprised by the light. Many thought this was a severely bad omen while others dismissed any superstitious ideas out of hand. Jamaal had no idea what it meant, but he needed to get back inside to check on his wife. Cautiously he would also ask if Simon would indeed accompany them on their pursuit of Motu.

He had no doubt his friend would come along, but felt guilty since it was just as likely that young Mael would want to tag along. The boy had been through so much early on in life, and Jamaal did not want to be the one to heap more trauma on him when he had a chance to live out an actual childhood. As if to remind him, he could see Mael and another young boy talking and gesticulating boisterously as they traded stories of adventures recently experienced. Jamaal couldn't help but smile. This was just the kind of joy he did not want to be even partially responsible for extinguishing. "I'll talk to him." he assured himself as he made his way back into Salim's.

Once inside everything had changed, and he could not tell if it was for the better or worse. One thing could not be denied. It was a bit creepy. Nearly everyone in the tavern were eerily silent save for a few people mumbling as they tried to figure out what was amiss. Kanaa was now standing with Simon and the two tetsuo monks. Finally noticing T'Ome standing in front of Eron, Jamaal could see what had everyone so enthralled. The massive warrior was staring at the ceiling with his shoulders held back and his bulging red arms were oddly hanging at his sides. Looking around, Jamaal noticed that nearly all of the Djaemon present were standing in a nearly identical pose.

They were stuck it seemed, mouth agape, saying nothing. Slowly making his way to Kanaa, Jamaal asks "What part of the game is this?" Kanaa shook her head negatively and shrugged her shoulders. Simon offered "This is no game that I've heard of or seen, but all of the Djaemon seem to be the only ones playing. With the exception of those two." Following Simon's line of sight placed their focus on the

Djaemon who had come to Kemet with the suspected exiles from the Isles of Esikrwada who claimed not to be from the isles. The other was the male server who seemed a bit scrawny to be a Djaemon, but no one seemed to question it.

Max and Sparks, the supposed exiles in question not truly from the Isles calmy walked over with their Djaemon friend. "Um…what's up with your homeboys Argos?" Max asks. Lofin, his friends and Daniel the lesser also gather with the unaffected to observe and speculate. Lofin asks "Argos is it? Why are you not in the same condition as your fellow Djaemon?" Argos shrugs as other focus on him before turning their attention to K'mbo who is similarly not afflicted with whatever was happening. Before anyone could ask him, he scampers out of the tavern.

Just as he exited Mael and Kenzo stumble back in nearly knocking K'mbo over. Mael blurts "The Djaemon outside are acting…strange." The two boys saw that the Djaemon inside were somehow behaving just like their kin outside who reacted to the spectacular light that passed overhead briefly. Lofin chuckles as he explains "The one who ran out was no Djaemon at all, but merely played at being one. None of you knew? I thought perhaps this was a purposeful ruse." Max mumbled something about "redface" but Sparks elbowed him in the ribs before he could get it out.

The Djaemon were all remaining eerily still. Eron the so-called silver-tongued savage was at a loss for words. He simply stood in shock staring at his former foe in the drinking competition that was in full swing before all the Djaemon just froze. At first, he thought it was a ploy when the big red warrior was about to lose, but he soon realized if that were the case, they were all in on it. Hard to pull off when there were now members of other Djaemon clans in town. Cautiously Kenzo walked up to T'Ome since no one else had the nerve to approach or attempt to move them. The boy decided someone should try and snap them out of it.

Just as Kenzo's small hand was about to grasp T'Ome's forearm the warrior took a deep breath as if he had been holding it the entire time. Simultaneously the other Djaemon did the same, shaking their heads as if to clear them but when their eyes opened, they glowed red. Kenzo called out to T'Ome and D'Na but they didn't seem to hear him or if they did, they were not responding. Almost as one the Djaemon turned and began to slowly walk out of Salim's. The rest of the patrons were befuddled and dumbly followed them out to see a throng of other Djaemon filing out of Kemet proper.

Some of the other Kemet city shields men came behind the last of them when Zaniah exited the tavern with Akil and Rahil. The twins signed a question to her and she replied "No, stop them from doing what? Leaving isn't against the law. Let them go. I only wish we knew why they left in this…manner." A lot of the citizens had come out of their homes to witness this strange exodus of the Djaemon who had only just recently entered their city. Something that had never happened in the numbers witnessed, and never under what could be termed as friendly circumstances.

Daniel the lesser along with Olorun, Orunmila and Olofi still in disguise came out of Salim's. Olofi had just arrived outside in time to hear the city shield commanders' comments. Looking on with everyone else Olofi concludes "Serat calls them." Max who looks obviously confused says "By Serat you mean the blood god they worship? Like this is not some metaphor." Turning to Argos he adds "Families can be weird but your family is really weird bro."

Chapter Twenty-Six

The normally quiet, dismal night side of the lunar body that rests on the other side of Nyumbani reflecting the light of Izulu is alive with the raucous stomping of Serat, the blood god. Pacing back and forth in his lair deep beneath the surface turning recent events over and over in his mind. Specifically, he mentally relives the visit from Olorun, and it's not clear yet whether or not he should be offended. His senses scream that he should be. The other gods who occasionally make appearances here are suspiciously absent, and the constant swirl of reclaimed Djaemon souls are miserably lacking of any rational acumen.

There is no wellspring of advice from which Serat could draw insight on this. That fact only serves to fuel his rage. Each step sends shockwaves through the celestial body and scatters red glowing souls that would otherwise float and flit about lazily. The blood gods' movements disturb and disrupt what would usually be a serene yet oddly desolate environment. Thinking more on the random visit from the sky god Serat grumbles to himself "How dare he place his hands on my personage! Does he think me weak? To question me at all is an accusation! What I have a hand in is none of their concern! The Djaemon are the spawn of my flesh! I am no thing created from their machinations and prayers. Quite the opposite. I'll have to show them who the true influencer is. The blood of gods would be the ultimate sacrifice! Let's see if we can find homage for me from higher sources."

Making his way to the surface, Serat gazes down upon Nyumbani as a large cloud of red souls follow him creating another light show that mortals looking up at the night sky would see. Peering down at his hands Serat grows his nails until they become talon like. Reaching up he rakes himself causing blood to flow from his chest and abdomen. As the black blood pools, the glowing souls begin to swarm to it like a giant cloud of crimson lightning bugs.

Crouching in a horse stance Serat begins weaving his hands back and forth. The blood raises off the dusty lunar floor swirling with the gathered souls. Soon the strange mixture begins to flow in time with the movements of the blood god's hands. He flails his hands wildly in a circular motion overhead. More souls billow out from beneath the surface to join this ethereal mixture of sanguine energy. After a long moment of revolutions, Serat has a whirlwind of blood and souls hovering in a wide ring above him. Finally, he forcefully points his large arms towards Nyumbani and it causes the red halo above to extend into a bridge of sorts toward the planet.

It takes a while for the large ribbon of sanguine light to reach the surface proper and when it does, Serat takes a mighty leap to surf his way down. Screaming his way through the initial atmosphere breach, he rides his makeshift bridge all the way down. Those that caught a glimpse of this saw what appeared to be a large red comet headed for planetfall with its tail dissipating as it fell. Peering at the fast-approaching landscape Serat is deciding where to land. Spotting a desirable coastal area, the blood god need only point in the direction he wants to go, and the crimson wave of souls guide him there.

There is a resounding crash as he touches down on solid ground disturbing a large host of wild life in the greymoor woodlands as well as startling many communities in the vicinity for a vast distance around. With Serat safely on the ground the souls evaporate, their mist returned instantly to his lair on the lunar celestial body. The moon turns red then to a shade of pink before returning to its glowing white or grey as the souls retreat once again below the surface.

Without speaking a word, Serat had mentally put a call out to all of his children on Nyumbani. He could feel some of them that had already begun their journey to him from all corners of the world. There was a minute number that were not compelled for reasons unknown to him. Perhaps they were disconnected somehow. Serat could feel that some had been twisted in some fashion and weren't totally…alive. That made little sense to the blood god but he knew what he felt, and that was the most he could make of it. No matter he thought. It didn't matter how many arrived, it would be enough.

Soon there were large caravans of marching Djaemon, all nearing his location gazing up at his massive frame. The terrifying form of Serat stood with open arms welcoming his children. Some of the Djaemon were snapped out of the trance his compelling had placed them in, and they could finally see with their own eyes the hulking embodiment of their faith in all his scarred glory. Others were overwhelmed at this falling instantly on their faces or knees in supplication. An ever-growing red army was mobilizing before Serat and this pleased him to no end. Their faith, adulation, and prayers began to strengthen him.

D'Na, and T'Ome are mentally conscious but unable to control their bodies as they literally march overland from Kemet along with those of their clan who went to witness the closing of the proceedings that were scheduled to happen before Motu escaped. D'Na felt as if she were simply sleep walking yet the difference was that she was somehow still aware of what she was unintentionally doing.

Using her eyes, she could tell some of the other Djaemon were still deeply entranced and likely unaware of what they were doing. All of their eyes still had the ghastly glow that suddenly appeared in that tavern. She could also see that nearly all of their clan that was left behind had made their way here as well. After searching as best she could she found K'Ain. Their king did not look to be aware. His luminous black and red eyes glazed over staring only ahead to where his feet were mindlessly carrying him.

When she looked at T'Ome, she thought she saw a hint of cognizance in him, but she could not be sure. She then noticed that it wasn't just their clan on this involuntary pilgrimage. There were a variety of Djaemon from a diverse number of clans represented, and even some of the clan less. Her feet had to be blistering from the nonstop march, and she was unbearably exhausted yet she could not stop. Soon out in the distance she believed she saw their final destination, and she could not quite let her mind grasp what her eyes were seeing. Serat, the blood god, in the living flesh towering above the landscape.

Their patron deity loomed large with the greymoor woodlands painting a surreal backdrop. D'Na grew up learning all the traditions, participated in all of the rituals and was a leader within her clan, but if she were to look deeply within herself, she honestly never truly held strongly to the beliefs. It was simply all she knew. The swath of clan less now marching mindlessly along with them would have been at odds with the Djaemon from Gcina Okubomvu. K'Ain was king to one of the most renown Djaemon clans in the world.

D'Na's pride in that alone would have instantly influenced her to at least think these unnamed to be beneath them. At most they would have sent them into oblivion as tribute to Serat, or died trying. Despite their lack of faith or any outward evidence of it, they were here alongside many clans that had indeed pledged their loyalty and way of life to the sanguine order. How could that be? She thought. T'Ome was unsuccessfully struggling against the compulsion which clued D'Na that her hunch was correct. Her clanmate was aware. She wondered how many others were having a similar experience.

Soon it started to matter less and less. D'Na realized the closer she got to Serat other thoughts and feelings were closing in on her mental autonomy. Somehow her faith was strengthening leaving no room for the doubt that was plaguing her mind moments ago. The pain in her legs and feet were gone despite the physical evidence she could clearly see on her and those marching along with her. As the mass of marching Djaemon warriors got closer as Serat ushered them into his presence, all they could focus on was the majestic tapestry of scars running throughout his body and visage.

Suddenly he laughed and the sound boomed over the lands somehow further strengthening the metaphysical bond with them. The call was far too strong for any of them to even attempt resistance. D'Na, T'Ome and any others that were the last to hold out were finally overcome. This close to the font, it was hard not to be carried away by the current. As one they fell to their faces in prayer which would have sounded like rhythmic growling to anyone close enough to hear them. With the number of Djaemon gathered, one would not have to be close. This strange sound carried far and wide.

At last Serat's hardened visage gazed down on his children and they felt what he felt. His joy spread throughout the throng of Djaemon gathered and they rejoiced in it. A flash of bloodlust reverberated through all of their beings and he reveled in that shared communion. Serat thought of the disrespect he felt at being questioned by Olorun, and the Djaemon had vivid visions of deicide. Some were to the point of howling at the skies at the thought of the glory they would attain with such an achievement.

Serat had never before set foot on this world and wondered how far his talents would extend here. His souls were back in his usual domain. Raising his hands as if about to play maestro to an invisible orchestra, the blood god began gesticulating. The Djaemon sat in awe wondering what was about to happen. Within moments he found he was able to manipulate the very lands just as he could at his lair. Seeing this the Djaemon heaped many praises upon him. It reinvigorated him and the build became increasingly easy.

This became an oddly reciprocal experience as his elation began to funnel into his gathered children of renewed faith as he erected a towering fortress from the lands changing the immediate landscape around them. It was a large foreboding temple. The first of its kind as this was first formed by a deity. As great as any of the other monuments were raised by the most loyal to the order, they would pale in comparison. He certainly would not be able to sit or stand in any of the mortal made dedications to him. Here they could gather to bask in his glory. The sentiment led him to speak to his people at long last.

"My children!" Serat proclaimed and was answered with a chorus of mighty cheers that could shake mountains. The blood god continued "The gods that hold sway over these lands on which you have resided since your inception has dared to challenge me! Through you, my most beloved creations, I think it is time to return the favor. None of the beings that follow them and their ways are as deserving of the bounty this world has to offer than you! I wish to begin a cleansing. A culling of the weak that will place you in your proper place among the other mortals here."

Another resounding yet ragged cacophony of cheers went up. Serat goaded them further "With the number of their worshipers diminished their powers will wane giving me the opportunity to return to you the tributes you have offered to me throughout your many seasons on this forsaken place. I bid you to go forth and continue to wet your blades in my name knowing that I am at last here with you. Those of you that fall will not only go to glory but will come directly to me, and soon know the indescribable feeling of spilling the ultimate blood! Go forth my children…cut everything down in your path. I'll part with a bit of my strength as a gift to you."

A red wave of energy exploded from Serat and washed over the gathered Djaemon. Most who were on their knees rocked back with eyes closed only to open them as an intense bloodlust overcame them. Many howled in rage as their eyes glowed more intensely. Black blades were unsheathed as they all stood en masse and charged out of the blood gods fortress with reckless abandon. The mob of red hate and discontent began to cut a bloody swath of terror throughout the greymoor woodlands then spread out in all directions.

With each kill Serat could feel his strength grow, and when a Djaemon fell his or her soul immediately flew into the blood god from wherever it was clipped from the corporeal husk that had temporarily housed it. As the groups of marauding Djaemon came into contact with Djaemon not initially compelled, some were instantly recruited just by being in close proximity. Serat doubted any of the conventional warriors the other denizens of this place could offer up much resistance. Groups of magi were able to hold them off long enough to retreat without being overwhelmed but the ferocity and numbers were sufficient to overcome the tactical advantage magic afforded them.

In most cases the infamous magic users chose to disengage and regroup to figure out how best to deal with this unexpectedly large and unusually coordinated series of attacks. Serat knew it was only a matter of time before the Orisha would have no choice but to do what he had been indirectly accused of doing. They would finally have to openly have a hand in the struggles here. The blood god knew this would not be the first time, but most of those that did dip their toes into matters in this place went to lengths to hide their involvement. A silly practice to be sure.

Serat was uncertain as to how this would all unfold but one thing, he was sure of, it would not bore him. The mundanity of what his existence had become was partially to blame for the stoking of his rage. Olorun merely provided the tipping point. Gods were not meant to simply sit idly by observing their creations, or oversee their domains. Eventually the need to effect change within the universe would come calling, and the blood god was truly elated that it did. Now he wondered who would be the first to answer his challenge. Who would be the first to cross blades or test their limits of power against the god made for spilling the liquid that fuels life?

Feeling his power continuing to burgeon, Serat awaits the answer to that all important question. As the night turned to day, he could see the wait might not be as long as he expected. A gathering of flashes that could only mean a small exodus from Izulu heralded the incoming presence of other Orisha. Any mortals looking skyward in the early morning would see golden comets streaking towards the surface to different locations. There was a great impact near the outskirts of Kemet. Another splashed into the Iilwandle Ezinkulu, the great ocean.

Two more fell from the sky nearly in the same spot just outside of the Luhlaza woodlands as lightning struck the magical barrier raised by the reclusive Elinanye. Out of the crater near Kemet came Ogun no longer disguised as a master forger but in his true form, eyes aglow with a blade slung on his shoulder. He felt the presences of others within the city but he wanted to meet with the new arrivals first. The god of war and iron was confused. Was he to remain on Izulu when he received the summons from Olorun only to find the creator himself gone when he arrived? He was still unhappy with the possible infringement on his domain in this dimension. The sky god knew Ogun's whereabouts so the summons was unnecessary.

Ogun quickly leapt over the Mulanje mountain ranges to get closer to the other presences he felt. As soon as he crossed through the Pantu grasslands he could feel Oya and Shango approaching. They were of course bickering as usual. When they caught sight of him, they stopped and pretended as if they were conversing normally. He wasn't fooled. Without a word they turned south towards the coast and walked the shore until the waters began to broil. When they became their most tumultuous Yemaya sprang from them to land beside them.

For a few moments the gods of thunder, and war stood with the goddesses of the sea and storms. Shango, Oya and Yemaya waited to see what Ogun had to say. Finally, Ogun states "I don't know exactly what Serat is playing at here, but I for one cannot let it stand. We know Olorun likes us to abstain but this is an unforeseen circumstance. I know and can feel that the creator along with his aspect is here and one other I can't quite identify, but if they will not quell this intrusion before it gets out of hand then I will."

Oya adds "You're right. Let us go to Olorun and see what he has to say now after that ridiculous inquisition. He cannot tie our hands now." Yemaya nods her agreement feeling the loss of life from some of her most loyal coastal worshippers far to the east. Looking at Oya,

Shango shakes his head saying "I cannot believe I am actually agreeing with you!" The two of them share a brief laugh before taking to the skies forgoing the walk to Kemet. Ogun runs at high-speed leaping over large land masses while Yemaya dives back into the seas preferring to travel by water for as much as possible.

The group of Orisha would gather to decide what was to be done about this new incursion by another deity no less. War between mortals could have long lasting adverse effects but war between gods could destroy entire worlds. Olorun would no doubt advise caution, but Ogun would likely fall into his lesser-known nature. Iron was forged for a great many things including useful tools, but the most common tools were often also used as weapons.

Serat had come to bring war, to spill blood and have it spilled in his name. While siphoning the power of some, he may just be bolstering the power of one who had come to remedy matters here. Ogun was unsure if the blood god was even aware of what he was setting in motion, and part of him didn't care. He knew deep down that if what the sky god proposed wasn't satisfactory, he would indeed handle things himself.